MOUNTAIN MAN PREQUEL

MOUNTAIN MAN

MAN

PREQUEL

KEITH C. BLACKMORE

Podium

Cover design by Podium Publishing

ISBN: 978-1-0394-4990-9

Published in 2023 by Podium Publishing, ULC
www.podiumaudio.com

MOUNTAIN MAN PREQUEL

1

"So, how's it going?"

Gus turned at the question and looked the professor straight in the squinty eyes. The late afternoon October sun beamed down with a bug-searing vengeance that made it feel like July on Mercury. Shirt doffing weather in the house painting business, even though Gus never took his shirt off. Folks got particular about men stripping down on their property these days. And Gus's full-figured man girth made him a little gut shy while on the job. As a result, his tan pretty much stopped mid-bicep. Even though he kept clean shaven, he usually skipped his jelly roll jolliness because all he needed were homeowners gawking at the overweight Sasquatch painting their house. Plus, there was Toby. Toby would make jokes all day long about his hair and cracks. And those skin nooks and crannies would generate a kiln-like heat. All Gus needed was to be mocked while sweating miserably. So, he wore two T-shirts, stretched tight over his two-hundred-seventy-five pound plus frame, and tried to stick to the shade where he could.

But sweat still seeped out of him, as if he'd been locked in the devil's own sauna.

The professor, however, had no problem with the heat.

Dressed down in a black fishnet tank-top and showing off way too much chest and midriff (and a respectable four-pack), the professor was a little too comfortable with the late-season heat wave. Hair flourished on the man. Tufts of it sprouted from the guy's shoulders, and miniscule tumbleweeds peeked out from his ears. The guy was an oversized hobbit on 'roids. He also wore, and goddamn him for doing so, a pair of much-too-short cutoff jeans, showing off a pair of hockey player legs. Those thick tree trunks rippled with power, and for all those reasons, Gus strove to look the guy in the eyes, totally avoiding the skimpy denim cutoffs and the barbarian thighs.

But mostly the cutoffs.

"Going good, good," Gus informed the professor.

"Not painting today?"

"Ah, no, not today," Gus said, looking to the sky. "Today we just scraped everything down and primed it. Lots of dead paint peeling away from the wood here. And the wood's old. We slapped down drop cloths and went to town, scraping away what we could. The dormers make things a little tricky. These old Victorians look nice, but it can be slippery getting at some places, especially at the top of a thirty-foot ladder or on a roof with a sharp incline."

The professor nodded at every word, listening intently, and studied the top of his house as the sun crawled past its peak. There was a window up there, one of five on this side.

"See you did some scraping up there." He pointed.

"Yeah," Gus said. "Lots of things going on up there. The soffit and facia are really old, but they're holding. Easy to see the old layers of paint. We can save you a few bucks by painting over it again, but you'll have to replace it in a couple years."

"What are those?" the professor asked.

"What?"

"The soffit and do-flicky."

The professor taught political science at the local university in Annapolis, and for all intents and purposes, didn't seem like a bad guy to work for. He left the crew alone while he did his thing inside the house, apparently enjoying a day off, while Gus and company prepped it for the painting to come.

But for a guy who taught poly-sci, not knowing what a soffit and fascia was surprised Gus a little. Still, he didn't make a big deal of it. Gus didn't completely understand the parliamentary system either. So, he pointed to the eaves. "See that? The fascia's the part facing outwards. The soffit's the part underneath that runs back to the house there."

The professor nodded, squinting, taking it all in. "I see, I see."

"Never did any painting before?" Gus asked.

"No," the professor shrugged and smiled. "Not for me. I leave that to professionals like yourself."

Gus didn't detect any condescension. "Well, anyway, Toby and I did the scraping today. We'll be back first thing in the morning, weather permitting, and slap on the first coat."

"I know what that is," the professor said.

Gus smiled back. "We'll get that on in a day or two. Put on a second coat on Wednesday or Thursday. All weather permitting."

"I think it calls for sunny weather."

Gus heard the same thing. "Where was all this in July?"

"Oh, it was up there," the professor winked. "Just hiding behind the clouds."

"Too bad."

"We're getting it now, that's the important thing."

Suppose so, Gus thought, though the long days of summer were long gone. "We're just going to clean up here and get moving."

"Done for the day?"

A car pulled into the driveway out front, distracting the professor. The wheels stopped with a squeak, as if too much pressure had been applied.

"Excuse me," the professor said, suddenly concerned. "That's my wife getting back home."

"Everything okay?" Gus asked.

"Not sure. She called me about twenty minutes ago saying she was coming home early. She's not feeling well."

"That's too bad," Gus said with a frown.

"You'll be back tomorrow morning?" the professor asked as he neared the house's corner. A car door slammed out front.

"Yeah."

"What time?"

"Nine okay?" Gus asked.

"That's fine," the professor yelled, as he disappeared around the house.

Gus stood in the afternoon light, holding his hips, and hoped the professor's missus was indeed okay. There was a wicked flu strain on the go. Before he could further follow that thread of thought, Toby walked around the other corner of the house with a rolled-up drop cloth.

"She's sick?" he asked, also squinting, with his mouth half-cocked in a question.

"Apparently," Gus answered.

"Oh, too bad." Toby said as he went to a garbage bin settled on the back lawn, near the work shed. Gus moseyed on over to his fellow painter just as he heard the house door slam. Toby emptied the drop cloth and huffed at a dust plume.

"There a lock for the shed?" Toby asked, shaking the fabric clean.

"Unknown."

"So, we just leave everything in there?"

"Yup."

"Think it'll be okay?"

Toby had a penchant for asking unnecessary questions.

"Yeah, it's only drop cloths," Gus said. "The good stuff will be here tomorrow."

A violent retching came from inside the house, slightly muted because of the walls. The volcanic voiding etched frowns across both their faces.

"Jesus, that didn't sound good," Toby remarked in a low tone.

Gus warned him with a scowl. "We're still on site."

"Yeah, but—"

"If we can hear them—" *They can hear us*, Gus warned with his eyes.

Toby shut up. He folded the drop cloth to manageable proportions and slow-pitched it into the work shed, right over where Gus had placed his, just before a parked lawn mower.

"Let's get moving," Gus said.

Toby closed the door and locked an imaginary padlock. Gus went back to the truck, eyeing the side of the house with a rueful frown. Truth was, he didn't like what he'd just heard. The professor's wife sounded sick. *Real* sick.

Three vehicles were in the driveway. Two were sedans, a white one pulled up behind a black one. Next to both, and almost as long, was the company's yellow Ford pickup. The truck was a monster of a rig with a crew cab with the words Brush-it Ink on the canopy's side. Gus never liked the company name, but he was somewhat buzzed when Benny came up with the idea and didn't argue long enough against it. Now that the business cards and the flyers were all done up and out there the name was pretty much set in stone.

Unless they came up with some big money jobs.

Which Benny hadn't secured yet. Not yet. But he was working on it.

Gus slid between the truck and black sedan, his expansive ass and rolls brushing against the sides, and carefully opened the driver's door. He sucked in his gut, cringed at the barest contact of truck door to sedan, and squeezed himself in, trying to remember if he had parked so close to the car or wondering if the professor had snuck out and returned, snuggling his ride a touch closer to the truck. As soon as Gus was aboard, he fidgeted until comfortable, which was hard to do when your clothes clung to your sweaty ass. When he reached that right position, he pinched his jeans away from his boys and gave them an adjustment.

Toby came around the other side of the Victorian, avoiding an open flower bed of purples and yellows just as Gus started up the engine. The guy's face darkened visibly as he approached the cars, and he took his time circling both sedans.

"What's wrong?" Gus asked as his friend pulled himself aboard.

Toby shut the door before answering, signaling that they were officially off the job site. "Bitch heaved by the driveway."

"*Whaaa?*"

"You didn't see that shit?"

"No, I walked in between."

"Good thing," Toby grimaced. "She must've dropped a pound of some real nasty-lookin' spaghetti. That's one place the grass ain't gonna grow no more."

Gus cringed.

"She must've gotten out of her car, keeled over, and fuckin' barfed like she was being goosed or something."

"Ew."

"Shit's disgusting."

Gus put the truck in gear. "You sound like you never got sick before."

"Yeah, but it's different when a woman gets sick. I don't know why. I feel sorry for them. Kids too."

"Didn't sound too sorry a second ago." Gus said.

"I know. Ironical, ain't it?"

Ironical. Watching his mirrors and the rear camera, Gus reversed out of the driveway, checked traffic, and eased out into the street. "Well, hope she's all right."

"Fuck," Toby ejected. "I just hope that shit's not catchin'. All I need is to get sick and miss work for a few days."

"I think you're covered," Gus said.

"By who? Worker's comp ain't gonna cover you for a few days," Toby declared with quiet scorn. "They'll fuckin' stare at you like you got three hairy dicks. *Little* hairy dicks. You have to be gut shot, tea-bagged and left for dead on a highway before they'll even slip you the paperwork, and even then, there's questions with that not-quite eye contact. You know what I'm sayin'? Like they're lookin' at that spot right between your eyebrows or checkin' out your teeth? I can't afford to miss a day or two or three. Need them hours. Livin' paycheck to paycheck over here."

"Whose fault is that?"

"All mine," Toby admitted. "Just sayin' is all. Jeez, you're a shitty listener."

"Maybe you need credit counselling?" Gus asked, cocking an eyebrow as he drove along a wide street with the odd car parked on the side. Tall elms filtered the waning daylight, crossing the asphalt and grass in shadows. A tall Baptist Church rose on the right, the brickwork beautifully obscured by colorful leaves.

"Credit counselling," Toby scoffed, miming jacking off before tossing his hand at the windshield with a Shakespearean flourish.

Smirking, Gus returned his attention to the road. Toby was in his early thirties, with naturally blonde hair and a complexion unmarked by acne. He was slim, regularly went to church on Sundays (sometimes hungover, but he got there), and looked to all concerned like a quiet, respectful, God-fearing man who worked five and a half days a week when he could. Toby could've been a poster boy for bright, blue-eyed Mormons who traveled overseas, spreading the word of the Lord to people on subways and sidewalks—if said people could spare just a minute of their time.

But when you got to *know* him ...

Toby had missed his calling. He should've been on a stage somewhere, packing in crowds of thousands just to hear his raw comedic afterthoughts and filthy observations, which quickly shredded any previous conceptions of the wholesome-looking young man.

Man *child*, Gus corrected himself.

Toby wasn't a bad person—just uniquely Toby.

At that, the man heaved out a couple of blank dry-heaves and shivered for effect, as if ingesting bad medicine.

"Remembered the puke, did ya?" Gus asked.

Toby nodded. "Just glad I wasn't around to see that slop comin' out of her. That would've stayed with me all through supper and breakfast tomorrow. That shit gets me every time, and in a bad way. That and people who insist on calling me Tobias. You don't know what's on the go these days. And that flu shot they give people? You know what that is, right? That's nothing but dead viruses shot straight into your bloodstream. Dead. Fucking. Viruses. Non-living matter. Think about that."

"I'm pretty sure they're not dead fucking viruses."

"You get a flu shot?"

"Regularly."

Toby shook his head. "You're in denial then."

"I'm also not sick," Gus continued. "And if they were dead viruses, that's not a bad thing. What do you think your immune system does to viral strains?"

"It shits it out."

"It does *not* shit it out."

"You're not gonna to drop this, are you?"

"I'm not—" Gus did a quick double-take in Toby's direction before refocusing on the road. "*You* brought it up."

"*She* brought it up." Toby said thoughtfully, planting an elbow on the windowsill and taking chin in hand. "Literally. I wonder if she stuck her fingers down her throat?"

"Now I'm going to be thinking of that."

"You know what she does?"

"What? For work?"

"Yeah."

"No."

"She teach? Around kids? That's the *worst*, man. Especially the young ones. The amount of snot she has to wade through in a day." Toby cringed. "That's all kindergarten is, man. One big human petri dish. Filled with fluids. Fluids drippin' down, sniffed back, and coughed out. Sometimes picked and eaten. It's a wonder teachers don't wear hazmat suits."

"Keep it up and I'll drop you off at the nearest playground." Gus checked his side mirror.

Toby was silent for seconds, then, "Hope she didn't puke in front of her kids."

"I don't think she has kids."

"I mean where she teaches."

Gus rubbed an eye. "I don't think we established her place of work."

"Be embarrassin' if she did," Toby continued, lost in the scenario. "Like shittin' yourself in church or something. Worst with kids, though. You *know* they'd be gigglin' their little evil asses off. And pointin'. Ohhh teacher, *ohhh*. Try goin' to bed tonight and not havin' that nightmare, eh? God, that would be embarrassing. Shittin' yourself right there. Even worse if you wore white. Or a dress. Or a white dress. Or a white dress to an interview for a job you wanted. Fuck. Wouldn't that be something? Gettin' the shitarrhea durin' a fuckin' important job interview? Like, the *very* job you'd trained and studied for your whole life and you forever fuck yourself out of it with an unexpected lapse of sphincter control? Christ, that would be embarrassing. So embarrassing. Can you imagine?"

Gus could *not* imagine it. "Why not a white suit?" he muttered, hating himself for even participating in the conversation.

"Why not a suit?" Toby repeated, spreading his hands as if completing a magic trick. "Why not a suit? Excellent point. Hey, wear whatever you want to an interview. Wear a fuckin' tutu if you want. I'm just sayin', is all. That's all."

Gus sighed and stopped at a red light. Thankfully the windows were up so no one else could hear. As an afterthought, he scratched his balls.

"So, name something embarrassing for you," Toby asked out of the blue. "Since we're on the subject."

"*You're* on the subject," Gus pointed out. "*I'm* thinking about getting out here and walking home."

"Haha," Toby said. "You're funny, sometimes. Come on, it'll be fun. Something embarrassing. It'll be fun. Really."

Shaking his head, Gus wouldn't budge.

"C'mon," Toby persisted. "You got them. I know you do. We all do."

"Look. I don't wanna remember any of my embarrassing moments. Takes me forever to fuckin' *forget* about them."

"How do you improve upon yourself if you don't remember the embarrassing times? Or better yet, the circumstances that might've directly or indirectly resulted in an embarrassing moment? How do you take that awkward instance and turn it into something good? Something positive? Empowering, even?"

"I don't."

"You should."

"I ... will not."

"*Do it*," Toby insisted. "C'mon. You should. Really."

Unwilling to participate any further, Gus stared ahead.

"All right," Toby relented, hands raised. "All right. I'll get this started. Just to establish a comfortable zone. For disclosure."

Christ almighty, Gus thought. Up ahead, the light turned green, and he accelerated.

"Okay," Toby continued. "So, I had this uncle, okay? And for the longest time, he thought ... well ... Jesus I can't believe I'm going there. Fuck. Well, anyway, he thought I was retarded."

That was met with resounding silence on Gus's part. Then, "He what?"

"He thought I was retarded."

The frown returned to Gus's face. "That shit's cruel."

"I know, right? But that's what he—"

"No, I mean, calling folks retarded. Seriously. That's not right. Or fair to folks who are actually, uh, mentally challenged."

"So, what should I say?"

"Just say that your uncle thought you were mentally challenged. I think that's politically correct. Not retarded. And not handicapped. I've even heard of developmentally delayed. No, wait, these days I think it's special. Yeah. Special."

"Oh, sorry. Okay, I'll say special, okay? How's that?"

"S'all right," Gus muttered. "Sorry for interrupting. On with your story, please."

Toby paused and backed up. "So, anyway, my uncle, right? He thought I was special y'know? In a retarded sorta way. I was only six or seven at the time. Had trouble saying my words. 'Trees' came out as *Twees*, y'know. Skunk was *snunk*. Anyway, turns out I was just a little ADD. But back then, I mean, really, no one knew about ADD. Or could afford gas detectors. So, I was just … you know, going from between being super fuckin' hyper or chemically zoned out."

"Just stick with mentally challenged," Gus sighed, defeated.

"Okay. That, then. Maybe he thought I was a little … you know. Maybe a lot. Anyway, my uncle took it upon himself to test me."

"He was a doctor?"

"Mmm no, he worked at a post office."

"Okay. Close enough."

"How is that close enough?" Toby looked genuinely perplexed. "That shit's nowhere near close. Not even in the same city block."

"Continue with the story, please?"

"Okay, so, I mean, he meant well and all, but his, ah, methodology was a little—look at the ass on that."

Two women wearing shorts walked on the sideway. The masterfully executed segue distracted Gus, even though the ladies did nothing for him. He was spoken for.

"Anyway," Toby resumed without missing a beat, "he decided to do a few tests to see if I wasn't MC. In any way."

MC. Gus saw what Toby did there. "Any of those tests involve electricity?" he asked. "Or drinking anything purple?"

Toby sat back. "I can see this was a mistake."

"No, continue, please. I'm listening. About an embarrassing time in your life. As a child."

"You're mocking. There's a difference."

"No, I was listening. Really. Go on. You were saying how your uncle thought you were crazy and—"

"MC. He thought I was MC."

"MC squared."

"No, just MC." Toby raised a finger. "There's a difference."

Gus drew a hand over his face and scratched at his chin.

"See, you can barely hold it in."

Gus's shoulders trembled ever so slightly.

"Don't you do it," Toby warned, turning his false wrath upon him. "Don't you do it! No wait, *do it*! For Christ's sake, *do it*. Let it all out. Last thing we both need is you shittin' yourself."

So, Gus laughed.

2

Swaths of orange and indigo airbrushed the sunset as Gus slammed the company truck door. He locked it with a *tweet tweet* and walked toward the stairwell of his apartment building. Traffic streamed by on the nearby road. Kids chattered and screamed on a distant playground. He'd dropped off Toby fifteen minutes ago, not quite on the other side of town but close enough, and was lucky enough that city traffic wasn't heavy. He'd driven home with the windows down, tunes playing, passing through dying streamers of sunlight, appreciating the dusty evening and the cooling of the day.

Three sets of stairs later and sweating once again, Gus was home.

He locked the door, stripped in his bathroom, and hopped into the shower. Copious amounts of body wash were applied and rinsed away. Shampoo was scrubbed into his scalp, not too hard, however, as his hair was thinning in the back. Ten minutes later, Gus dried off his oversized bum, pulled on a pair of boxer briefs (black ones so as to hide any accidental skid marks) and plopped down in his living room's sofa chair. Being three floors up, he had a decent view of a nearby soccer pitch where, sometimes, young university students would catch some sun or kick a ball around. He craned his neck, saw the field empty, and dropped back into his seat. The phone soon filled his hand as he dialed Tammy.

Three rings later, she picked up.

"Hi," she greeted, sounding sleepy.

"Hey," he said, a smile coating the words.

"You home?"

"I am, indeed. You coming over?"

"I am not."

"*What?*" he blurted.

"Can't, honey. Sorry. My sinuses are killing me, and I've already puked twice."

"What?"

"Yeah, I picked up something somewhere."

"Shit, that's too bad. That's *terrible*. I was looking forward to seeing you naked. I mean later."

Tammy giggled and *tsked*. "You shit."

"How about I come over there and nurse you back to health?"

"You'd do that?"

"In a heartbeat. Already completed all of them important S's."

That brought around another giggle, finished off with a sniffle. Tammy knew what they were. "All three of them?" she asked, the connection making her voice all soft and crackly.

"All four. You should see the places I washed."

"I bet."

"Even washed behind my ears."

"Glad to hear it."

"And my dick."

"Gus, not that I'm adverse to your shower routine, but I'm really not up for dick talk on the phone right now."

"No dick talk. Got it."

"So, yeah, I think it's best you stay where you are tonight."

"Awww."

"No, really. I don't want you catching what I have. Just in case."

"Awww," he repeated in a more affectionate tone. "Well, that's sweet. You're too sweet. Listen. I'll pop over anyway. Fix you up some soup or something. Doughnuts. Chocolate ice cream. Hot rum toddies. Fill you up on fluids."

The very mention of the word summoned images of snot-nosed preschoolers, grinning and stretching glistening lines from nostrils to gob-tipped fingers. Gus cringed. "What I mean was—"

"You're risking infection, dear."

"I know."

Truth of the matter was, Gus would risk anything to be with her. Their relationship was only seven months and a bit old, but he was ready to marry her. Marry her and do what he could to make and keep her happy. The only reason he didn't pop the question right there and then was … he wasn't sure how she felt about him.

"I could bring over a fan," he suggested.

A puzzled pause. "You don't have a fan."

"That Japanese hand fan. I'll use that on you. All night long if I have to."

She chuckled, light and lovely. "You might have to. I have the windows closed and the air conditioning on. Still warm here."

"See? Then it's settled. Best I be around anyway, in case you need a lift to the hospital or something."

"I'm not *that* bad," Tammy groaned. "You mentioned soup?"

"You want soup?"

"Yeah, I want soup."

"Soup you shall have."

"Minestrone?" she asked.

"No chicken?"

"Not tonight."

"Then minestrone it is. No chicken tonight. And you shall have crackers. Unsalted. See you in a half-hour."

"Sure, see you."

Click.

A half-hour and he meant it. Gus held the wireless phone and collected his thoughts. Tammy sounded sick. Her folks lived down around Yarmouth. There was no else one around except her friends, and he was pretty sure he just beat them out. Getting sick wasn't a big issue for him. Unlike Toby, he had a few bucks stashed away in case of medical emergencies. Financial planning one-oh-one, have at least six months salary stashed away in an account solely for end-of-the-world scenarios. Just in case. So he missed the odd social gathering where alcoholic beverages were being served. Perhaps he didn't partake as much as his friends did, but that didn't appeal to him anymore. He was no longer in his thirties. That time of his life was behind him, and besides, he was never much of a drinker anyway.

He stood up and glanced out his wide window toward the soccer pitch. A figure was out there, standing in the middle of the field. Gus stopped and narrowed his eyes, straining to see. It was a woman, that much he knew, her back to him, wearing shorts and a T-shirt. She looked like the pointy part of a sundial the way her shadow stretched toward the east.

The handset buzzed in his hand, jolting Gus like he'd been caught thinking dirty thoughts. He wasn't, of course. So, he glanced at the number, frowned, and answered the phone.

"Gus?" a man asked.

"What's up, Benny?"

"Listen, got a job to do tonight."

"Can't do it."

"Listen," Benny protested. "It's good money. Real good. One night. Over at Mollymart. The manager there wants her office painted. Just her office. I've already talked to Toby, and he's on it. So's Gord."

"So you got everyone," Gus said, turning away from his window and looking at the not-so-sturdy entertainment unit his television rested upon. "I just made plans to see the missus."

"Look," Benny insisted, "this is big for us, okay? This is *Mollymart East.* Big chain coming online. Joan Miller is the regional manager. The fucking regional manager. She's like second in command for the whole company. You hear me? We make a good first impression and it might lead to a few more in-shop jobs and then even more stores in the chain. One night of your life to make a good impression and we get Mollymart to open its purse strings. Its *considerable* purse strings."

Gus sighed. "Benny, I'm tired. I stink. And it's getting close to suppertime. And I gotta get up in the morning to do that professor's house. And in case you didn't realize it, it was twenty-seven degrees outside today. I lost one ass cheek."

"Hey, you know why I wasn't there today?"

Gus rolled his eyes.

"It's because I was out pricing *jobs,*" Benny explained. "I was out looking for work for *us.* Knocking on windows and blowing down doors. I got this call at four o'clock, Gus. *Four.* Went right over there and met Ms. Miller on the spot. That impressed her. She told me that herself. Everyone else was, 'Oh we'll get back to you next week' or yadda yadda. Not me, and not us. But here's the thing, she wants it started and finished tonight. When the crowds aren't so heavy on the floor. The office is exactly twenty-four by seventeen. Nine-foot ceiling. No heavy prepping, and the three of you can roll the whole damn thing in two hours max. And here's the thing, because it's after our regular hours and a rush job, I told her our rates are doubled and a half."

That arched Gus's brow. "And she went for that?"

"She didn't even blink at that. That's what I'm saying. We show that we're fucking there when Johnny shits on the spot and we're in. I mean, Brush-It could be absorbed into the chain. Hell, we show we're punctual and capable enough to a regional manager? Who knows what might happen."

"We might get to paint more Mollymarts."

An over-excited Benny pounced. "We might get to—" the jets cooled almost immediately. "Was that sarcasm? 'Cause that sounded like sarcasm."

"That was uncorked smartassitude, yeah. Sorry Benny."

Silence on the other end, and for a moment, Gus thought the boss man was going to let him have it.

To his surprise, Benny did no such thing. "All right," he finally said. "I'll let that go. But only if you get your ass over to Mollymart by seven tonight."

"*Seven? Awww* Benny!"

"*Seven.* All hands on deck."

"Do you even have the paint? You can't get the paint today. Paint shop's closed by now."

"Wally's already on the case," Benny explained. "Four cans are on the mixer even as I speak, I shit you not. I stopped by there before calling you."

Despite his exasperation at the prospect of painting an office after hours, Gus had to admit Benny was on the case. "You got Wally to do that?"

"Guy owes me a favor."

"Must be a big favor. What about gear?"

"Already taken care of. You get your shower, something to eat, and get your ass over there, okay?"

Shoulders heaving, Gus looked to his toes. The night wasn't going to go well for him. He could sense it. "I made plans with Tammy."

"She'll understand," Benny countered. "Gus, this is potentially *huge.* I can't stress the fucking *hugeness* enough. You make this work, okay? One night. A quick roll. Three guys with rollers. You'll be out of there just after midnight, if that. I'll explain the situation to the professor and his wife in the morning. Double time and a half and the potential to be eaten by an up-and-coming grocery juggernaut."

That was the last piece to push Gus over. "All right. I'll … I'll do it. I gotta call Tammy first. Let her know. And take care of those S things."

"What's that?"

"Shit, shower, shave, shampoo,"

Benny chuckled in his ear. "You can cross off at least two of those things. It's a night job. Low traffic time."

"Yeah, I'll be there at eight." Gus said.

"Seven."

"Eight, Benny. You got Toby and Gord, so they can start at seven. I'll be there at eight. Maybe even a little earlier, but no later."

"All right, eight," Benny conceded. "See you then."

"Yeah. Later."

Disappointed, Gus hung up and did a slow turn in his living room. He didn't think about the little white lie he told Benny about needing to take a shower. The night was supposed to belong to Tammy and him. Their night. Without a Mollymart.

"Shit," he muttered and fumed, hating how things refused to work out at times.

In the end, he dialed Tammy's number.

"Hello?" she answered three rings later.

"Ah, yeah, hi babe, it's me. Listen, I'm sorry. Slight change of plans …"

3

Gus arrived at six forty-five, under the cover of darkness.

He wasn't sure if Mollymart East was built to the mall or vice-versa. Bright colorful signs lit up the starboard side, giving the building's vast expanse a grounded, intergalactic space freighter kind of vibe. A few vehicles were scattered along the parking lot, one even leaving as Gus turned into the mall's lane. Ignoring all the attractive lighting illuminating the various shops and restaurants inside the commercial mecca, he pulled up to the west side of the superstore and saw his crew waiting. Checking his mirrors, Gus drove toward them.

Gord spotted him first, then Toby. Both men stood against Gord's hatchback, wearing clean coveralls with paint rags hanging out of their pockets, looking like a pair of unimpressed thirty-year-olds.

Of Benny, there was no sight.

Gus parked alongside the little hatchback.

Temperatures had dropped to a pleasant twenty or so, with the night sky in full starry brilliance. A quarter moon rose on the horizon and, as Gus got out of the truck, a nice smell of burning leaves caught his attention.

He went to the back of the truck.

"He got you, eh?" Toby said as he appeared, leaning against the back of Gordon's hatchback. "Thought you were going for some honeytime with the lady?"

"She's sick."

"Ah."

"Gord," Gus greeted.

The little man nodded in typical Gord fashion. Though the painter stood at only five seven and a half, the man had a reserved air about him, as if he

17

were destined for life beyond the stars, and certainly beyond his current plot in life. He sported a profound beard, meticulously trimmed, had his scalp buzzed down to a black fuzz, and had a dark complexion that made him look Italian. Regardless of the detached vibe emanating from the guy's very pores, Gord was professional to the extreme.

"Gus," he replied in turn, in that whispery gunslinger voice of his that won over the ladies. "Got the gear in there?"

"Some," Gus said and faced the men. "Y'know, never noticed before, but in these lights," he said and waved a finger around the parking lot, "dressed like we are, we look like we should be making ice cream or something."

The others didn't disagree.

"Where's Benny?" Gus asked.

"Should be here soon," Gord said, narrow eyes gleaming. "Not seven yet."

No one questioned if Benny would be on time or not. Benny was always on time.

"He's got the rest of the gear," Gus informed them. "What we need, anyway."

Gord grunted, and the three men stood silent for a moment, each thinking about better places to be that night.

Off in the distance, a police siren rose and drifted away. Living room lights and street lamps lit up a subdivision across from the mall. A pair of shadows speed-walked along a sidewalk, their arms chugging. A dog started barking and wouldn't shut up.

"Christ, what a shithole," Toby muttered, as if he'd woken up and realized where he lived for the first time.

Gus and Gord had the good sense not to comment. Gord, in particular, looked to his sneakers without interest, just killing time before it killed him back.

"I mean, seriously," Toby rumbled in a disbelieving voice. "Look at this place. Subdivision over there. Another one that's one street back of the place. On lots Gus could barely fit his ass onto."

Gus frowned at the dig but wasn't completely offended. He'd had shit slung at him all his life because of his size, and in bigger, more sustained clumps.

"Fifty years ago, the churches drew the faithful," Toby continued. "Now it's fuckin' malls."

No one joined the conversation. A group of teenagers slammed the doors to a jacked-up pickup and walked, giggling and joking, toward the main entrance. The three painters watched them because they were the only interesting thing in the parking lot.

"Didn't this place have roof issues back in 2020?" Gord asked.

"It did." Toby answered.

"I don't think malls are doing that well," Gus added after a time, hooking his thumbs into his overalls. Brush-It men had to look the part.

"A lot of folks shop online, nowadays," Gord added.

"Online shopping," Toby scoffed. "You're fooling yourself, Gordo. Picking up sweatshop goods at discount prices. You should be ashamed of yourself."

Gus kept his mouth shut, but he knew one thing: Gord hated it when Toby called him Gordo.

Gord cleared his throat. "So, you prefer to shop at mega corporations striving for market dominance by undercutting all the smaller family-owned businesses and forcing them out of business?"

"I don't shop here," Toby said defensively.

"Yeah? Where do you pick up all your designer shit?"

"Flea markets, man. The underground economy."

Gord didn't seem that impressed. "Best keep that to yourself."

"Where do you shop, Gus?" Toby asked.

"For what?"

"Shit."

"I don't buy shit."

"Groceries then?"

"Co-op. I get a member's discount."

"Oh. How's that working for you?"

Gus shrugged.

Gord took to studying the building. "Place doesn't even have a laundromat."

"Or a movie theatre," Toby pointed out.

Gus looked at the place. "Oh, we're on this side. There's a Big Wings on the back."

A car pulled into the parking lot on the far side, gracefully turned, and turned its low beams on the three painters.

"There's our boy," Toby announced.

Red tail lights flaring, Benny stopped his mid-sized SUV alongside the Brush-It truck.

"Six fifty-eight," he announced, slamming the door behind him. Benny rounded the corner and shook his head at his foreman. "You're way early."

"Didn't wash my dick," Gus said. "Saved myself a few minutes."

Benny frowned. He wasn't fond of dick jokes.

"Where's your overalls, Benny?" Toby asked.

"Yeah, Benny," Gus agreed suspiciously, taking in the owner's pressed blue collared shirt smartly tucked into beige no-wrinkle pants. He had a crease down the right side of his scalp that positively glistened.

"I'm not painting tonight," he replied in an *I-ain't-touchin-that-thing* tone, and upon seeing Gus's jaw twitch, he quickly added, "I'm *management*. I'd only be in the way. Besides, there's no need for me. Three of you can roll this in no time. You'll see when we get up there."

"What's that I smell?" Gus asked.

Gord and Toby sniffed, sniffed and scowled, and exchanged questioning looks. A wary Toby leaned forward, sniffing all the way, toward Benny ... who rolled his eyes.

"That cologne, Benny?" Toby asked in mock alarm. "Is that a faint yet very masculine eau de shit water?"

"You going somewhere, Benny?" Gus joined in, confirming the aftershave with an air-clearing wave.

"You got a *date*?" Toby pushed with roguish delight.

Benny was at a loss for all of two exceptionally long seconds. "All right, you guys. Back off. Just back off. And no, I don't have a date, all right? Just thought I'd get cleaned up for the night."

The men took in that explanation when Gord piped up with that gunslinger's voice of his. "I call bullshit."

"Yeeeah," Toby said, stretching out the syllable. "I second bullshit. She's a babe, isn't she, Benny?"

It was dark, so Gus couldn't determine the level of embarrassment on Benny's face, but the man fluttered as if kicked in the head.

"No swearing on the job," Benny warned with a finger.

"Job's over there," Toby said. "We're in the parking lot. So fuck it."

"So we are," Benny allowed and indicated the rear of his SUV with his chin. "All right. Gus, scratch your balls now and get it over with. Gord, do what you do. And you," he directed at Toby, "just keep your mouth shut. You leave your cell phone at home?"

"You're changing the subject," Toby said.

"Because you know the only phone to be on site is the company phone."

"Aw Benny—"

"No 'aww Benny' me—you're lucky I kept you on after Mr. Murphy caught you playing poker online. In his kitchen, no less. I mean, really? On a job site? Keep doing stuff like that and I'll have to draw up an official document for that kinda behavior. I don't understand you Toby. You don't see Gus or Gord trying that stuff."

"Look," Toby said seriously, "It was a bad time in my life. I'm over it. And thanks again for keepin' me on."

"Thank these two. They're the ones who vouched for you. Now start grabbing shit and come on."

With that, the boss picked up a notepad, took a tablet in his hand, and walked for the Mollymart's automated doors.

No sooner did Benny turn his back when dirty smiles erupted all around, including Gord. Benny was getting good at changing subjects, especially when deflecting attention away from himself.

The lads loaded up on painting tools and supplies. There was a fresh batch of plastic and cloth drop sheets. Carrying what they could, they followed Benny to the entrance.

"She's a babe," Toby whispered slyly, a paint can hanging from each hand and a drop cloth under each armpit. "The Miller chick is a babe. You just wait."

Gord didn't comment. Gus honestly didn't care. He was spoken for, and Gord was married. Toby was single for all intents and purposes and regularly participated in social safaris and exploring the urban wild. As did Benny.

A pair of four automated doors opened. A long shopping cart bay was located to the right, just behind a waist-high dispenser for sanitizing wipes. A second set of inner doors opened for the guys, between shelving units containing bagged loaves of bread. A few candy machines were against a wall, along with a huge pop machine with an enlarged bottle decorating the front. Florescent lighting as sterilizing as the hand wipes glared overhead. Inside the second barrier of doors, well out of range of the sensors so as not to send the system into a spastic fit of opening and closing, stood Benny.

Talking with the regional manager of Mollymart East.

Who just happened to be a babe.

Raven-haired with business glasses to match, meaty hourglass figure, classy black skirt four fingers above the knee, and a blue shirt with the top two buttons undone, and a set of boobs that were lifted like attentive puppies smelling barbeque. She was a little heavy around the middle, with angular hips that seemed almost fabricated.

Joan Miller was a solid seven point five.

Don't objectify, Gus told himself, hearing Tammy's voice in his head. *Don't objectify. Do* not *objectify*.

He glanced around, casually inspecting the immediate supermarket displays of fresh fruit, a deli on the right, and then Toby's profile—a decidedly *muted* profile, but that sleepy façade didn't fool Gus.

Toby was objectifying.

Toby was objectifying *hard*.

Gord was not objectifying. He looked like he was sleepwalking. Truthfully, Gus could not read the man or his undoubtedly deep-running thoughts. Gord would kill in Vegas.

The three painters passed through the inner doors, their strangers-in-a-saloon swaggers halting before the professional-looking couple. Benny was smiling, not so much that it would hurt to look at him, but the harsh lighting made his teeth gleam wetly. Gus thought they looked good together, suspecting both to be in their late thirties, no doubt already past comments of how their identical blue shirts made them twins.

Twins.

Gus didn't think that was Freudian in the least.

Benny turned away from the lovely Ms. Miller, a delighted expression of *ah, here are the lads* forming.

"Here's the crew," Benny said.

They met amongst a veritable tossed salad of uncut fruits and vegetables on display.

"This is Toby, Gord, and Gus." Benny introduced them, flicking a gun-finger at each. "The heart of the company."

A smiling Ms. Miller nodded at them. "Nice to meet you all," she said in a reserved and oddly nasal baritone.

"They'll have your office done by midnight," Benny promised. "At the latest."

Gus hated it when he did that.

"Wonderful," Ms. Miller said. "Well then, I'll leave you to it. Good evening gentlemen. I'm very much looking forward to seeing the office tomorrow morning."

All three smiled pleasantly in return.

"Benny," Ms. Miller said, wiggling her fingers at him in a flirty goodbye. She walked away from them, through an aisle where red, ripe strawberries were on one side and bananas on the other. Little signs sprouted from the fruit, announcing specials.

"This way," Benny said, drawing the three men in another direction. "*Toby.*"

Toby turned back from the departing regional manager, his face contorted with awe as if he'd just snarfed back a jalapeño. Benny motioned for them to follow him.

The four men entered a long aisle, and Toby slipped by the others to better position himself next to Benny. "Holy shit, you goin' out with her tonight?"

The boss man's head stared straight ahead.

"You dog you," Toby said.

"Keep your voice down," Benny warned.

"Hey, I'm just impressed. She's got it all. Weird voice, though. Sexy, but weird. Like a luxury liner's horn."

Benny shook his head, wanting no part of such a conversation. He pointed to a wall of mirrors one level up, presiding over the meat section and allowing a generous view of the Mollymart East shopping experience.

"Quit tryin' to change the subject," Toby said. "This your first date or what?"

"Listen, Toby, the only thing you need to concern yourself with is that office right there. And finishing the job before midnight. That's all. Do that and I'll see if she has a sister."

Toby wasn't looking at the aisle anymore. "You'd do that?"

"On condition you get the job done."

Shelves of canned mixed vegetables, carrots, and peas passed by, failing to tempt Gus in the least. Thank Christ they were walking down the canned food aisle and not the snack aisle. He wouldn't have made it past the first bag of Doritos.

"I feel motivated," Toby exclaimed happily and glanced back at Gord and Gus bringing up the rear. Gord looked half-asleep already.

At the aisle's end they turned right, walking around a tower of boxed crackers, both unsalted and salted. Open coolers dotted the rear lane in an easy maze of frozen foods. Signs displayed prices for cod nuggets, fillets, and other various goods. Behind the coolers and occupying the rear wall were well-lit shelves brimming with a grand assortment of packaged chicken, pork, and beef. The guys walked by it all, approaching a wide swinging door waiting with the words EMPLOYEES ONLY stamped upon its surface.

An open window where the surgical-looking meat cutting facilities were lay just beyond the door, the lights dimmed for the day.

"She give you a tour of the place, Benny?" Toby asked.

Benny pushed the swinging door open and led the guys through, ignoring the question. The storage area was a cluttered maze of shelves filled with boxed goods and plastic-wrapped flats, with at least two walk-in freezer units near the back. A sign for washrooms hung over one set of doors as well. Benny turned left and hiked up a wide set of stairs, toward an open hall.

"Benny?" Toby persisted.

"Buzz off, Toby," Benny grumbled. "You keep on with this line of questioning and the sister's off."

That shut the man up.

"Okay, so," Benny pointed to the right as he reached the second level. "Employee lounge and lockers are here. Nice view of the floor on the left here."

And it was. Beyond a series of one-way windows, Mollymart's aisles were laid out in wide, well-planned lanes underneath an exposed pipe and ventilation system resembling a robot's digestive tract. Large signs hung over the sections, displaying a short list of the items found there. Parts of the main entrance could be seen, and anyone sitting in the half-dozen or so chairs lining the wall only had to turn and look over their shoulders to watch the shoppers do their thing.

A single modern table with a blue and white vase was the only decoration in an otherwise drab-looking waiting area. The walls were painted in a brain-numbingly plain eggshell white.

"Must be the shop's colors," Gus commented.

"Think a place like this would invest more in their fuckin' colors." Toby said.

Benny stopped and glared a warning.

Toby held up his hands in apology. "Sorry. That one slipped out. There's no one around. I'm sorry."

Not pleased, the boss man went to the office manager's door at the end of the waiting area.

Toby looked back at Gus and Gord, widening his eyes in exaggerated fear.

A sign with "Regional Manager" had been fixed above the frame, and the black door looked like it should've belonged on a 1960's mansion somewhere in the countryside, where the first line of defense was an impenetrable barrier. Benny stopped, turned the knob, and swung the office door open wide.

The waiting-room whiteness continued inside and all the way around the room, so did the hip-high one-way glass on the left wall. Light from the floor shone through, causing the office walls and furniture to gleam. A huge hardwood desk, regal, and probably able to stop a battleship shell, was set before the opposite wall. A high, plush leather chair was behind the reddish-brown desk, and expensive wooden cabinets were behind that. A sleek-looking personal computer, the kind that could function as a tablet if needed, rested upon the desk. Green leaves crept along the top of the cabinets, indicating someone with a gardener's touch. A thin, well-kept carpet covered the floor, while pictures of Caribbean beaches and cruise ships lined the right wall, no doubt distracting Ms. Miller during times of boredom. Traces of a subtle fragrance hung on the air, distracting Gus as he entered. He didn't know what it was, but it was nice enough to make him wonder where he could buy some of the same. Tammy loved that shit.

Benny flicked on a light, illuminating the dream a little further.

The men gawked. Most of the offices they'd painted before were small business oriented, placed in the back of service centers or in the basements of homeowners.

This was an office.

This was an office of a regional *manager*.

"Whoa," Gus said for them all, taking in the polished majesty of the work area.

Toby immediately went to the desk, pushing aside a pair of wheeled chairs parked in front. He slid a hand across the wooden surface. "Mahogany. Sweet cheese and rice, Benny. This is mahogany."

"The cabinets aren't," Gord deadpanned, but his eyes wandered.

"This desk probably cost more than I make in a year," Toby stated with barely suppressed awe, his hand searching for the furniture's pulse.

"Which is why we're going to handle it all like live ordnance," Benny explained. "Got that? Extreme care. Everything gets covered twice. Nothing heavy on the desk or the cabinets. We move everything to the middle of the room and work around it. No banging this stuff through that door. Everyone good?"

Nods all around.

"Leather sofa too," Gus said and pointed, the piece just behind the door and tucked into the northeast corner. "Easy to miss when you see that thing first."

"I want one," Toby said, "and one of these." He rubbed his hands over the desk.

"All right, set up here," Benny said, closing the door and indicating the corner between the windows and the door. "This is base camp."

"She doesn't like the colors?" Gus asked, inspecting the walls.

"No, she doesn't approve."

That got the three men to trade looks.

"Stop that," Benny told them. "She's in a head office here, not an ice cream container with glass. I mean, look at this place. It's totally vanilla."

"She got a minibar around here?" Toby looked behind the desk. "Holy mustard pickles, she does. Right there."

He pointed to one end of the cabinets where a black refrigerator occupied the bottom section.

"That's a fridge," Gord clarified.

"Bet there's wine coolers in it. Or scotch. She a scotch drinker, Benny?"

Benny didn't answer.

"What's that smell?" Gus asked.

"Sandalwood," Gord answered and ignored the looks. "Incense."

He pointed to an end shelf on the right end of the cabinets, where a wooden tray that resembled a miniature ski rested, with one hole situated in the curl of the wood.

"You sure?" Gus asked.

"I'm sure," Gord said, gravitating to the wall of windows.

"What color she want this, anyway?" Toby asked.

"Rose," Benny answered. "Apparently, it's a color of energy." He cleared his throat. "And action."

"Lust too, Benny," Toby remarked in a passionate tone, his face twisting into a caricature of desire. "*Lust.*"

Benny frowned. "Should've fucking known a fruit-loop like you would know something like that."

"Hey," Toby said. "Color psychology is a science and a hobby of mine. You be surprised why companies choose the colors they do. Not just picked at random, buddy-boy. We're all being manipulated by color schemes and patterns and we don't even know it. And where's that swear jar?"

"Door's closed," Benny said in a voice that dared Toby to say one syllable more.

Gord was behind the desk, inspecting the floor. "Got one of them plastic mats back here so the chair rolls easier."

Gus joined him, seeing the mat go all the way to the window. Ms. Miller, when she sat behind her desk, could roll herself over to the sill and just people-watch if she so desired.

Benny's phone jingled. He dug it out of a pocket. His face drooped. "All right, I gotta go," the boss announced, reading his message.

"Go?" Gus asked. "Go where? Thought you were going hang around here. Help move furniture."

"No, we went over that."

"He's got … other plans," Toby said in a whispery sizzle.

"And yeah, matter of fact, I do got other plans," Benny said, not appreciating the joke.

"With Ms. Regional Manager."

Red-faced, Benny opened the door. "You guys know what to do. All done by midnight. Not a scratch on anything and not a drop. And keep off the couch."

That last line he aimed at Toby.

"I'll check on things in the morning." And the boss man was gone, closing the door behind him.

In the resulting silence, the painters waited, their thoughts secret. When a good ten seconds passed, Gus pointed to the Mollymart shopping floor.

Benny was passing through the toilet paper and diaper aisle, walking as if he desperately needed to find a washroom.

"Why's he walking that way?" Toby asked.

"Looks like he's gotta take a dump," Gord added.

"The man's got other plans," Gus repeated.

Benny disappeared for a moment, the angle obscuring him, but a few seconds later, he reappeared. Ms. Miller was walking beside him, the back of her lovely head and Benny's easily identifiable as they passed through the inner doors and waltzed out into the night.

"That sweet smelling devil," Toby remarked. "God bless him."

"Well boys," Gus stated in a dusty drawl. "I'd say we're on our own."

"You say we're alone up here?" Toby asked.

Gus nodded, pretty certain that they were.

"Jesus fucking Christ for that," Toby blurted. "I was about to explode there. And for the record, I'm fucking that couch before I leave here this morning."

"You are not, sir," Gus said.

"Well, I'm jacking off on it. At least."

"If I see one drop of pudding on that leather," Gord said in that rattlesnake voice of his, "I'll roll your shitty-ass self into one of the freezers downstairs."

Toby scoffed with an airy *phttt*. "One drop. Who do you think you're talking to? I'll leave at least a bucket. Probably three. What do you say there, Gustopher?"

27

Gus watched the floor below, noting there weren't too many shoppers around on a Monday night. "Right about now, I say let him fuck it. Might as well get some revenge for agreeing to this. Fuck the couch, Tobe. Go balls deep. Ass fuck it if you want."

The furniture's dark cushions and supple crevices drew Toby's eyes. "I like how you think."

Gord ignored Toby and walked around the desk while eyeing the megastore's shopping area below. "Big store, all the same." He checked his watch. "Seven-thirteen."

Gus met his co-worker's eyes. "Go time?"

"Yep."

"How long to completion, y'think?"

The little man tabulated the time in a second. "The paint's dark. One coat will do. Four hours. Four-thirty, tops."

"That's what I was thinking."

"Tobe?"

"I concur."

"All right, then," Gord nodded at his co-workers. "Let's grease this crack."

4

"*Pah-wah*," Toby intoned while standing before the one-way glass, fingers clawing at the heavens. "I have *pah-wah*!"

"You have a problem," Gus stated, going for the desk. "Ya fuckin' nut. Grab the end of that."

Toby did as told, and together with Gord, the three of them grunted and pushed and pulled that monstrous slab of Amazonian wood to the center of the room. The desk didn't go easily, resisting the men to its best, albeit inert, ability as a dead weight. It dragged on the carpet and hooked in places. By the time the piece was out of the way, Gus was sweating as if he'd just been chased by rabid dogs.

"Holy shit," he panted, slapping the wood. "The old girl's a ton."

"I'd torch the fuckin' thing if I thought I could get away with it," Gord said, red-faced and stretching his back.

Toby sized up the door. "How they get the thing up here? That's a pretty tight fit."

"Just barely," Gus figured. "Okay. Couch is next."

The sofa was not quite as heavy, but the men struggled with it all the same. They transferred the piece to the waiting room, and that little bit of exercise drained them as well. Then went the chairs, coffee table, and anything small enough to go outside the office, contrary to Benny's instructions. A rocky slope slowly appeared in the waiting area.

"Gonna have a heart attack," Gus said, wiping his brow. "Right here. Just ... splat. You think I never did this before."

"You're fat," Gord told him plainly. "*Too* fat. And that's coming from me. And just so you know? If you do drop dead, I ain't giving you mouth-to-mouth."

"I'll give you mouth-to-mouth there, Gustopher." Toby offered.

"Fuck off."

They flipped chairs onto each other, unloaded the cabinets of various manuals and boxed software before walking them to the growing mass. A little island of furniture formed in the room's center.

"Time?" Gus asked.

"Twenty-five minutes," Gord reported. "The furniture took longer."

"We'll make it up on the rolling."

"We should."

"We will," Gus assured him. "We got a race track here."

Paintings were taken down and placed outside the room, but the nails remained. Gord switched on a small vacuum, and he sucked the cobwebs and dust bunnies out the corners while Toby and Gus wiped down walls and molding. The power outlet covers were removed and labeled. The shade for the fancy light fixture was taken down, immediately brightening the interior. Plastic drop sheets were unrolled over the mound of furniture and allowed to tumble onto the carpet. The guys overlapped the plastic with cloth, just for a little cushion, tugging the sheets tight to the baseboards. They plugged tack holes in the walls and trim with fast-drying putty, then scraped and sanded. Gus was happy to see there weren't too many holes. Toby made two trips to the Brush-It truck to gather up a final milk crate of tools, supplies, and a pair of stepladders. When he returned, Gus and Gord had almost finished prepping the room, covering the floor and furniture with protective layers.

"Took you long enough," Gord said. "Lose your way in the hand cream section?"

"Yeah, looking at the brands your wife likes," Toby smoothly responded. "I also might've had a little chat with one of the cashiers."

"We're on a clock, Toby," Gus reminded him, none too pleased.

"Sorry, sorry. I'm here now, so let's paint this box."

They started in. Paint cans were popped open. Stir sticks appeared. Trays were laid on the drop cloths.

Toby stopped at a milk crate and extracted a long tube filled with sealant. He affectionately rubbed the mini rocket-sized container. "Gotta nice tube of caulking here." he said. "Isn't this a nice tube of caulk? Brand new caulk too. Look at this. Seriously. I mean, who doesn't like a brand-new caulk? Who *wouldn't* want a brand-new caulk? Nice and thick. Nothin' better. Uh oh. There's a problem. This caulk's *uncut*. Can't have that. Where's the knife? Gotta slice the tip off this thing. Can't work with a carrot caulk. That shit's not right."

Gus and Gord exchanged looks.

"There's no need for caulking," Gus said, refusing to partake in the very old joke.

Toby looked mortified. "No caulk?"

"No caulk. Already went over it. Everything's been filled."

"Filled with caulk?"

Gord wearily shook his head as he inspected a roll of painter tape.

"Maybe I should go over everything again," Toby continued. "I mean, if there's any cracks, I gotta put caulk in 'em. Cracks gotta have caulk and then a little wet finger action. You know what I'm sayin'? Gotta have 'em. It's my job. Wet finger action and caulk. Lots of caulk."

Gus did not encourage the man.

"So there's no need, huh?" Toby said. "Well, goddamn. That's disappointing. Filling cracks with caulk is pretty much the best part about this job. Who filled those cracks with caulk?" an indignant Toby suddenly demanded, fists on hips. "Who filled *those* cracks with *my* caulk?"

"The last crew, I'm guessing," Gus muttered as he inspected a three-inch brush and then a one-inch.

"Did they give it a proper caulking?"

Gus stopped to rub at an eye. "You're wearing it out now, you know that, right?"

"Did they give it a proper caulking?" Toby insisted.

"Looked fine to me."

Toby relaxed. "Everything's filled? You're sure?"

"Pretty much."

"Filled with caulk." Toby reflected, and smiled a second later. "Nothing better, is there?"

Gus didn't say a word.

"That boy ain't right," Gord muttered.

Gus agreed and waved a brush at the man. "Toby, stop messing around and get to work."

Toby held up one hand while kneeling at the milk crate. "I'm puttin' the caulk down, Officer Gus. Okay? My caulk is back. Back in the box. I have holstered … my caulk."

"We gonna cover all these windows?" Gord asked, changing the subject.

"There's five," Gus noted. "Leave the middle one undone."

"Hey, dickhead," Gord fired at Toby. "Get over here and help me cover the windows. And then you can check the place over."

Toby nodded that he would indeed.

At exactly nine thirty-nine, the room was ready.

Brown paper shielded the office windows, except one. Drop cloths protected the floor and remaining furniture. Tape and paper covered the baseboards, molding, and sills. Tape also masked the outlets and any unmoveable permanent fixtures. The office resembled an enormous, somewhat unfilled, gift box. A paint bomb could go off inside the place and nothing important would be stained, not that the guys would make a mess. They might dribble here and there, but for the most part, they rarely lost more than a drop. The cover was down, just in case.

Stepladders were set up. Toby poured paint into trays and smaller containers. He and Gord would start cutting in corners and brush around the room while Gus would work below.

The room quieted as the guys settled into the calm before the rolling. Gord's face screwed up as he inspected the deep pinkish hue while Toby emptied a can.

"What's wrong?" Gus asked, sensing something other than latex paint.

"Rose," Gord replied.

"Yeah?"

"Rose paint," Gord clarified.

"Yeah, so?"

"The ceiling too?"

Gus checked the four cans. "Yep. All rose."

The facial creases of Gord's disapproval deepened. "She weird or something?

"Maybe she likes rose," Toby interjected in mid-pour.

"Wasn't talking to you, y'freak," Gord muttered, then to Gus. "I mean, I like yellow, but I'm not gonna go full-on Chiquita."

"What's wrong with Chiquita?" Gus asked, scrutinizing the paint.

"Nothing's wrong with Chiquita. Chiquita's fine. I like Chiquita. But the whole room? This place is gonna look like the inside of a twat."

Gus supposed that was the case, but he didn't add to the conversation.

"Hey," Toby threw in, "if I'm inside a twat for eight hours a day, five days a week, pink is the color I wanna see. Pink. No black. No blue. And sure as hell no green or yellow."

Instead of firing back at the guy, a glimmer of amusement appeared on Gord's face.

"Don't listen to him," Gus said. "And rose is the only color here, so rose it is. Benny's out with the lady even as we speak, so I'm not going to think too hard over why she wants rose. It could be worse. A lot worse."

Paint brush and paint can in hand, Gord listened while readying his stepladder.

"Think about it," Gus said as he went to the nearest corner with his own brush. "It's only one coat. Worse case scenario—"

"The bitch don't like it and we get to do it again," Toby finished.

"Exactly. So, to me, rose is just rosy. You guys ready?"

Gord had one foot on his ladder in the rear left corner, where the desk would be returned. Toby was in the other corner. Both would work clockwise.

"Ready," Gord said.

"Ready," Toby repeated.

Gus frowned at the contents of the milk crate. He bent over and rooted around clean rags for cleaning up any potential excess, paint knives, and an assortment of spare brushes.

"Missing something?" Toby asked.

"Can't find the timer."

"In the other crate, there?" Gord asked.

Gus peered inside the second container. He held up a green-handled hammer—affectionately called "the whammer"—while searching the innermost corners.

"No," he reported after a second. "Nothing. Well, shit."

"It's in the truck?" Gord asked.

"Yeah. Must be. And if not, there's a spare anyway."

"Don't really care for the timer," Toby said. "Like it better without. Less stress."

"More efficient with the timer," Gord explained, sounding more patient than he was. "More focus. Better painting. Proved time and time again."

Gus flicked a thumb across his nose. "I'll get it. You guys start. Only take me ten minutes out and back. No trouble. We'll have this place done in no time, anyway."

"I need a beep of some kind," Gord said. "Can't start without a beep."

"When I close the door, that's your beep."

That satisfied the painter.

"Don't you make any time with those cashiers," Toby warned.

Gus left. He didn't see the men start.

The remaining furniture had been stacked into an angular briar patch to one side of the waiting room, allowing Gus to walk by the clutter without worry. In a few seconds, he pushed his way through the swinging doors and walked through an aisle loaded down with household goods. He believed the time somewhere around nine forty-five or just past that, and for a Monday night, he figured anyone out were ones who worked weekends.

He briskly marched past the fruit section, empty of shoppers. Though the job should be finished before midnight, there was still the issue of moving all the furniture back into place, which would best be done in the morning, allowing the paint to dry. Gus sighed to himself. Either Benny was a little too quick, or he forgot to mention something.

The deli tempted him fierce when Gus waltzed by the assorted meat trays, the glazed hams, and the ready-to-eat barbeque chicken. He wondered where that food would go if they failed to sell. One of the greater mysteries of the universe. Unsold food. A man and woman wearing white aprons and hats muddled about behind the deli counter. The woman met his eye before returning to her work.

Upon exiting the superstore, a nice breeze moved across Gus's freshly shaved chin. He counted a dozen cars on the parking lot, most stopped close to the main doors, but others were spread out. The odd vehicle cruised along the main road while engines revved somewhere deeper in town. Gus walked to the Brush-It truck. The horizon above the vehicle was softly lit with stars.

He stopped for a moment, just appreciating the view.

Toby had called the city a shithole. Taking in all that celestial beauty of the night sky, Gus disagreed with a contented smile. He wondered about Tammy. An asshole of an inner voice reprimanded him for taking the job, chastised him for not thinking it through enough, but Gus heard Tammy's words as well. He promised he'd take her out someplace nice when he got paid. Pizza Hut, maybe.

The timer, a little white handful with three blue buttons, was in the glove compartment, and Gus had no recollection of placing it there. He grabbed it and secured the vehicle.

A ghostly dirge of sirens came from somewhere in the valley, causing him to stop and wonder. The cops had a busy one on their hands this night. And it wasn't even a Friday.

Taking another look at the heavens, Gus walked back to Mollymart's main entrance. He glanced over his shoulder once and saw a silhouette racing along the street in a flat-out sprint. The sirens ceased, and for the briefest moment, the frenetic, far-off slap of sneaker soles hitting sidewalk perked his ears.

Interspersed with—

Gus slowed, not quite certain of what he was hearing.

But it sounded like panting.

Very heavy, very energetic panting—belonging to a dog, perhaps a minute into chasing down a rabbit.

But then the sirens started and the automated doors slid open.

Gus entered without giving the sounds another thought.

5

Back in the office, the guys had made good time.

Gord had cut in nearly most of his wall while Toby was finishing his own section.

"Got it?" Gord asked upon Gus's return.

Gus held up the device and inspected the completed work. "Looks good, boys. Looks good."

"What's it like outside?" Toby asked.

"Cooler. Cops are on the prowl. Heard their sirens somewhere over the hills."

"Not even Friday," Gord stated stoically. "Set the thing up by the phone there. My timing's all off now. Feel like I was rushing or something."

"How'd you guys get into timers anyway?" Toby asked.

"Before your time," Gus answered. "Ask Benny about it. He read an article on increasing productivity levels."

"Increasing stress levels."

"There's good stress and there's bad stress," Gus continued. "For example, say if Ms. Miller also said she'd pay us an extra hundred bucks or so if we finish the room by midnight, that's positive stress. Negative stress would be, say, if Gord there promises to kick your teeth in if you don't finish the office at the same time."

"Shit works," Gord said. "That's all I know."

"Prefer a radio or something," Toby noted. "Background noise."

"Here's some noise for ya." Gus placed the timer on the covered-up desk, next to the company cell phone. Sharp little beeps sounded as he set the device for thirty minutes.

"You guys ready?" he asked, picking up his own brush and paint.

Nods from his co-workers.

"Start," he said, tapping the button.

The men returned to painting, plunging the room in an eerie calm where the only sounds came from the silky glide of sure roller and brush strokes. Gus commenced his work at the windows, cutting the trim with a smaller brush, drawing a rosy line straight down the side while the others swished their way around the room. With a hand so rock-steady it might've been in a plaster casing, Gus went down the length of the window, dabbing his brush in his little paint can when needed. He secretly loved his job. For all the shit he sometimes had to put up with, and the occasional weirdo he had to work with or for, Gus loved to paint. Loved working with latex. There was nothing better than applying a fresh coat of color to something. Despite his dislike of the heat, he preferred working outdoors best, but only on cloudy days, when the sun couldn't penetrate as much. When the winds blew across the Fundy shoreline and carried that fresh smell of mudflats and salt water, well, there was nothing better. Setting and prepping a place was really the worst part of the operation, and cleaning up wasn't much fun either, but everything in between, the actual slapping paint to a surface, that was as fine as dark chocolate.

Thirty minutes in, the timer went off.

"Break time," Toby announced, leaving his brush across the paint can's top.

Gus studied his work. Sharp, damn near perfect. Two windows left to cut.

"Five minutes," Gord announced, and set the timer again.

"Just thinking," Toby started, standing at the base of his ladder. "We gonna eat anything tonight?"

"Wasn't planning on it," Gus admitted.

Gord shook his head. "I didn't bring anything."

"Plenty of grub down there," Toby pointed out. "I think I spotted a couple of roast chickens at the deli."

"They got sandwiches too," Gus remembered.

"They any good?" Gord asked.

"Don't know. I don't shop here much."

"I don't shop here at all," Toby said.

"I go to Finnegan's," Gord said.

"There's that Big Wings on the back there."

"I ain't goin' to no chicken wing place," Gord said. "It's either from below or nowhere. A sandwich will do me."

Gus looked out the only uncovered window. There were three people down there shopping, the tops of their heads visible. One of them browsed near the front, amongst the fruit and vegetables.

"What do they do with the food if they can't sell it?" Gus asked.

"Probably dump it," Gord said with a frown.

"Think so?"

"Yeah."

"Better to give it away, isn't it? Homeless shelters. Old folk's homes."

"Maybe they do," Gord said. "But I'm guessing they dump it. Sell whatever they can, inspecting what's left over from the day before and tossing the rotten stuff out. Not saying they do, but that's my guess."

"You know that we lose or throw away up to thirty percent of grown food before it ever gets to market?" Toby piped up, nodding at the floor outside the office window. "Thirty fuckin' percent of a harvest. Fuckin' crime when you think how many people go to bed hungry. And you know why?"

Gord and Gus waited, knowing Toby was going to tell them anyway.

"Because it fuckin' looks funny."

"What?" Gord asked.

"That's fucked up," Gus added.

"That's what they do, swear to God," Toby said. "If a potato looks like it's shaped like a crooked testicle, they chuck it. Carrots with two dicks? Into the garbage. Anything that doesn't conform to our perfect image of what vegetables or fruit should be becomes garbage and gets tossed out. Ain't that something? If it's got a little brown bruise on it and someone thinks we won't buy it, it doesn't make it to market. If the shape isn't appealing, gone. And don't get me started on table scraps. That shit's nasty. They fill up your plates with whatever, way too big portions, and whatever's not eaten, into the can."

"Huh," Gus said matter-of-factly, wondering if Toby wasn't making a subtle point about him being overweight.

"Yeah, right," Gord aimed at Toby. "I bet you toss out your food scraps."

"I do not. My fridge is packed with leftovers. I'll fuckin' pinch the mold offa strawberries if I got to. Same for everything. I cook in small portions, man. I cook in small portions. You know there's folks up in northern Labrador and Quebec where they pay damn near two grand a month on their groceries? Two grand a month. You think about that next time you order a pizza."

"Hey," Gord squared his shoulders, "if I'm payin' for—"

The buzzer went off, signalling break time was over and effectively cutting Gord off. He frowned and reset the timer.

"So, we gonna get something to eat later on or what?" Toby asked again.

"After that little rant?" Gord asked.

"Hey," Toby ascended his ladder. "I was just sayin'. Bringin' some awareness into your lives about your food. Don't kick the messenger in the nuts. I didn't mean we not eat while we were here."

"No, we're not getting anything to eat," Gus said, annoyed at the man. "Just because the job's supposed to be done quick. We do it quicker without eating."

"I'm feeling hungry now."

"Goddamn it, Toby," Gus moaned. "Just paint, okay?"

"I wouldn't mind something later," Gord said. "I did see sandwiches down there."

"The subs?" Toby asked. "I saw those too. They looked good."

"Jesus Christ," Gus muttered, not surprised at the quick, morally tormenting change of conversation.

"Just sayin," Toby said. "Gotta eat sometime. Can't do anything about wanton waste tonight. And we're here. Bet there's plenty down there with special discount stickers on them. Those are the ones that are about to be tossed. So, essentially, we would be doing our part by picking up those."

"I don't know if he's serious or not," Gord muttered. "But I'm leaning toward full of shit."

"I'm already there," Gus said.

"Everyone on their mark," Gord announced and started the timer.

They resumed painting. Gus started on the window right of center. He'd worked with Toby for five years now, after a string of guys didn't work out or who moved on to better things.

There was Austin who went into refrigeration. Joe Miner left for Alberta and hadn't been heard from or seen since. Jane Sweeter married a car dealer and started working on the lot. Gus remembered Darce, the football player, one of the guys who didn't work out. Nice enough to work with and eager, but once he got on site and realized he occasionally had to climb a forty-foot ladder, well, he discovered he could only manage the first rung. Fear of heights in the painting business was rare but understandable. Not that Gus had any problem with climbing. He even offered to take care of the high stuff and Darce could work below—but Darce still left the next day. Gus wasn't sure if Darce was second or third string or if he ever made it to the CFL. There were others who moved on or didn't work out for one thing or other, but Gord was the rock in the little company. A no-nonsense, pitter-patter kind of worker who could've gone out west like a lot of tradespeople but decided to make a go of it locally.

"How long we been working together now, Gord?" Gus asked as he sized up the paint levels in his can.

"Long enough that you should know not to ask," Gord said from where he worked.

Touché.

"No, really."

Silence.

Which was Gord's respectful way of saying don't ask.

"Ten years?" Gus continued, ignoring the timer completely. "Fifteen? Twenty?"

"I want to get out of here before midnight, Gus. Not discuss old times."

"Just wondering is all."

"Eleven. Eleven years. And I feel blessed every fucking day."

Gus pouted at that. Gord could be a sarcastic bastard when he wanted to. The man was solid at what he did. Dependable and reliable and owned a stake in the company, but a sarcastic bastard at times.

Gus dabbed his brush and sized up the window's side. He'd wasted a minute or two, but he'd get them back.

When the unfocused periphery of his eye caught movement. He arrested his painting and looked to the floor.

There, zooming up the middle of the canned fruits and vegetables aisle like a meatheaded missile, was a guy.

And the guy was screaming.

Spires of canned vegetables exploded.

Cardboard displays of unseen merchandise toppled.

The screamer plowed headlong through the lane, a human freight train with flailing arms, and suddenly *stopped,* as if clotheslined by the waist. The savage's three note wailing instantly became a neutered *guh*! and a shriek of rubber on tiles as his head dropped from sight.

"The fuck was that about?" Gord asked in offended amazement.

"Think it was a meth-head," Gus answered, lifting his chin to better see. Which he couldn't, as the screamer was completely out of sight. Probably curled up on the floor, cupping his lower guts—or worse, his boys—and writhing in pain.

"Makin' that noise?" Toby asked.

Gord crowded onto Gus's right side. Gus had to shield his brush from the glass to avert disaster.

"Jesus," Gord muttered.

"He slammed into something," Gus explained. "Damnedest shit. He was streaking down that aisle like a bolt of lightning and *bam*! Dropped out of sight."

"Maybe a gang banger," Gord said. "Coming up from the south. See it all the time on the news. Only a matter of time before they got—"

"Where?" Toby asked over Gus's right shoulder. The three painters filled the window and looked to the floor.

"Down there," Gus pointed.

"Fucking bangers," Gord said.

"I don't think it was a banger."

"Can't see shit," Toby complained.

"Maybe it was a meth-head then," Gord said. "Or worse. Some other synthetic shit that hooks you just by being in the same room. Drives you crazy."

A shopper tentatively leaned around one corner, fearful of what he might see, and checked on what happened to the scream. The scene resembled a timid mouse attempting to navigate a maze laced with pointy traps.

A scrotum-tightening shriek blasted the aisle just as a dark head popped into view. The head wobbled a bit as if he wore bedsprings on his soles. An arm lashed out, wildly, sending a brief squall of silvery cans onto the floor. The bounce and rattle of metal echoed throughout the store.

"That guy's fucked up," Toby said for them all.

The screamer spotted the shopper peeking around the corner.

And broke into full-on offensive tackle mode.

"Oh shit," Gus hissed as that charging head and shoulders came into greater view.

The shopper immediately retreated and ran, shocked by the stampeding person.

The screamer banked on a dime, failed to anticipate the lack of friction on the megastore's tiles, and launched himself over a large cooling unit. Inertia carried the body to the other side of the cooler, where the screamer, still screeching as if something pink was caught in a zipper, struggled to rise. The man stood awkwardly, mashing boxes of fish nuggets underfoot, and attempted to free himself of the cooler and its contents.

He took one step forward and fell to the floor.

Face first.

"*Oooo*," the three painters gasped as a collective, hearing the solid connection of face on tile.

The screamer promptly bounded to his feet, unaffected by the fall. He regained his bearings and sprinted after the last known position of the fleeing shopper, who was already well into the cereal and baking goods section.

"The hell?" Gord said.

The shopper shouted for help, shouted for someone to call the cops.

The screamer scrabbled after him. Not only was the screamer loud and resilient, he was *fast*, and quickly gained ground on his quarry.

Other heads began appearing around the edges of the scene, drawn to the developing chase and unrelenting cacophony. The shopper exited the baking aisle, heading toward Mollymart's entrance. People near the front stopped and wildly looked around, attempting to ascertain the danger level.

The shopper bobbed around the fruit displays.

The screamer went over the fruit displays in a violent spray of citrus matter. Oranges crashed to the floor. Lemons and limes bounced.

The shopper darted out the inner doors and disappeared.

The screamer rose, unhurt. A different voice shrieked, distracting the screamer. Three people fled to and crammed themselves through a red door. The last person glanced fearfully back at the rampaging individual, quickly closing the distance.

The door slammed shut just as the screamer struck it.

And struck it.

And continued to strike it, beating out a furious rhythm of meat and bone. While screaming.

BOOMBOOMBOOMBOOM!

"The hell is he on?" Toby said in mystified awe.

"Banger could be on anything," Gord supplied.

"Oh shit," Gus whispered, feeling his guts twist and churn.

The screamer put his hand through the door's surface, and though the distance had to be well over a third of a football field, there was still no trouble seeing the wooden surface of the door go from flat to gloss. The screamer bucked and wailed and struck the door again. Fluid splashed.

"Is—is he bleeding?" Toby asked.

"That sick bastard is definitely bleeding," Gus confirmed.

The screamer stopped pounding. He turned, face covered in a frightful scarlet sheen. Something moved beyond Gus's line of sight, but the screamer picked up on it immediately. He took off from the door, arms chugging at his sides, and periodically blinked in and out of sight as he passed a line of checkout counters and upright coolers.

A woman squawked and ran, flushed out into the opening.

6

The woman bounded around a tall cooler filled with juice cartons and eggs.

The screamer followed.

A metallic *tonk*! reached all the way back to the regional manager's office.

Gus didn't wait for Gord or Toby. He was already moving for the door. The boys were right behind him. They descended and raced through the store, closing in on the last place of sighting. A handful of other people were gathering around the juice coolers.

Faces—concerned and freaked out—turned when the painters arrived.

In the middle of the floor, a woman sat squarely on a significantly smaller screamer person. She was hefty—brown haired and big boned—and she held, by a long handle, what appeared to be a huge black cast iron frying pan. Blood dripped from the pan to the floor, into an expanding pool that contrasted with the white tiles. Six other people surrounded her and her prisoner.

But that wasn't what got Gus's attention.

What got his attention was the screamer.

The guy's nose was a squashed strawberry that dribbled and spewed red, and even though the woman had clocked the screamer's ticket with a full on frying pan to the face, he still moved.

Or at least tried to move to the best of his limited ability. His head raved left and right, up and down, sending bright drops flying and spattering metal and tiles.

And he continued to scream.

"Shut up," the woman warned in a voice not to be challenged. She looked down while shifting her considerable butt to keep her captive in place. "Shut up or I hit you again! Shut *up* I said, you!"

But the screamer did not shut up. In fact, the screamer became increasingly wormy, as the subduing effects of the frying pan wore off.

One of the male shoppers stepped back from the circle. "I'm calling the cops." He said and went to a corner where two lines of freezers met.

The screamer howled at the words, but facedown as he was, with perhaps a three-hundred-pound-plus woman planted on his center of gravity, he could do little else. His arms waved, wide arcs that created bloody wings upon the floor, but his joints prevented him from doing anyone harm.

Realizing his situation, the screamer pulled in his arms. He squirmed and planted his hands as if about to attempt a push-up.

"I *strike*," the big woman warned and readied that cast iron mallet.

The screamer ignored her. He thrashed underneath as if he were the world's angriest trampoline.

As promised, the big woman struck.

The frying pan clanked into her prisoner's profile, subduing him instantly. The gathered shoppers flinched at the unexpected connection. She ignored them and lifted her weapon, inspecting the guy's pale and bloodied face.

A red bubble popped on his mashed lips.

"He's alive," she grimly informed the onlookers. "For now. Did you call the cops?"

The man near the freezers held up a finger, indicating he was still on the case.

"The hell is going on?" asked a dark-haired woman in her early twenties, wearing a set of librarian's glasses.

"He's crazy," the Frying Pan Woman said with the slightest accent. She had a chubby face, a plain and clear complexion, and angry eyes that matched her hair color. "Running around like that. Screaming like crazy man. Crazy. Just crazy."

"You're gonna get arrested," said a third woman.

The Frying Pan Woman scowled in dismissal. "Self-defense."

"Actually, it's not," said a younger man with mousey facial features and wearing glasses with square frames. "He was chasing her," he pointed at the third woman, who looked positively white from the ordeal. "And when she rounded the corner, she—" the finger went to the sitting woman with the frying pan, "clocked him."

The screamer stirred.

"Jesus Christ," another of the men muttered. "He's coming around."

"You got the cops yet?" Frying Pan Woman asked in a loud, earthshaking tone of voice. *Natural projection* came to Gus's mind.

"Can't get through," the caller in the corner reported. "All the lines are busy, and I'm getting recordings."

"He's coming around," Toby pointed out. "Get ready to whack him again."

"She already whacked him like three times," the third woman protested. "I wouldn't be surprised if she hasn't given him brain damage."

"So, what?" Frying Pan Woman asked with a glare. "He was going to hurt us."

"He didn't hurt anyone," the other woman countered, setting her feet.

"He scared the shit out of me," muttered one of the men. A portly, ruddy-cheeked soul, getting control over his fright. By the size of his paunch—barely contained in a blue striped shirt where the tails hung over his belt line—he'd consumed more than his share of burgers.

"Me too," said another man.

A fourth woman raised her hand.

"Look," the third woman said and drew breath to go in full-on lecture mode. Gus could tell she was going to clarify procedures to adhere to and the consequences that might possibly ensue if those procedures were not followed to the letter.

Trouble was, the screamer's eyes popped open, red-rimmed and furious. A low whistle of a whine issued from him, one that grew into a power chord of absolute hatred. He again attempted to free himself from the two-ton jailor sitting on his back.

"So, you want me to let him up?" Frying Pan Woman asked The Bitch, as Gus so thought of her.

The Bitch backed up, suddenly unsure of herself, watching the struggling screamer.

"Huh?" Frying Pan Woman asked, now actively keeping him down. "Because if you say so, I'll let him up. Where you're standing, I think he'll go straight for you. Maybe you know something about the law eh? Maybe he'll ask you to be—to be his witness or something eh? What do you think?"

But The Bitch had sidestepped and distanced herself from the scene, just in case the Frying Pan Woman did indeed release the screamer.

"No?" Frying Pan Woman inquired. "Okay then." She took a firmer grip on her weapon of choice. "You got the cops yet?"

"No cops!" the guy in the corner replied.

"Well, I can't *sit* on this prick all night," Frying Pan Woman exclaimed. "You, cashier!"

Heads turned. Two cashiers stood a dozen steps back. A man and a woman in their late twenties. The guy resembled a walking cadaver, with sunken cheeks and a thin mustache. His name tag designated him as "Walt." The woman was slim, bespectacled, with short-cropped platinum hair. Her names tag said "Rebecca."

"You got tape or something to tie this guy up with?" Frying Pan Woman asked.

Walt nodded and ran.

Just as Frying Pan Woman lurched to one side.

Her arms went out for balance and one leg kicked out as the screamer underneath her, yowling like a trapped cat with a microphone, seemed to get a second wind.

Gus stomped on an elbow, pinning it to the floor, hating the feel of flesh and bone under his sneaker. Toby, cringing with a mixture of revulsion and determination, planted himself down on the screamer's back legs, trapping them under his backside and grabbing a pair of kicking legs. He fastened his arms around the limbs and held on.

Gord joined the guy in the freezer corner, to better supervise calling efforts.

The guy with the paunch stood back and held up his own cellphone, recording the events with glassy-eyed wonder.

Gus wanted to slap that thing out of his hand. "Get some paper towels or dish towels or something!" he yelled, struggling to keep one arm pinned. "Clean up this blood!"

But Paunch Guy with his camera only backed up a step and did no such thing.

"Don't get any of that on you," one of the women warned. "He could be infected with something."

"Great," Frying Pan Woman said. "You infected with something, you sonnavabitch? Huh? If you are, I'll fucking *flatten* you right here. Just like the shitty-assed bastard you are. I don't give a shit."

The mousy guy with glasses joined Gus, stomping on a spidery hand slicked with blood. The screamer flexed and yanked himself free, so the mousy guy clenched teeth and planted shoe heel to elbow.

Gus questioned him with a look.

"Sorry," Mousy Guy said. "Just tryin' to not get any of that blood on me."

That was a good idea. There was so much shit on the go that who knew what might be going through one junkie's veins.

Except—

The screamer tore his arm out from underneath Gus, throwing the painter off-balance. He teetered toward the juice coolers but righted himself before gravity pulled him down.

The screamer had his *third* wind, and while scalding them all with near-black eyes, he tried to get up once again.

"Jesus!" Frying Pan Woman blurted as she *gonged* the screamer once more. Then again. Then a third time, swatting the guy like he was a cockroach refusing to die. She filled her lungs to deliver a fourth blow, lips drawn back with furious intent.

"*Knock that shit off!*" Gus ordered her.

That verbal command unlocked something in her. She stopped swinging that unforgiving iron slab and stared at Gus for seconds, seconds in which the intent to subdue or worse left her eyes. She glanced at her prisoner and visibly paled.

Half the screamer's face had split apart from his temple to mid-cheek, while his eyes were vacant and staring. Blood left his nose in wheezy spurts, as if someone were squeezing his lungs like near-empty ketchup bottles. Grunts left the bleeding form that twitched every second or two. The fingers of his right hand shivered as if his spine had been spiked. The screamer didn't make as much noise as before, but after the barrage he'd just sustained, it wasn't surprising. There could've been a halo of little birds circling his head, and that wouldn't have surprised Gus.

Interestingly enough, the screamer's wheezes became snores.

A despondent silence descended over the onlookers, gradually broken by footfalls rushing toward them.

Walt the cashier arrived with an armload of supplies. He had hand towels, sanitizer, and rolls of masking tape. Not duct, which Gus would've preferred, but he didn't complain.

"Holy shit," Gus swore, reaching for the towels. "Got any gloves in there?"

Walt shook his head. "I can get some though."

"We're good, I think."

The screamer snorted and coughed. A blast of organic jam hit the floor. His eyelids fluttered.

"Ew, Christ Almighty," Frying Pan Woman said, drawing back. "Gross."

"That's head trauma," The Bitch said, watching the events from afar. "You cracked his skull with that … that weapon! You better hope he doesn't have family because I can guarantee—"

"Shut the fuck up," Frying Pan Woman shot back.

Gus took the tape and pulled away a length. "You get this from the shop?" Walt nodded.

"Good man."

"You guys aren't *really* going to tape him up," The Bitch grated in a disbelieving voice. "No way. I mean, I can't believe you're doing this."

The four people on the screamer paused long enough to quietly reflect on the situation and assess their actions in the next few seconds.

And on cue, the screamer's snores ceased, and his limbs became weakly animate.

"Do him up," Gus ordered. "Just in case."

"*What?*" The Bitch wailed. "You recording this?" She aimed at Paunch Guy doing exactly that. To his credit, the Paunch didn't break filming to acknowledge her.

They covered the bloody parts in hand towels. Gus grabbed one of the guy's bare wrists and balked in horror at how the skin had split apart around the knuckles, revealing milky bone. Then he started rolling, lashing the wrists together, feeling the strength returning to the screamer's limbs. Tape ripped as it was applied. The woman with the librarian glasses backed up five feet, staring at the prisoner like he was a sack of dead and decomposing rats.

Gord came over. "Wrap up those feet too. And I mean *wrap* them. He's coming to, Gus, he's coming to."

The screamer *was* coming to, and Gus was no rodeo hand trying to tie off a struggling calf.

"Tape his mouth up," Gord directed.

Gus and Frying Pan Woman did a double-take.

"I ain't going near that mouth," Gus informed his co-worker.

Frying Pan Woman grabbed one of the unused hand towels and wrapped it over the screamer's head. "Tape that," she said. "It'll soak up the blood."

So, Gus did, covering up those black eyes in doing so, and remembering a time when he went fishing further down the valley and hooked an eel. The screamer wasn't squirming like that, but he was warming up, and clearly not as injured as they thought.

"All done back here," Toby reported.

"Wrists are done," Gus said, inspecting the thick layers and wondering if he'd gone overboard on the tape.

"I'm getting off him," Frying Pan Woman announced. "All right?"

"Yeah," Gus said. "On three we all let go, okay?"

They agreed.

"One, two, *three!*"

The crew released the screamer and quickly cleared the area.

The bound man became a full-on firehose filling with water. He straightened and contorted, yowling at his restricted movement. The towel taped to the guy's head hid everything except that bloody mouth, and that wasn't pretty to look upon in the least. The screamer twisted and mewled, rolling into the cooler's base. There he settled down but didn't completely relax.

"Gimme some of that," Gus said, taking the hand sanitizer from Walt's hands. "And get some more towels, would you?"

The cashier nodded and ran off again.

Gus squirted generous gobs of lotion into his palms before handing the container over—and realized for the first time how fucking *big* the woman who had sat down on and restrained the screamer was. She was perhaps two or three inches broader across the shoulders, and what Gus initially thought might've been fat was now in doubt. She moved quickly, didn't lumber, and carried her mass quite well. If he had seen her from behind, he might've thought of her as a small footballer regulated to second string defense.

"What?" she asked him, plainly, in a tone that very clearly implied he speak his mind.

Or else.

"You're a big one," Gus said.

Frying Pan Woman frowned while slathering her hands—which were large and tough-looking.

"I still can't get anyone on the phone," the guy in the corner reported.

"What?" Gus asked.

The guy shook his head. "They're not picking up. Goddamn it. We're on our own until we can get through."

"How long will that be?" asked the female giant on Gus's left.

"Until we can get through to someone," Gord repeated.

"I can't hang around here," The Librarian said. "I got places to be—things to do."

"No one's going anywhere," The Bitch informed them all. "This is a crime scene, and if anyone leaves, I'll make damn well sure the police know about it. Especially *you*," she directed at Frying Pan Woman. "What you did to that poor man was unnecessary, violent, and sickening. You're going to prison for what you did. I can guarantee it."

"Oh yeah?" Frying Pan Woman retorted. "Next time, I'll let him have your screaming ass, you ungrateful bitch. You weren't crying boo-hoo when he was coming after you through the aisles."

"That doesn't justify what you did."

"Bitch, are you *crazy*?" Frying Pan Woman said, pausing her sanitizing of those big farm-type mittens that passed for hands.

"No one's leaving," she warned and pointed a finger at Paunch. "He's got everything on camera there. The police will want to talk to everyone involved, and right now, *everyone* here is involved. I'll blow the whistle on anyone who tries leaving beforehand."

"Maybe I'll just sit on you for a while, huh?"

The Bitch tensed, poised to evade the larger woman if necessary.

"Easy, now," Gus said to Frying Pan Woman. "Just relax for a moment."

"Me relax? Tell *her* to relax. I put that crazy bastard down, and *I'm* getting shit on for it? Especially since he was going after her?"

Faces turned in The Bitch's direction.

"That true?" Gus asked.

"That doesn't make any difference," The Bitch responded indignantly, color rising to her cheeks. "I would've lost him anyway. The point is she exercised lethal force in subduing that poor man. Lethal force. You saw her. She whacked him with that frying pan five or six times. She would've kept *on* whacking him if you hadn't stopped her. He's got it all on camera."

Again, she pointed to Paunch Guy, who remained detached, observing events through his phone.

"Hey, dickhead," Toby said to the guy. "Give it a fuckin' break, will ya?"

But the guy ignored the request.

A bang distracted everyone then.

The screamer was twisting, *writhing* with serpentine fury on the floor. He twisted his arms and legs into painful-looking contortions that popped and strained joints. He slammed his head against the cooler's base. Dark flowers bloomed through the towel. The gruesome sight rendered the small group of shoppers and painters speechless, and they stood well back from the prisoner.

"So, we wait for the cops?" someone asked anxiously.

"Yeah," Gus said.

Frying Pan Woman said it for them all. "What do we do with him, then?"

"We keep him here."

"Buddy," the big woman said, "that one ain't gonna wait for the cops."

Gus met Toby's gaze, then Gord's.

"You guys got a freezer?" Gord asked the cashiers.

7

They loaded the screamer onto a wide dolly, which Walt fetched from the storage area of the superstore, or what he referred to as "out back." A burly guy with a shaved head and a name tag of "Nelson" came with the rig. Rebecca broke open a box of disposable plastic gloves and handed them to the folks handling the screamer. There were no protective rails on the dolly, so Gus and the Frying Pan Woman walked alongside the rig as Nelson pushed it through an aisle, toward the final destination of the freezers.

The Bitch chastised the little group every ten feet or so. She gave orders, directing them to tuck the screamer's arms up and in, or to get his legs. Twice the guy squirmed off the broad bed, until they taped him down to the dolly.

Paunch Guy followed them all, recording everything for the police to watch when they arrived.

"Just how cold is the freezer?" The Bitch asked.

Walt and Nelson exchanged looks. Nelson had unnaturally bright blue eyes, the spooky kind, which had to be contacts.

"Minus one," Nelson reported, steering the dolly well away from the product-laded selves.

"What? He'll *freeze* in there."

"So, we'll put a blanket on him," Toby said from ahead of the dolly, aiding the steering by keeping the rig straight. "You got spare coats or something back there?"

"We'll find something," Nelson replied.

"That's *inhumane!*" The Bitch lashed out. "This isn't Siberia! The hell are you people thinking about?"

"I'm gonna shut her up," Frying Pan Woman vowed through clenched teeth.

"Look." Gus glared at The Bitch. "It's like this. The guy's violent. Potentially dangerous. That's clear enough. We agree on that. There's no other place to put him that'll hold him where he won't get out."

"Well," Nelson drew out, attracting the attention of all. "There is a safety release inside the door."

"What?" Gus asked, taken aback.

"Just in case someone was inside and the door closed on them. Just a palm-sized plate that releases the lock. You can't really lock yourself inside."

"See!" Bitch exclaimed. "This is all totally unnecessary. Put him in an office or just keep him out back. There's no need to stick him in the freezer."

"And he's not going into any of the offices here," cashier Rebecca said. "Or the lounge.

"Can we turn the freezer off?" asked one of the shoppers following the group.

"Can't turn it off or warm it up," Nelson explained, the dolly's crossbar at his chest. "There's thousands of dollars in frozen food back there."

"What about barricading the door?" Gord asked with a coolness that Gus didn't share.

"Oh sure, we can do that fine. Few flats of bottled water, lock the wheels, no problem."

"Okay, that's settled," Gus said.

"You people are in*sane*," The Bitch scolded as they exited the aisle. A short weave between a set of coolers and they bumped their way through the same double doors Gus and crew entered earlier.

"This way," Nelson stuck out his goateed chin, pointing to a freezer at the back of the storage area.

"This is crazy," The Bitch protested. "You have no right to do this!"

"I think it's called a citizen's arrest," Gord said. "And that's enough. You've said your piece, and you're outvoted. The cops can sort everything out when they get here."

"Still not answering," reported the one guy with the phone.

Unreal, Gus thought and kneed the struggling screamer back from the dolly's edge. The bound man grunted at the contact, then attempted to howl through his masked tape. A new sound, part wail, part squeal, erupted from the prisoner.

Prisoner, Gus thought. *I guess he is that.*

"Is he choking?" The Bitch demanded, outraged at the very thought.

That attracted concerned looks from all.

"Get that tape off his mouth!" The Bitch yelled, wide-eyed and waving that finger. "Get it off him!"

Gus was getting tired of that finger.

Gord stepped to the screamer, shoved the head back, and unravelled the tape. Bloody froth soaked the material, and as the layers got peeled away, the screamer's chomping increased, chewing the remaining tape into wet pieces.

Gord managed to keep his fingers and retreated from the sight.

"Bet you're glad you wore gloves," Toby smiled.

Gord didn't answer, but his scowl said *fuck off.*

When they reached the freezer, Nelson went around the group and opened the door. Chilled vapor puffed into the storage area. A snow-white cave lined with shelving units lay beyond. Cardboard boxes of every conceivable shape and size containing various foods filled the shelves.

They pushed the screamer to his temporary resting place.

Rebecca appeared seconds later, holding up full-length red aprons, a pair of what appeared to be meat cutter's coats, and a jacket. All of which she handed over to Gus and the Frying Pan Woman. They placed everything onto the screamer, taping it down in places, all the while the man's squirming became stronger. Gus was getting increasingly nervous with the guy. The blood had stopped flowing, but the screamer seemed even more pissed off than before.

Gus draped the jacket over the screamer's torso and head. Once finished, they retreated from the freezer, where Nelson waited to close the door.

"Can't believe you're doing this," The Bitch said once again, not ten feet back from the crowd. The Paunch continued to record all with a surreal, almost clinical indifference.

"Hey," Toby released. "That guy came running in here, creating a public disturbance and looking for a fight. He chased your sorry ass until she clocked him with the frying pan. He's lucky he's still conscious, if you ask me. If he'd come running at me, I would've broken something."

"Shut the fuck up, Toby," Gord muttered.

"He'll kick that off himself," The Bitch complained. "Those coats. They're too thin, anyway."

"Then he'll kick it off himself," Frying Pan Woman said for them all, confronting The Bitch.

"Close it," Gus said in a tone not to be fucked with.

Nelson pushed the door close, sealing the icy prison with a metallic sounding *clack*. A solemn silence fell over the gathered people, as if they were just witnessing a body delivered to a tomb.

"All right," the stock guy said, breaking the quiet. "Those water flats over there, on those pallets. Push them on over, and I can lock the wheels."

Lying upon a broad-wheeled pallet and pushed against a wall was a formidable pile of perhaps twenty cases of bottled water, with each case containing eight four-liter jugs. Gus and company did the deed, rolling the heavy pallet right up against the freezer door. Once in place, Nelson locked the wheels. The boxes reached the lower window of the door, allowing anyone interested to look in on the wormy figure covered in a colorful patchwork of fabric.

"You can barely hear him in there," cashier Rebecca noted, leaning over the topmost case.

"All right," The Bitch said, digging through her handbag. "Now that he's locked away, I'm taking names here. In case any of you think about sneaking out before the cops come. They'll want statements from everyone, and if you aren't here, I'll make goddamn sure they know who you are anyway. And he's recorded all your faces, so give me your real names or you'll only make it worse for you."

"Lady," Gord said evenly, "you're starting to get on my nerves."

"I don't care," she said with a note of indignity while producing a pen and little notebook. "You have no authority over me. You can't tell me what to do. And everything's been recorded."

"Even the parts where you're being a total bitch?" Frying Pan Woman asked.

But The Bitch ignored her.

"Names," she said, "and don't make me ask for IDs."

As if being nabbed by a hallway monitor, the little group hesitated and glowered.

"Names!" The Bitch insisted, her eyes widening. "*Now.*"

So, they gave them up, not knowing any better, but knowing that the collective had restrained a potentially dangerous individual.

Frying Pan Woman was Anna Hajek, and spoke with the barest accent that suggested she was second generation something from somewhere Eastern European. Her defiant glaring informed Gus that Anna was going to exact revenge in some form or fashion upon The Bitch.

Carol Freeman was the twenty-something librarian with the glasses.

Rene Albertson was the third woman, who Gus couldn't remember as saying a word since the initial whacking with the frying pan.

John Maple was the guy with the square glasses and mousey complexion.

Perry Fletcher mumbled his name, not taking his eyes off his cellphone's recording feature.

Vlad Raymond was the guy continually trying to summon the police.

And that was all.

"And who are you?" Anna challenged The Bitch. "Better say it now. Record it."

"Mel," she released.

"Mel who?"

"You tone it back a bit," Mel barked.

"You don't tell me what to do," Anna warned. "Not ever. You're not the boss of me. I gave up my name just for the camera. So answer the question."

"Grant," Mel said with obvious dislike.

"Well, Mel," Anna said, "you better hope the cops get here soon, because I got better things to do than hang around here all night."

"All right," Gord said, his low voice inducing silence. "We're all gonna wait for the cops. Right here."

"For how long?" Rene asked him, the first words she'd spoken.

"As long as it takes. That right, Mel?"

Mel took her time answering. "Yes. That's right."

"And we keep an eye on him while we wait," Gord explained, jerking his head in the direction of the freezer. "Just in case."

"None of you have the authority to detain a person," Mel said. "None of you. You're violating his rights as a human being."

"You mean like you're detaining us?"

"That's different, idiot."

Gord's eyes narrowed. "Yeah," he finally said, weary of the exchange.

"Hey," Vlad Raymond exclaimed, straightening as he pressed the phone to his ear. "Yes, I need help. Just a second."

He motioned for silence and switched on the speaker mode.

"Yes," Vlad said, "I need police at the Mollyma—"

"Sir," a female voice cut in. "I'm sorry sir, but we're currently experiencing an unusually high number of calls, and we are unable to send a unit to you at the moment. Maybe within an hour. Possibly longer. What's the reason for your call?"

Vlad blinked, processing the question. "I'm at Mollymart. A young guy came running into the store, terrorizing the staff and the shoppers. We, ah, restrained him—"

"Forcefully," Mel said, receiving a round of hot glares.

"—restrained him," Vlad resumed, "and we're holding him in one of the store's freezers."

"He's in a freezer now?" the voice asked, a tad hurriedly.

"That's correct."

"You're calling from Mollymart?"

"Mollymart East, yes."

"Please hold."

Vlad rolled his eyes and shook his head at Mel's outburst. He was a thin man, late thirties and balding, wearing a checked collared shirt and beige pants. A mole dotted his left cheek, half a finger from his nostril.

"Your name?" the voice asked.

"Vlad Raymond."

"Mister Raymond, there's been a unit dispatched to the Collingwood subdivision, which is located just across from Mollymart's parking lot and main entrance. I've been unable to reach the officers sent to Collingwood, and as all of our other units are responding to calls, I'd suggest crossing the street and looking for them, if you are able to do so."

The fuck? Toby mouthed to the others.

Gus couldn't believe his ears. The night he needed a couple of cops and the Annapolis PD was unable to comply. Annapolis wasn't a big city, and while it had its share of crime, hearing that the cops were overloaded with calls for help on a Monday night surprised him. And made him just a little more nervous.

"Uh, all right," Vlad said, looking helplessly at those standing closest to him. They looked back, equally dismayed by the news.

"If you are able, Mr. Raymond," the voice went on, the words coming without pause. "Otherwise, I'd recommend staying indoors for the next while or so. Or if you are able, return home and stay indoors. Listen for updates on whatever electronic devices you might have with you or have access to."

"But—"

"Thank you for your call."

Click.

In the abrupt absence of the voice of the law, a scuffling and yowling could be heard from the depths of the freezer.

"Listen for updates," Toby muttered for them all. "The fuck's that all about?"

"And what was that about staying inside?" Gus asked. "The hell's going on?"

"She sounded busy," Carol Freeman commented, adjusting her librarian glasses.

"No one can get to us." Toby said, looking to his co-workers.

"She didn't say that. She said within the hour. Maybe," Gus said.

"Or we can go over to the subdivision and look for them," Gord said. "Collingwood's just over there, across the main drag."

"No one's leaving here," Mel warned them.

"You want the cops?" Gord put to her.

"Of course," she scoffed, minus the *duh*.

"Well then, you heard the operator. They're busy. Real busy. If we want, we can cross the street and look for them. That's just over there." Gord pointed in the direction of the main doors. "A couple of us can head over right now."

"What was up with that?" a dismayed Toby asked. "We could go look for them? *We*? We're not a search party. I mean, holy shit!"

"That was weird," Vlad agreed.

"So, what do you want to do?" Gus asked Gord.

The painter looked at him, then a few other faces. "I don't want to spend all night here. As it is, dingbat in there," he jabbed a thumb at the freezer, "has pretty much fucked our chances of getting out of here by midnight. Let's you and me head over to Collingwood and see if we can find those cops. We'll take the truck."

"You're going over there?" Mel asked.

"Yeah," Gord faced her. "We're going over there. You guys can stay here with your smartphones in the meantime. Can't do anything until we get this sorted out, and for that we need the law. Agreed?"

Mel hesitated. "Yeah. Agreed."

"All right then." Gord looked at Gus. "You up for this?"

"Yeah, sure," he said, but the expression on his face said otherwise.

"It's only across the way there."

"I know, I'm just …" Gus rolled his shoulders. "I'm just a little worried about what's going on when the APD is telling us to go look for their units."

"That's fucked up, dude," Toby stated, no longer feeling bound to self-censor his language.

"That *is* fucked up," Gus echoed.

"All right," Gord said, taking charge. "Someone needs to stay here and keep watch on the dingleberry in the freezer. The rest of you can do what you like."

"But we stay here," Mel added sternly. "All of us. Until the cops arrive."

"No one's going anywhere," Gus said to her.

"You got the keys?" Gord asked him.

"Yeah."

"Then let's go."

8

They left Toby with the main group. The man had the look of a person who knew he was being used as a guarantee that the others would return. He took it well, however, and didn't try to talk his way into going along with his fellow painters.

Gus and Gord walked briskly toward the front of the store. Gus was thankful to go, but he was also worried about what was happening in the city for the police to be so utterly occupied. There weren't many shoppers in the superstore, but it was only Monday night. Not even the weekend.

"Glad to get out of there," Gus said, just barely keeping up with his co-worker's pace.

"I know," Gord said. "Freaky shit."

"That Mel woman was getting on my nerves."

"She's a righteous one."

"Yeah."

"Collingwood's not a big place. I figure that, for some reason, those cops have moved on and just haven't bothered to contact dispatch."

Gus frowned at that. "Ain't that weird too, though? I mean, I'm not a cop, but shouldn't they call in first for whatever? Just to check in? Get a heads-up to command and then maybe go to the next call?"

"Suppose," Gord agreed, thoughts elsewhere.

The inner automated doors parted with a low rumble for the two men. They passed through the vestibule, where rows of shopping carts waited to be used.

The outer doors opened.

Gus and Gord stopped just beyond the threshold and stared.

Under that clear night sky dusted with stars, the suburb on the opposite side of the mall's parking lot and the main road appeared as a collection of pointed roofs and soft-glowing street lamps. But somewhere beyond that condensed barrier of bungalows and two-story houses, a police cruiser's lights swirled with disco-ball brightness. A repeating halo of red, white, and blue flashed across the peaks of houses and the night skyline, churning as if brewed by badness itself. There was no noise, no commotion, and that, in itself, bothered Gus.

"Jesus," he said quietly. "A UFO land over there or something?"

"Pretty-looking, ain't it?" Gord said, taking his eyes off the whirling light show and inspecting the roads.

"It's eerie," Gus whispered, wary of saying the words any louder. "I mean ... it's fuckin' *eerie*. Can you—"

Screeching tires from far away cut him off and distracted both men. There was a sudden crashing boom, a crumpling of metal, and then silence. Gus listened, listened hard, and thought he could hear voices somewhere to the west, but then a night breeze blew by, loud enough to wipe the sound away. The chill that enveloped him had nothing to do with the wind.

"The hell was that?" Gord questioned.

Gus had no answers, so they stood there outside the closed automated doors and waited a little longer.

In Collingwood, over that row of houses, the lights spun and beckoned. Nothing else moved. For a police cruiser, parked wherever it was, to throw up that amount of light in a residential area, one would think there would be more activity. The inactivity bothered both men.

The streets should have been teeming with people. There should have been cars and people and dogs all over that place. Yet, there was nothing of the sort.

"What do you think?" Gord asked.

"I dunno, man," Gus said. "This is fucking weird. I think I mentioned that earlier."

"You said eerie."

"Yeah, well, eerie and weird. I can say both."

"Still wanna go over there?"

Gus slowly shook his head. "No. No, I do not. Not at all. But I guess we gotta."

"Something might've gone down," Gord suggested. "The cops might not be able to move. Or to help."

"So, what can we do?" Gus asked. "I mean, seriously? What if it's a terrorist situation? Huh? That's a little beyond our capabilities."

"It's not a terrorist situation."

"Oh yeah? How do you know? I even remember you saying just last week it was only a matter of time before something happened out here."

Gord chewed on that, staring off in the direction of those spinning lights.

"Hey," Gus said. "You see that?"

"See what?"

"Just at the turnoff there, for the subdivision. Thought I saw ... well ...."

Gord waited.

"People. Running between the houses."

Gord squinted.

"I don't see shit," he stated in that quiet calmness that once again convinced Gus the man had been a lawman in a previous life, adept at breaking up fights in western saloons.

"Coulda sworn ..." Gus started and pointed. "Wait. What's that? You see that?"

The far end of the parking lot was lit by street lights, but beyond that, against a wall of presumably dark hedges and other garden decorations, Gus's eyes detected movement. A lot of movement. A rustling of colors lurking just beyond the light.

"The hell's that?" Gord muttered, staring at the same thing.

Gus shook his head, mystified. "Looks like ..."

A wall of people wandered into the fixed cones of light marking the fringe of the parking lot. A patchwork of summer clothing and bare flesh, they resembled a search party combing the area for lost clues. Except these people weren't looking down, and they weren't walking.

They were running.

Toward the Mollymart entrance.

"Whoa," Gus said, taken aback as a line of perhaps twenty figures, hunched over and dappled with light, rushed onto the parking lots. To the left, more silhouettes filled the road, their arms chugging as they ran, fallen sleeves and wrists flashing in the night. More people came the other way, running down the darkened highway, racing underneath the street lights.

"What the hell." Gus muttered, his heart pounding out the message his brain wasn't quite yet ready to acknowledge.

"Maybe we should forget about this," Gord said, taking a step back.

And if that suggestion wasn't enough to break Gus, the sound did. What reached his ears turned his knees to painter's putty and gave his bladder a dangerous squeeze. He blinked as if a string of neurons went off behind his eyes like firecrackers. The people weren't wailing like the screamer they'd just imprisoned. Nor was it a battle roar of some medieval army's front lines charging a drawbridge.

Those people were *panting.*

Like a pack of hounds too exhausted to bark, yet still doing their damnedest to close the distance between them and the rabbit before it disappeared into its hole. And all that frantic throat singing, punctuated by an occasional gasping note of fatigued rage, grew louder as they crossed the parking lot. The faces were indistinct, the distance smearing their features, and hands clawed at the air.

Gus backed up for the automated doors. Gord followed.

And when they moved, the people storming the parking lot screamed, or *tried* to scream, releasing breathless whistles one might hear from over-boiled kettles. They sprinted for the two men with a frightening urgency.

The automated doors couldn't open fast enough as Gus retreated, and he thumped through the portal. Gord was right behind him, casting uncharacteristically fearful looks over his shoulder. Both painters rushed through the inner doors and stopped in the fruit and produce section. They glanced back. Beyond the glass panels, that ghoulish, stampeding line became bigger, and more distinct.

"Oh shit," Gus whispered. His eyes widened, realizing their predicament.

The *doors.*

They would open for *anybody.*

"What's that guy's name?" Gord asked in a near panic.

"Walt!" Gus said. "WALT! REBECCA! REBEEEEECCCCCCCA!"

"Stay here," Gord said. "I'll get them."

And Gord took off, weaving amongst the fruit bins and shouting for the pair.

Thanks a lot, Gus thought, looking over his shoulder. The pack was halfway across the lot, storming toward the doors. He had no idea what their problem was, but he was certain they intended him harm, much in the same way as the screamer. A cold realization gripped him.

There was no time.

Gord and Rebecca would not return in time to lock the doors. It was a footrace the screamers would win. Fear got Gus moving. He approached the inner doors and they dutifully opened for him. He waved at the unwanted mechanical result as if shooing away a swarm of mosquitoes. He studied the doors, noted the steel kick plates and bars crossing the glass, all facing the parking lot.

Then he zeroed in on the key hole.

He needed a key, but that only prompted a second troubling question.

How do you lock doors automated to open when you approach them?

A key wouldn't just do the job.

Somewhere behind him, Gord bawled for Walt and Rebecca.

The charging screamers were well past the halfway point, racing toward Gus.

Adrenaline firing, he spotted a covered switch panel on the far wall. He bolted for it, slipped, and righted himself on the fly. He flipped open the lid, revealing about twenty or so switches.

Gus flicked off the first two.

The lights winked out in the vestibule and in the fruit and produce sections.

The pack was three-quarters of the way to the outer doors. They were an animated line of contorted faces and wide-eyed fury, a livid mob bearing down upon the mall's entrance as if channeled by an invisible funnel. The sight of them amplified Gus's fright. He flicked four more switches, his hand blurring over them, and killed more lights inside the store. He squawked in horror, swiped everything back on, and frantically studied the panel, willing his brain to work. Was it a combination of switches? Was it something different? What was he missing?

"*The other side!*" a voice yelled out to him from the rear of the supermarket. "*The switch is on the other side! One switch!*"

Gus rushed for the other panel. He passed along the inner doors which again promptly widened for him, hearing the snarls and glimpsing furious faces not twenty feet away.

There. Partially hidden behind a tall fern was a wide circular panel of stainless steel. A single horizontal switch lay directly in the center of that dead metal sun.

Gus slap-swiped that switch.

A mechanical snap then, and the outer doors remained closed as the screamers rushed within ten feet of the sensors.

The mob didn't stop. Showed no inclination of slowing.

A cringing Gus staggered back as the foremost screamers slammed face-first into the armored door with a blunt smack of flesh on tempered glass. There was a meaty salvo of impacts. Noses exploded. Foreheads burst apart.

Profiles flattened in alien caricatures. A row of teeth visibly shattered before withdrawing with a hideous shriek—a split second before the face was rammed into the glass again by a screamer from behind. The charge stopped in its tracks.

The doors remained closed.

The glass held.

"Sweet Jesus." Gus wheezed and backed up into a slanted bin of grapes. He sunk his hands into the plastic bags, the fruit bursting underneath his fingers, but even that didn't distract him from what was happening outside the main doors.

Hands hammered the glass and steel plates reinforcing the doors.

Heedless of their facial wounds, the screamers pounded the barrier, beating out a rage-fueled rhythm while demanding entry. Fists and open palms pummeled the glass. Some hands had their fingers snapped back upon connecting with the edges of the steel bars before the smashing into the door. Blood splashed across the barrier, quickly becoming smears.

Walt and Rebecca rushed past Gus, causing him to jump. Rebecca went to the door-switch wall while Walt disappeared in a nearby office. She pushed aside the fern and checked the control. She slumped at the result. A second later, the inner doors closed and locked with a barely heard snap of metal, securing the vestibule completely, and adding that extra layer of protection.

Walt appeared through the office doorway. "Inner doors are locked," he reported.

Gus slumped in relief.

"You okay?" Gord gripped his shoulder, giving his co-worker a comforting shake.

"Think I shit myself," Gus said wearily, taking stock of himself.

Gord withdrew his hand.

Gus pulled his arms out from behind his back and inspected his palms.

"Grapes," Gord stated, seeing what Gus had backed into.

"Grape guts."

"Yeah, grape guts."

"Thank Christ."

Gus numbly cleaned himself on his painter clothes while peering out at the gang demanding entry.

Rebecca stepped out from the fern while Walt moved to the secured inner doors. The four of them gazed upon the angry group of people not fifteen feet away. Those people continued smacking their hands and faces against glass covered in grisly swirls and rivulets that made lines for the floor.

"The fuck is up with them?" Gord asked with subdued disgust.

"Are they insane or something?" Walt wanted to know.

"They're fucking zombies, man," Rebecca stated with quiet authority.

That stunned the men.

"Zombies?" Gord asked.

"Zombies."

"They could just be infected with something," Walt said, unable to take his eyes off the ongoing carnage outside.

"Which would result in zombies," Rebecca smoothly concluded. "Call them what you want. Infected. Diseased. Stricken. It's all the same. But, I mean, look at them."

They did.

The beatings intensified, or so it seemed to Gus, who no longer felt safe. As he watched, a spread hand slapped the not-so-clear glass, followed by a fleshy profile that slunk up and down the surface, biting as if attempting to chew its way through. A single black eye rotated with sickly vigor.

"Ah …" Gus signaled, "just how strong is that glass?"

"Pretty strong," Rebecca said.

"How strong?" Gus grated in a very-much-need-to-know tone of voice.

"They'd have to use a hammer to get through," Walt explained. "That's tempered glass. Five-eighths of an inch thick. Framed in stainless steel. It's strong enough."

"How do you know that?"

Walt shrugged. "I read a lot."

"So they can't get in?" Gord asked.

"Not like they're doing now," Walt said, staring at the spectacle. "Unless they drive a car through."

"Plenty of cars out there," Gus muttered.

"You seriously think they're going to hot-wire a car?" a composed Rebecca asked.

On cue, one of the screamers attempted to head-butt the door. The resulting burst of splitting skin was as rosy as it was spectacular. The others hammered away with open hands and fists, taking up position along the glass paneling extending to either side of the armored entrance. A row of what appeared to be bare knuckles thundered into the glass's tempered might, rupturing skin to the muscle and bone underneath.

The other trapped shoppers appeared on site, drawn by that Taiko-drum clamor. Anna Hajek's towering frame stopped beside Gus. She spared him a worried glance before focusing on the gruesome spectacle outside the Mollymart entrance.

"What's their problem?" she asked stoically, as if she was a word away from going out there and breaking some faces.

"They're zombies," Rebecca supplied.

Anna's expression twisted into a disdainful *what the fuck?*

"What're they doing?" Carol Freeman moaned, as if trapped in a nightmare.

"Trying to get in," Rebecca informed her.

"But they can't, right?" Anna demanded with an icy reserve that suggested she'd been through much worse. "They can't get in?"

Rebecca shook her head, but Walt didn't appear so sure as he positioned himself behind a bin displaying fresh apples for sale.

"Oh, shit," Vlad said, flinching at the power of each connection and wincing at the damage to the strikers. "Why the hell are they hitting the glass like that? Can't they *feel* that?"

"I doubt they feel anything," Rebecca said. "Like I said. They're zombies."

That drew looks from the new arrivals.

"How do you know?" Anna demanded.

"Shit's on TV all the time." Rebecca deadpanned as a hammer-fist walloped the tempered pane, failing to distract her. "Too much of it, really. It's like someone knew this was coming and decided to run a bunch of instructional videos, just to get everyone ready. I mean, whoever *wanted* to get ready, that is. Make the show educational, yet interesting enough that you'll pay attention to all the survival details and be all ready for the test on Tuesday. Or something like that. I watch one or two of the more popular ones, but not all of them. Think there's like four or five on now."

They all stared at Rebecca.

"Six or seven," Walt quietly supplied. "That *Dead* one is still on."

"That's a good show."

"I watch it all—"

A zombie face smashed into the glass and stayed there for a second, quashing all conversation. The face turned, squishing an already broken nose, expanding one nostril from the pressure. If the other zombies weren't smacking the doors, Gus had no doubt he would've heard that squeegee note of skin dragging across the glass.

The face withdrew, only to ram the doors again. That time a shard of shattered cheekbone slipped up and into the eye it was no longer supporting with all the force of someone stabbing a fork into a soft-boiled egg.

The screamer—zombie—did not react to the blinding wound.

"Oh … shit," one of the men muttered.

"Ew," groaned another and turned away.

"Holy shit," Toby whispered.

"All right, that's just disturbing," Mel Grant said, holding her forehead as if checking for a fever. "I mean, that's just wrong."

Anna regarded her with a scathing glare. "Why don't you get a little closer? Maybe get tubby there to record that too."

If he heard, Perry didn't show it. He hung back, keeping his camera aimed at the door. Recording everything.

"Shut up," Mel snapped.

"You shut up," Anna retorted. "Why don't you try calling the cops now, huh?"

Both women faced off, ready for the other to say something. Mel eventually broke away first. Anna did so a few seconds later. They all watched the store's front.

"Five-eighths of an inch thick eh?" Gus repeated, trapped in the same nightmare as the rest of them. The outside glass was beginning to look like one side of an aquarium badly needing to be scrubbed.

"Tempered glass," Walt reminded him with a nod.

A grim collage of faces and hands pressed onto it.

9

Vlad Raymond immediately went back to calling the police.

"Let's get back, out of sight," Anna suggested, watching the display of sheer singlemindedness happening outside the glass.

"Should we switch off the lights?" Gus asked. "Maybe, if they're zombies, they won't hang around the front there."

Anna considered the suggestion.

Walt looked to Rebecca, who stood with her arms folded. She dipped her head, indicating it wasn't such a bad idea. Walt hopped to the light switches.

"So, what do we do then?" Anna asked.

"Nothing we can do," Gord said, "except wait for the cops."

"I think the cops have their hands full tonight," Gus said. "But we did see a cruiser's lights in the subdivision across the street."

"Move back from the glass, people," Mel Grant said, already walking away. "Let's not give them anything to think about."

Gus, Gord, and Anna exchanged looks, not appreciating the woman's authoritative tone in the least. Still, it wasn't a bad idea. The men moved first, but Anna lingered a bit, watching the zombies outside. The lights went off in the vestibule, then the first row inside of the store.

Mel stopped and regarded the big woman. "You coming, or what?"

"I'm staying," Anna said.

"They'll *see* you," a frustrated Mel yelled. "And if they see you, they'll stay out there, so get back here."

Walt turned off the lights over the fruit and vegetable section. "Should I leave the others on? Gonna get really dark in here."

"Can you leave on a few here and there?" Anna asked.

"Yeah. I can do that."

"Do it. And do you have a chair in that office up there?"

"Yeah."

"Bring it down. I'll take a seat behind the fruit somewhere. Out of sight."

"What's your problem?" Mel suddenly lashed out, marching back to Anna and ready for a fight. "Didn't you hear me the first time? You want them to hang around outside all night trying to get at your fat ass? In case you haven't noticed, we have a *situation* here, and people's *lives* are at risk."

Gus and the others stopped halfway down the aisle to watch.

"I don't take orders from you," an offended Anna said, raising her own voice. "And let's get this straight right now—you're not in charge of me. And one more crack like 'fat ass' and I'll slap the stupid out of you. I didn't like you before, and now I sure as hell like you even less."

"That's a threat!" Mel yelled, pleading triumphantly to the others. "She threatened me!"

"Walk *away*, bitch!"

"Don't you *dare* talk to me like that!"

"Are you like a really smart person who has moments of stupid? You want to go back out of sight and leave this whole area unwatched? Huh? What happens if that glass breaks? Or if the cops show up? Or maybe you think we'll hear something all the fucking way at the back of the shop?"

Give her credit, Mel Grant didn't back down, but she didn't have anything to say to Anna's barrage. She stood there in the towering presence of the bigger woman and held her ground.

"One person's enough, and I'm volunteering for the first watch," the big woman said. "That good? Huh? I'll be back in thirty minutes or so and then someone else can take my place. Got a funny feeling you'll be the very last to volunteer. So, get out of here before I lose my patience."

"If they see you—" Mel blustered, raising a finger. Gus thought she liked pointing a lot.

"*Get out of here!*" Anna exploded.

The smaller woman flinched. Mel planted her feet as if riding out an earthquake, but Gus was certain she was getting ready to run, in case Anna made a swipe for her.

"I like that one," Gord muttered nearby, sizing up Anna.

Gus had to admit, he liked her too.

Just then, all but a single light winked out overhead.

Mel Grant's silhouette turned and marched back to the group of onlookers. She walked with either angry energy or frenetic fright; Gus couldn't rightly see her face to decide. She bumped Perry with the camera on the way past, who righted himself without a word and kept on recording.

"She wants to be up there, so let her," she snapped in a tone that warned everyone not to challenge her. "Everyone else get back and get out of sight."

So they followed. Gus, Gord, and Toby paused just a few seconds, long enough to see Walt return to Anna with a chair. She took the piece from him, led him back a bit, and sat behind a bin of what might've been grapefruit, if Gus wasn't mistaken. Or honeydews. Something big and round.

And there she sat.

"Hey you," Anna said, looking in Gus's direction.

"Me?"

"Yeah, you. Don't let that bitch take charge. Put everything to a vote if you have to, but don't let that one take charge. Not while I'm out here. Got it?"

"Yeah," Gus said for the three painters.

Walt distracted Anna then, as he spoke to her before shooting a final look at the storefront glass.

"Get going then." She shooed him away.

The cashier walked past the painting crew, and they followed him out back.

"This is some *Evil Dead* shit happening here," Toby managed in a scared whisper. It was the first complete sentence he'd spoken in a while. Gus would've been more impressed if the circumstances were a little more mundane.

"Those ones at the glass," Gord said. "Some of them broke their wrists, but they kept on swinging. You see that?"

Toby nodded.

"I saw," Gus stated, remembering the fingers flailing about like the fat strands of an old-fashioned mop.

Up ahead, Rebecca and Vlad held open the swinging doors while the rest of them passed through. Walt was the last to enter.

They gathered just inside the storage area, amongst tall shelves packed with cardboard boxes and other assorted, glossy-looking packaging. The lighting overhead remained on, being on a different circuit than the ones outside.

"Okay, everyone here?" Mel said, looking over the group.

"Everyone except Anna," Rebecca pointed out.

"I know where she is," Mel snapped and took a second to reset herself.

She looked at Rebecca. "Okay, you're the authority on zombies. What should we do next?"

The cashier took a moment, perhaps a little surprised at the attention. She adjusted her glasses and organized her thoughts. Walt gravitated toward her side. The two of them together didn't resemble anything like the smiling Mollymart East workforce so frequently advertised on television.

"Nothing really," she eventually said. "The doors are locked, so we're safe for the time being. The rest of the mall is closed, except for maybe Big Wings on the other end, but we lock our doors leading into the mall, and mall security locks up the doors on their side. Drew working tonight, Nelson?"

"Yeah," the stock guy replied, his hands clasped over his head, applying pressure to his temples. Gus thought he looked a step away from freaking out. In fact, a quick look around informed him that only Nelson and perhaps Carol Freeman appeared on the verge of screaming. The rest, while nervous looking, were ready to deal with the situation.

"Okay," Rebecca said, sharing a nod with Walt and his sunken cheeks. "Then everything was locked up at nine on the nose."

"Big Wings closes at eleven," Walt said.

"Big Wings does not," Nelson said in an agitated voice. "It's Monday. They close at nine just like everyone else."

"Oh, that's right," Walt remembered.

"Okay then. Big Wings is closed," Rebecca said. "So then Drew might still be around?"

"What time is it?" Nelson asked.

"Eleven oh two," Vlad said, who had given up on calling the cops.

"He's gone," Nelson said. "Long gone. Like we should be. Goddamn it. I just *had* to work tonight."

"Now we know what's going around the valley, anyway," Rebecca said to Walt.

"What's that?" Gus asked.

"The flu," she said.

"And I had to take the shift," Walt groaned.

"We all did," Rebecca added, then to the others. "We're not supposed to be here. The other cashiers called in sick. Even the assistant manager's sick, so Mrs. Miller left me in charge for the night."

An unchecked flower of horror spread across Gus's chest. The muscles in his calves and thighs tightened and thrummed with blood as cold as arctic ice.

"What did you say?" he asked for them all.

71

Rebecca met his eyes. "You don't know?"

"Know what?" Gord seconded, his voice betraying his own mounting horror.

"About zombies. Usually caused by a superbug infection or something occult-based. A lot of people called in sick today. We're pulling a double shift, in fact." She indicated to herself and to Walt. "Figured we'd be swamped, but no one really came around. In fact, the place was dead by mid-afternoon. There were a few shoppers around tonight, by which I mean mostly you, but that's it."

"Thomas was here earlier," Nelson said. "He looked like shit though. I was the only one around to cover for him."

"Yeah, but otherwise, most people were home sick with something, right?" Rebecca put to them all.

Uneasy silence answered the question.

"Oh, Jesus Christ," Vlad stated bluntly, holding his forehead.

"What do you mean?" Mel demanded. "What do you *mean*?"

Rebecca shook her head. "I mean, looking at you all, I figure you're the only ones *able* to come here tonight. That you're the only ones *not* sick. Am I right?"

Vlad immediately took to his phone again. Carol Freeman clawed at her own shoulder bag in a hurry to locate her phone. Mousy John Maple blinked and breathed as if he were going into labor. Even a shocked-looking Perry Fletcher lowered his cell phone and aborted his recording duties, staring in horrified wonder.

And the back area became a flurry of activity as those with phones tried to get in contact with loved ones at home.

A bug-eyed Gus backed up against a metal shelf, feeling the room begin to go into a very violent spin cycle. He grasped a metal post for support and looked up to see the smiling, winking expression of the Woodchuck Giant gracing the box filled with canned corn giblets, assuring him that everything would be all right. Everything would be just fine. Don't you worry.

"I gotta get home," Mel Grant announced in a shaky voice for all to hear, as if governing peasants. "Ethan and the kids were home sick all day. I ... I came out for juice and NyQuil. I gotta get home."

She started walking double-time for the doors.

"Wait a minute," Rebecca said, blocking all escape. "You can't go out there."

"You get the hell out of my way," Mel barked.

But Rebecca held her ground. "They're already out there."

Mel balked. "So how do I get out of here?" she demanded.

Rebecca didn't answer.

"There's the door at the back here," Nelson provided, eyes darting left and right anxiously. "Goes out into the loading bay."

"It's not safe," Rebecca said.

"I gotta get *home*," Mel fired off, turning her urgent countenance upon the stock guy. "Show me the door."

Vlad Raymond was shaking his head, not getting any answer.

Video man Perry Fletcher had abandoned his task to stick a finger into one ear while dialing a number.

Gord looked to Gus, the concern clear on his face. "I gotta call Mary."

I gotta call Tammy, Gus thought feverishly, feeling that familiar unpleasant squeeze on his arms now, his pulse quickening.

"You got the phone?" Gord asked.

"No," Gus replied, struggling for breath.

"Where is it?"

"I …"

"Upstairs," Toby said. "Next to the timer."

Gord ran for the stairs leading to the Regional Manager's office.

Toby stayed behind and grabbed Gus's shoulder. "You okay, man?"

"No."

"Yeah, I can see that."

People were yelling at each other now. Mel Grant and Nelson were walking away from the group, down an aisle loaded with boxed food supplies. Others followed, and the arguments went with them.

"How are you going to get anywhere?" Rebecca was shouting. "Drive? *The zombies are in the parking lot.*"

"I gotta call Tammy," Gus said to Toby.

"Okay man. You good to walk?"

Gus nodded and did just that. He was a little wobbly on the first few steps, but then he picked up speed. Rebecca and Walt spared them both a glance before seeing where they were headed. As long as the painters weren't going for an exit, they left them alone and continued following the main group. Of the ten or so people, only Carol Freeman—the woman with the librarian glasses—and John Maple—wearing his square frames—remained in place, divided on their course of action.

Gus pulled himself up the stairs, his thoughts swirling around Tammy and her safety.

When they entered the manager's office, Gord whirled and held up a hand. He had the company phone at his ear, listening to the calls going through to his house. The voices of the other shoppers drifted up into the office, receding, but Gus ignored them. He walked to the windows. With the overhead lights mostly off, the main floor resembled a darkened maze ready for the rats. He looked for Anna but couldn't find her. Shadows flittered in a violent dance beyond the locked inner doors.

"They're still out there," Toby said at Gus's side.

"Yeah."

"You think they're zombies?"

"I dunno," Gus replied wearily, but he'd seen enough horror movies with them. There was a very good chance they *were* zombies.

"I think they're zombies."

"Goddamn it," Gord blurted behind them, pulling them both away from the windows. The man held the phone at his waist, staring at the screen with distrust.

"Can't reach her?" Gus asked.

Gord looked up. "She's not answering."

"Maybe she's asleep?" Toby offered.

Gord glared. "I let the phone ring for damn near a minute. She's not answering."

"Try again in a few minutes," Gus suggested. "Can I ...?"

A frustrated Gord handed over the company phone. Gus thanked him with a nod and dialed Tammy's place. He slapped the device to his ear and waited.

One ring.

Two rings.

Three.

"Maybe she's in the bathroom or something?" Toby suggested to Gord. "Is she sick?"

"She's not sick."

"So, there's nothing to worry about. She's doing something and can't hear the phone."

Five rings. Six.

"Mary has the phone near her all the time," Gord explained. "She's not five feet from the thing. She plays games and shit on it. Chats on Facebook."

Toby lapsed into silence, turning to Gus.

Eight rings.

"Anything?" Gord asked.

"No," Gus answered. "Nothing. Ten rings now."

"She was sick?" Toby asked.

Gus felt his guts flop onto the floor. "Yeah, she was sick."

"Well," Gord said, "that settles it. I'm going home."

"Hold on, now. You live on the other side of town. And there's the thing with all them zombies outside."

"I gotta get home, Gus."

"Okay, so what are we gonna do here?" Gus wanted to know. "Crawl out a window or something? Out a back door?"

Gord glared at him, then at Toby, then back to Gus. "We gotta go. I'm serious. I'm worried about Mary. If she didn't answer, then that means she couldn't answer. The woman brings the phone with her to the can, for Christ's sake."

Gus deflated, holding his head, thinking thoughts about Tammy. "All right, then. Let's go."

"You should call Benny," Toby said.

"Huh?"

"Call Benny. Tell him we're leaving the job. He'll need to know."

"Oh. Yeah," Gus said. "Suppose so."

He dialed the number. Below, the main floor was empty. The inner doors were still sealed and holding.

The answering service picked up on the third ring.

"Benny, it's Gus. Ah, things are getting a little freaky around here. We think we have ... zombies. Running around the parking lot. We're bugging out. Gord wants to get back to Mary, and I want to get back to Tammy. Okay then, hope all is well with you. Later."

He winced when he finished the call, knowing how it sounded. Benny would call back any second and give him an earful. He knew it.

Except Benny didn't.

"Okay, that's done," Gord said. "We get out of here now."

"Can't go that way," Toby said, gesturing at Mollymart's vestibule.

"Then it's the back."

10

The three painters descended to the first level and followed the shouting match. They found the shoppers and Mollymart employees gathered around a black door with a horizontal push bar across the middle. A single caged light bulb loomed above the frame. Faces turned when the painters arrived, the stress already working its evil magic on their features. Some of them appeared in worse shape than others.

"You didn't go out there?" Gus asked Mel Grant, who looked like she was one nerve away from tearing someone's head off. She stood next to the door, opposite the stock guy Nelson, who'd taken up position on the left.

Mel ignored the question.

"What's the problem?" Gord asked.

Nelson looked to Mel, then to a nearby Rebecca, looking like a student wanting to spill the beans on some very naughty behaviour.

Something slammed into the door from the other side, causing all to recoil.

"The fuck was that?" Gord wanted to know, as another blow hammered the door.

"We opened the door," Nelson said. "And right across the lot, running up the sidewalk, was a pack of those things."

"Well, shit," Gus sighed.

"How many?" Gord asked.

"Don't know. Maybe six or seven?" Nelson replied.

"We can fight our way through."

"Nuh-uh," Rebecca said in a warning tone. "You step out there, and you risk infection. Or worse. They might just beat you up, or they might try and bite you. Maybe even eat your ass. Who knows what they'll do. But any contact and you risk becoming infected."

The pounding on the door didn't relent in the least.

"We're trapped in here," Vlad said. "Until the cops arrive, at least."

"This place," Walt said, spinning a finger, "was built right in the middle of a bunch of subdivisions. Easy shopping for hundreds of families."

"And those things out there now," Rebecca said, "hitting the door? That's a lot of noise. They'll attract others."

"So, what do we do?" asked a stressed-out John Maple, pushing his glasses up on his face.

"We're stuck here," Rebecca said simply, "until help arrives."

"You mean we're under siege?" Toby asked, seemingly unbothered by the prospect.

"It's not too bad. The place is locked up. There's no latch on the other side of that door, so no one can get in. You have to have a key, or someone has to know you're out there. No one can get in through the front or the loading bay doors. So, yeah. We're pretty much under siege until help arrives."

"We stay in here," Walt said over the assault on the back door. "All night if we have to."

"In a supermarket," Gord said with a dubious air.

"It's all we can do right now," Rebecca explained.

"Can't stay here all night," Mel mumbled.

"And you can't go outside either," Rebecca told her. "And remember, you were the one wanting all of us to wait for the cops, so get used to it. Keep trying to call your families if you can. Otherwise, we should move back from the door. Maybe post a guard here as well."

"I'll do it," Nelson said.

"No," Rebecca said. "One of these other folks. We might need you for something else."

"What else?"

But she didn't answer him. "You," Rebecca said, indicating Perry Fletcher. "You got that phone. You want to hang back here and keep an eye on things? For a half hour or so?"

To Gus's dismay, Perry looked to Mel for guidance and received none. "Okay," he said. "What do I do?"

"Just watch the door. Shout if anything weird happens."

"I can do that."

"Okay then, everyone," Rebecca said, "let's move back to the front.

Maybe head upstairs. There's a lounge up there. We can sit and wait and keep calling for help, if you'd like."

The quiet woman called Rene reached for Mel's shoulder, who flinched and flashed a *don't-you-dare* look. Mel walked beside Rebecca, who led them back through the brightly lit aisles of the storage area.

"Should you turn off these lights?" Gus asked.

"No need," Nelson said. "No one can see them back here. The only place they can't see them. And it's a different circuit."

Two minutes later, at something like eleven thirty-five, they gathered in the employee lounge. Carol Freeman and the very quiet Rene sat knee to knee on the great leather couch Gus and company had moved from the office, while others stood or paced while attempting to contact loved ones. Toby pulled away a few office chairs and righted them while Gord continued trying to reach his wife. Gus glanced down at the dark shopping floor occasionally, remembering that Anna was on guard.

"What else do you know about these things?" he asked, turning to Rebecca who stood with her back against a wall.

"Well," the cashier said, "only what I read in books and watched on TV, so you really can't go by what I'm saying."

"What?" Mel Grant said, stopping in her tracks.

"Truthfully, I don't know what they are. All I'm saying is that those people outside are displaying characteristics that matches what I've read and seen about zombies. They don't look or act like they feel any pain, and they're pretty pissed off. No one's tried to eat anyone, so there's that, but with the flu bug on the go and a lot of people being sick, I think it's safe to say that the bug did this to them. Drove them crazy. After that, I'm just speculating."

"How do you kill them?" John Maple asked.

"Kill them?" Mel Grant repeated in horror. "You can't kill them. They're *people*."

"Like that person we got stashed in the freezer back there?" Gord entered the conversation.

"Yeah, like him?" Toby asked.

Mel shook her head and went back to brooding.

Rebecca waited for seconds before answering. "Okay, I'm biased because I think they're zombies. I'm calling them that for convenience sake, since I watch the TV shows and read the books."

"Convenience sake," Mel said with a wry chuckle.

Gus thought the woman was close to losing it.

"I don't think they're dead," Rebecca said. "Or undead. Whatever. I think they're still alive. Infected and totally ... what's the word ... unaware of their actions. But alive. So, using that logic, anything should be able to kill them."

"There was that guy that broke his face on the door outside," Vlad said while miming an exploding eyeball. "That was pretty hardcore."

"Yeah, didn't seem to bother him," John Maple said, nodding in agreement.

"In the movies and TV, all it usually took was a shot to the head," Rebecca explained. "Destroy the brain. Some books said to destroy *parts* of the brain, and some movies had it where you could chop them up into pieces and you still couldn't kill them. Unless you burned them."

That silenced her audience.

"But the majority seem to go down from a head shot. Smack them in the head. Break the skull and the brain."

"If they're zombies," Gus said.

"Well, yeah."

"Doesn't matter anyway," Vlad said. "Nothing we can do about that. No one has anything to smack them in the head."

Gord looked at Gus and walked off into Ms. Miller's office.

"There's rolling pins in the household section," Walt pointed out. "They're solid. You could break a head open with one of those if you had to."

"There's barbeque forks too," Nelson suggested. "Them long ones."

"Too awkward," Rebecca said dismissively. "Too hard to stab for an eye."

"Jesus Christ," Mel murmured and sat herself down, holding her head as if coping with the mother of all migraines.

Gord returned with the whammer in hand.

"Where'd you get that?" Rebecca asked.

"Tool crate inside."

"Got any more?" Nelson asked, sizing up the hammer.

"Just this," Gord said.

"Shit."

"What else do we have down below, Nelson?" Rebecca asked.

"What does it matter?" Gus asked. "No one here is ready to fuckin' assault a lunatic. And besides, what if they're all better by the morning?"

No one wanted to answer that.

"Not sure I can stay here until morning, man," Gord said. "I gotta get home."

"There's no choice," Rebecca explained. "You can't reach your cars, and more of those people will be showing up because of the racket downstairs. Unless you can think of a way out of here that doesn't include crawling through the septic tanks—and we can't, the pipes are too small—then we're camping out here. It could be worse."

It could be worse, Gus thought.

He believed her.

Then a loud slam from below made all of them jump.

11

Peeking out from amongst a bin filled with watermelons, Anna remained on her chair and kept quiet, taking in the faint smell of rind. She watched the developing shit storm outside. Because that's exactly what it was. A shit storm. A great big shit-flinging hurricane with flying chunks of offal just whipping around, spattering everything. And even if you cleaned the shit up afterward, the smell would still be there.

Anna was a farm girl from Falmouth, third generation Czechoslovakian-Canadian, fluent in three languages and with the barest accent that left a few people looking at her funny. Because of her six-foot-two frame and bulk that intimidated most everyone smaller, especially menfolk, not too many asked where she was from. She wasn't fast or sleek enough to play basketball, much to her high school team's disappointment, but she took to weight training, which she very much enjoyed, and was naturally strong from her days of wrangling livestock and tossing hay bales. During her college days, she'd worked the front door of the campus bar because of her size. She even saw her fair share of action, when some oversized boys thought that she couldn't and wouldn't throw them out on their asses.

Simply because she was a girl.

She proved them wrong.

In the days after her school years, she retained a lot of her muscle, which helped her plenty while on the farm—the family business, which her parents left her after they'd passed away. Her father had died of a massive heart attack, dying on his front step while pulling on his work gloves. Her mother, upon hearing her husband of thirty-seven years grunt as if he'd stubbed his toes something wicked, rushed outside only to gawk in horror at her collapsed partner. Her own heart stopped when she couldn't shake him awake. Or so the paramedics later deduced.

That had happened only two years ago, and Anna found herself alone and in charge of a three-hundred-acre dairy farm with a developing twenty-acre Macintosh apple orchard. If she wasn't tough before that, she'd been vulcanized after, determined to carry on the family business as her parents often hoped she would. She had two brothers and one sister, all of whom were married and moved away to other parts of the country. None of her siblings were interested in the farm. They'd wanted her to sell it, but that wasn't going to fly. Not while she still breathed. And so, she worked it. She hadn't found a man to join her yet, but that didn't bother her either. She was thirty-three years old, and if she had to, if she really had to, she'd just locate a male she found attractive, preferably of her size and intelligence, club him over the head, and drag him back to the house.

Problem solved.

Now, however, the people outside of the Mollymart entrance captivated her.

The glass held, but she wondered about that. The people out there (she didn't like calling them zombies just yet) weren't giving up. The pounding had slowed down somewhat, but only a fraction, as if they knew someone was still inside the building. Hands slapped glass for attention. Fists pounded. Faces dragged across the glass, attempting to peer past the morbid whorls and patterns staining the surface.

The broken hands fascinated and disturbed Anna the most.

Though the outer lights had been switched off, she could still see the appendages flopping around. Whenever the owner started hitting the glass, an outline of a hand would briefly flail above the blacked-out face. Then the person would slam that mitten of shattered meat and bone into the glass, draw it back, and repeat the entire process.

It was mechanical, in a way. Focused.

And the only thing failing was the flesh itself. The will was very much intact, and Anna understood willpower. She understood determination.

The people outside the door would get inside eventually. It was only a matter of time.

A chill fell over her when she reached that conclusion.

It was difficult to see how many were at the door, as they were constantly pushing each other out of the way. As far as Anna could tell, there were a dozen or so. But then at least three new attackers arrived on the scene and added their weight to the assault. She knew they were different because their vocal chords seemed fresher compared to the others, as some of those had toned down their howls to loud moans.

And they weren't as bloodied. Not in the beginning, anyway.

One of the new arrivals slammed his face into the glass just five feet away from the main doors. The sheet rattled from the impact.

The sheer mad-dog ferocity impressed Anna, despite her rising unease. She remembered a tussle she'd gotten into with a guy half her size, who was clearly on something illegal. The angry runt, as she'd thought of him at the time, had pushed her back against a wall in a rage-fueled display of strength. It took her and two other security guys to restrain the man, and even then, the cops arresting him actually asked for help getting the nutcase into their back seat.

An elbow hit the glass. A point of bone burst through the skin. More blood spurted. The person rammed their elbow into the glass repeatedly, as if they were assaulting a punching bag. The thickening gore and lack of light hid the damage, but Anna knew someone would need surgery and a shitload of stitches to repair that joint.

The elbowing stopped, and the person started slapping the window instead.

She couldn't take her eyes off the show, as horrific as it was. None of them were falling to the ground because of injuries or blood loss. She'd seen her share of blood, both human and livestock, so the sight of it didn't bother her in the least, but the amount being spilled outside was incredible. There was blood wherever they hit. Grisly spatters and smears covered the store front, turning the world beyond into a nightmarish chum. The glass below the waistline, where the people didn't seem to bother with, was lined in thick rivulets that ran to the ground.

They were still making noise, but not so loud, so there was that. But the fury remained. An unchecked rage powered those frames of organic matter and compelled them to do terrible things to themselves, heedless of the pain and damage.

Maybe they were zombies after all.

Nothing human could maintain such an effort or sustain such injuries.

She should've kept the frying pan, but after braining the guy, she'd left it on the aisle floor.

A figure shoved its way to the storefront and took a crack at the glass. Its fist held the first two strikes, but broke upon the third blow. No matter, the person kept on swinging. More zombies appeared, taking their best shot at the barrier.

Behind the camouflage of the melons, Anna took a new head count. She wasn't exactly sure about the number, so she countered a second time and thought about the result.

If she was correct, five or six new zombies had joined the fray. Mollymart's glass front wasn't quite filled with violent shadows, but close.

And they were all battering that tempered shield.

Anna became a little more nervous.

12

"The fuck was that?" Gus blurted a split second before Nelson answered.

"That was the freezer."

Heads turned. Faces tensed and slackened as people remembered.

The screamer from outside.

Boom.

The guy had freed himself.

Gus fidgeted with indecision, but then the Mollymart staff was running for the stairs. Toby and Gord got pulled into that sprint, so Gus chugged after them.

Seconds later, the group moved a box of water jugs to the side so they could access the window, but they didn't remove the barricade from the door. Once the top box was out of the way, Rebecca looked in on the prisoner. The taller guys peeked over her head.

"Can't see—" she said, but then a face loomed up in the rectangular glass.

Nelson shrieked. The others jerked back in horrified shock.

The screamer pressed his bloodied face across the glass, wiping it. Then he positioned himself right before the window and tapped the middle of the pane with his forehead.

"Oh shit," Gus muttered, knowing what was about to happen.

The screamer reared back for dramatic effect and slammed his forehead into the glass. A dewy blotch exploded from the point of meaty contact. The screamer kept his head to the window, as if stunned by the blow, before moving his head to the right. A broad mouth appeared in his scalp, lipless and drooling.

"Oh Jesus," a woman said. Gus thought it might've been the quiet one named Rene.

With drunken determination, the screamer righted himself. He moved unsteadily and still hadn't used his arms, so Gus wondered if the guy still had tape around his wrists.

His feet, he realized. *We taped up his feet too.*

And yet, the screamer was standing.

With all the might of a strongman rearing back a club, aiming to ring the bell at the top of a carnival's *test your strength* contest, the screamer leaned back and plunged his head forward again. Skin and blood flattened. Bone appeared through that oozing slit. The onlookers gasped and reeled at the backlit scene, the freezer's inner lighting revealing all in a grotesque frame. Hands went to mouths.

"Maybe we should open the door," Vlad suggested.

The screamer rammed the glass a third time with an audible crack that positively frightened Gus.

A line appeared in the window's surface like magic, no more than half an inch, but it was there.

"Oh my God," Mel Grant said, backing away from the sight.

The screamer, no more than a murky outline in the bloodstained glass, swayed and readied himself for a fourth strike. He smashed his head forward and missed that little crack by a couple of inches.

"We gotta stop him," Nelson said.

"No one goes in there," Rebecca warned.

"You heard her," Gord said, gazing on with steely reserve.

The screamer straightened, lined himself up with the window for yet another blow. He wobbled, then squared his shoulders, and through that messy portal, Gus saw that the next strike would be right on the money, and that either bone or glass would break and one of two things would come through. Gus wasn't sure he was ready for either brains or razor shards, so he retreated a step. Half the group did the very same, expecting the worst.

The screamer wavered and coughed.

The sound was unmistakable, and a thick sheet of … *something* speckled the bloody glass. It wasn't blood, but a spray of mucus as thick and pulpy as freshly pressed oranges splashed against the window. Then a second blast peppered the glass. Then a third. After that, nothing, but the coughing continued in great whooping klaxons.

That sound mortified the spectators outside the door.

The coughing stopped.

"The hell was that?" Perry Fletcher asked at Gus's side, startling him. The man had vacated his position at the rear door and rejoined the group.

"No idea," Vlad said, "but it's nasty."

"Stay back from the door," Rebecca advised, withdrawing a good ten feet from the freezer.

"What's wrong with him?" Gus asked.

"I'm not sure," she answered.

"But you have an idea," Mel Grant demanded.

"Yeah."

"Well then, *what?*" she yelled.

"Give her a chance, and maybe she'll tell you, goddamn it," Toby aimed at her, earning the woman's wrath.

"You don't tell me what to do," she told him.

"Lady, I don't think anyone tells you what to do, which makes you a pain in the balls."

A heavy blow struck the door then, followed by a yet another. The strikes distracted the confrontation, and while they could see a shape beyond the dirty window, details weren't easily distinguished.

Gus knew, however. "Holy shit."

"What?" Gord asked.

"It can't see."

Gord looked back to the window, his usual stoicism shaken.

"He must've blinded himself or something," Gus continued. "But he can't see the glass anymore."

As if to prove the observation to be true, the screamer bashed his head against the freezer wall, a good two feet to the left of that punished window.

Gord edged up to the opposite side of the window, shushing Rebecca's horrified expression with a hand. He tried seeing inside from that angle, craned his neck, and pulled back with a head shake. "Can't see shit."

"Listen," John Maple said from the rear.

So, they did.

The screamer wasn't hitting the wall or door anymore.

"Did he stop?" Mel Grant asked.

"Maybe he knocked himself out?" Walt asked, watching his co-workers.

"That door stays closed for sure now," Rebecca said. "No one goes near it."

"Switch the freezer off then," Mel Grant ordered.

"No," Rebecca said. "Don't do anything. That coughing you heard? Well right now, whatever's infecting that guy in there is riding the air currents, just waiting for a fresh body to take over. Open that door without the proper gear on, and you'll be exposed."

"Then what?" Nelson asked anxiously. "We turn into one of those things?"

"Probably."

That killed all conversation.

"What proper gear?" Gus asked.

Rebecca looked at him. "Considering what's going on here, I'd say hazmat suits. Anything that would prevent the pathogen from coming into contact with your airways. And that's just a guess. It might only have to come into contact with your skin. Your open eyes even. But it's in there, just swirling around."

"Can it get out?" Gord asked.

"Maybe through the vent system," Nelson said. "It all gets drawn up and shot out through the roof. But the vents all go out, so nothing gets in here."

"We're okay, then," John Maple said for them all. "Oh, thank God."

But Gus wasn't feeling anywhere near okay. Having those things blocking the exits was one thing, having one inside the megastore was another, even if the zombie was contained in a freezer. A damaged freezer.

"Maybe, uh," he gestured at the cracked glass. "Maybe you can put some tape on that? Seal it up. Just in case."

A heartbeat later, Mel Grant led the charge away from the door, realizing what Gus was implying. The painters remained, however, as did the Mollymart crew.

"Better this way," Rebecca said. "And yeah, good idea. Tape that up, Nelson. I don't think that crack's too bad, but do it anyway. Maybe the light out here shines through in there."

"If it were, the zombie in there would be smacking his head against the glass then," Gord pointed out. "And he ain't doing that. I think you're right," he directed at Gus. "He can't see shit in there. Maybe blackened his eyes or poked them out or worse."

"Ew." Toby shivered.

"He's calmed down, anyway," Gus observed.

"Or he smashed his head open," Rebecca added.

"What?"

"You heard me," the Mollymart woman said. "These things are totally clueless when it comes to personal safety. And he was really smacking that glass and wall. How long before he weakened this?" She tapped her own forehead, shaking her short platinum locks.

"All right," Toby said. "I'm convinced. They're zombies. They're all fuckin' nasty ass bitin' zombies. So, what's the plan?"

They looked to Rebecca.

"Stay here," she said in an apologetic tone. "Keep calling the cops. Maybe see what's happening on Facebook or Twitter. We can't be the only people seeing this."

Gord immediately tossed the company phone to Toby, who caught it. "Your unlucky day," Gord said. "See if you can find anything on them sites. You're the social media nut."

"Social media *master*," Toby corrected as he went to work.

"How long can we stay in here?" Gus asked.

Rebecca glanced at her co-workers and shrugged. "I dunno. But look on the bright side. We still have power and plenty of food on hand. So we're good that way. We wait for help."

"And if help doesn't come?" Walt asked worriedly.

Rebecca stared at the man and couldn't answer.

Which was when the double doors flew inward with a bang and Anna rushed into the room.

13

"They're breaking through," the big woman said as the inner doors swung closed behind her.

Rebecca led the charge back to the main entrance. Gus heard the commotion as soon as he entered the main shopping area. Through the shadowy cave that was Mollymart, dark figures moved and thrashed at the locked automated doors. His dread heightened the closer he got to the scene.

They stopped amongst the last few fruit displays and stared. Anna pointed, although there really was no need.

"Five-eighths of an inch thick, eh?" Toby said for them all.

The zombies outside ripped apart the outer doors. One had already punched out a spidery hole and used his still-working fingers to pull the fragments away. The glass came apart in stubborn chunks, not shards like Gus would expect, but more like a windshield. Once that initial hole had been made, the glass's integrity failed, and the zombies beat and ripped away the excess. The horizontal bars remained on the doors, but as Gus watched, a zombie—a man—oozed his way through the crusty opening at waist level. He yowled all the way, until someone shoved him face first into the glass-speckled floor. The screaming caused a few of the shoppers to cover their ears, but that wasn't what disturbed Gus the most.

Hacking coughs could be heard interspersed with that mind-freezing yowling.

The zombie tumbled inside the breached vestibule, got his feet under him, and launched himself at the locked inner doors. He crashed into the glass face first again, anointing the shivering doors. The zombie bounced back, steadied himself, and started clubbing the second barrier with his arms.

Rebecca held her face.

Toby held his face with both hands.

Nelson hefted a crowbar and moved to intercept.

"Wait!" Gus said, stopping the stock guy. "Don't—the doors are holding."

"I'll go out there and beat his head in," Nelson said.

"No," Rebecca said. "Don't open those doors. They'll get in for sure."

"They're *already* in!" Nelson insisted. "We can kill them off as they crawl through those openings."

"Listen," Gus said.

So, they did.

"The coughing?" Nelson asked.

"The coughing," Rebecca said.

"What about the coughing?" Anna wanted to know.

"You open those doors now, and whatever's in them will get to us," Gus said. "It's airborne. That right, Rebecca?"

"That's right."

Anna screwed up her face, angry and revolted at the notion.

Two zombies attempted to worm their way through the breach at the same time. Both were in a gruesome mess from scalp and face lacerations. The second one through was a male, and his T-shirt hooked on a jagged edge. The crystal shard unzipped a line along the zombie's chest, and a sheet of blood spattered the floor below.

"Oh, dear God," someone muttered.

Gus turned away, before he saw something he knew he would not forget.

Other zombies shoved the bleeding one through. They then struggled to get through the breach, piling into each other until a solid shadow mashed itself into the megastore's damaged front. A zombie, the one before the bleeder, rose and slipped, crashing back to the floor.

"They'll get in," Gus said. "Eventually."

"What do we do?" Mel asked Rebecca.

The cashier watched those writhing creatures, thinking on the next course of action. "We pull back. Fortify ourselves in the upstairs office."

That quieted the lot of them.

"Fuck that," Toby said for them all.

"I'm not doing *that*," Mel Grant echoed. "No *way*. Look, if they're coming through here, and that ruckus is attracting them, what are the chances of the other exits being covered?"

"She's right," Gus said. "If they're through, all we have to do is keep them here. Long enough to slip out the back."

"And circle around to the parking lot?" Mel Grant asked. "But that's where those things are."

"So don't get your car," Gus said. "Run home if you can. But the car's there if you want it. Someone could stay here, in plain sight so they—" he nodded at the zombies, "stay focused on the door. Stay here until the others are gone."

That silenced the group, while fists pounded the glass, causing it to shiver.

"They'll break through that door," Gord agreed. "Worse, once that glass splits, whatever the hell they're coughing up will get in here."

As if hearing the discussion, the first invader reared back his head and smashed it against the tempered glass.

In a burst of scarlet and organic wadding, the front of the skull flattened while elongating everywhere else, much to the shock and awe of the living trapped inside. Hands covered mouths, while some people whimpered in unchecked horror. It only took a second to realize the thing had broken its head and the resulting shards stretched and contorted the skin.

The zombie slumped, the legs just getting the message that topside was no more, and collapsed to one side before falling over onto its back. The thing did not rise.

"Holy shit," Gus whispered. He'd never seen anything as fucked up as what he'd just witnessed, and he knew he'd be having nightmares because of it.

"What just happened?" Anna asked with a calmness that Gus didn't share.

"I'd say that someone cracked their skull earlier on the first sheet of glass," Gord rumbled, studying the death. "And that tap finished the job."

Rebecca moved in closer, inspecting the fallen zombie. "He looks dead. Really dead."

One of the initial zombies squirming through the outer hole managed to rise, but the right arm wasn't working so good. So it slammed the functioning left into the head cheese and jam decorating the inner door. Another zombie slipped through the outer breach while more attempted to follow. Multiple forms tried to crawl through at once. It was like watching an old 1930s comedy movie, where the actors got caught shoulder-to-shoulder while walking through a doorway.

"We better go," Walt advised.

"Move back to the rear," Rebecca said and double-timed away. The shoppers and painters briskly followed. The painters were the last to go, watching the zombies crawl inside the vestibule only to be denied by the second door.

And the hammering increased.

The people gathered in the back, in front of a row of organic snack bins, where a grand selection of nuts and raisins waited in tall dispensers.

"Okay," Rebecca started, gesturing at Gus. "He's right. They're going to get in here. Just a matter of time. So, I vote that we get out of here. We can go through the inside entrance to the mall, get to another store, one with a back door that goes out onto the rear parking lot. Far and away from here. We see if the coast is clear. If it is, we unlock the doors and go for the cars."

"So, we get outside and creep around the mall to the cars," Vlad Raymond asked.

"That's right."

The danger of the plan hushed them, while arms, fists, and faces continued battering the doors in the background.

"We can't stay here," Rebecca said. "There's nothing strong enough to keep them out other than a freezer, and that's not going to work."

"I'm not barricading myself in a freezer," Vlad Raymond said plainly. Others agreed.

"Any other place in the mall?" Gus asked.

"We can see," Rebecca said, "But I don't think so. Everything's locked up."

"So, we break in," Toby said. "He's got a crowbar."

"And how do we close the broken door then?" Anna asked him.

Toby stopped with an *oh-yeah* scowl.

"I'm in," Gord said. "For the cars."

That set off a pensive round of agreement from the rest, as they weighed their chances of success and didn't like the odds, but even those odds seemed better compared with staying in the megastore. Even Mel Grant grimly consented in going for the cars, as if reality had dumped her into a ditch and drove off, leaving her to fend for herself.

"Does someone stay back?" Perry Fletcher asked.

Walt looked to Rebecca. Gus thought he did that a lot.

"No one has to stay back," Rebecca said. "And I'm not going to be responsible for picking someone. I think we can slip out the back without being detected. It's the parking lot that worries me. That's open ground."

"All the more that someone stays back," Gus explained. "Right? Stay in sight. Keep their attention off the parking lot."

"You volunteering?" Mel Grant asked him bluntly.

Faces turned to Gus. Thoughts of Tammy went through his head. He didn't answer.

93

"Think you can run?" Mel Grant asked again, with surgical directness. "You don't look like a runner to me."

Gus didn't feel like a runner. "I'll run fast enough when I have to."

"One last thing," Rebecca said and motioned them to follow her. They went to the household section, and she stopped before a selection of wooden rolling pins. There were seven hardwood pins, priced at an affordable $4.99 each. Another buck off if you had a Mollymart member card. She then took a box of disposal latex gloves from a shelf and ripped it open. Everyone received two pairs. Nelson went off to the meat cutter's room, and when he returned, he handed out disposable masks that covered the nose and mouth.

"Just in case," he said. He carried his crowbar, and Gord still had the whammer.

For seconds, the group of employees, painters, and shoppers stood and regarded their weapons and meager protection.

"Fuck me," Toby said in resigned disgust, shaking his head at his rolling pin.

"Got anything better around?" Anna asked.

"This is mainly a grocery store," Walt told her. "What you see is it."

"Isn't there a sporting goods shop in the mall?" Toby asked.

"There is, but they're closed," Walt answered.

"We could break in."

"We *can't* break in," the cashier said. "That's against the law."

"I'd say a goddamn zombie apocalypse is reason enough to break in," Toby reasoned.

Anna left the group and walked a little further down the aisle. She bent over and hauled out a cast iron frying pan. "I'll take this. Until I get something better. The other one did the job."

No one argued with her.

Thus prepared, the Mollymart employees led the pack to a side entrance that opened into the mall itself. The screaming and pounding from the main doors hurried them along.

There was a single door that led into a wide corridor where a series of outer and inner glass doors remained untouched to their right. Walt reached up and hooked a lever free at the top and bottom of the side entrance before sliding one section open just a crack. He listened and studied the wide corridor beyond. Overhead night lights remained on, casting a starry gleam on the floor tiles, spaced out evenly along the ceiling and forcing back the empty cave darkness of the mall. Bare wooden benches and kiosks selling afterthought items or lottery tickets were in the corridor, while a few huge ferns covered up the drab walls between shops. A pair of children's rides, a huge rocket for two and a one-kid car were just inside the main doors.

Walt looked to his right. "Looks clear."

"What's there?" Gus asked.

"That's the bank, and they open into the parking lot."

"Could we go out that way?" Mel Grant wondered.

"The Mollymart doors are only fifty, seventy feet away and on the same side," Walt explained. "Might be too close. We're heading to a store in the rear, with a back door."

"Lead on, Walt," Gord commanded.

The Mollymart man left the door to Nelson, who waved the rest through. Anna and Gus were the last to past the stock guy, and as Gus went by, Nelson let the door swing shut.

"Can't lock that from the outside?" Anna asked.

Nelson shook his head. "Inside job only."

The three of them caught up to the lead group. Gus looked back to the mall entrance. The doors were clear, and the starry reflections of the few overhead lights shone in the glass. He could see what was in the parking lot, and there were no zombies in sight. More importantly, there were no zombies seeing them leave Mollymart.

The darkened store fronts of the other businesses drifted by—a salon, a travel agency, a book shop. Gus passed by another pair of sparkly kiddie rides, one of a cartoon car and another of a moose, both offering rides for only a loonie. They turned a corner which got the group out of sight from any of the main doors.

"How far we going?" Gord asked.

"Not far," Walt said, his attention on the corridor ahead, where it eventually turned north, just past a display of indoor flower beds surrounded by an octagon of benches, where seniors would stop with coffees or teas during the day.

"What about there?" Toby asked.

Stanley's Sporting Goods was a blacked-out cave.

"What about it?"

"Those guys have a back door?"

Walt stared at the shop front. "Probably, but—"

"So, let's go through there. I see a rack of baseball bats. Feel a fuckton better about a bat than this." He held up his rolling pin. "And besides, they didn't lower that cage thing over the door."

Which was true.

Walt looked to Rebecca, who shrugged. "We're away from the front, which is all I care about."

With a resigned expression of *whatever*, Walt walked over to Stanley's Sporting Goods. Nelson hurried to the front, and brandished his crowbar.

"Stand back everybody," he told them.

And swung the bar.

Which bounced off the glass surface.

"Goddamn," Toby muttered as Nelson took another whack at the door.

And failed to break it.

"Give me that," Anna said as she stepped forward.

She snatched the tool from Nelson and backed him up. Anna rolled her shoulders, held the crowbar a batter's pose, and swung with both hands.

Perforating the glass in the center.

Crystal bounced and rattled off the floor. She bashed out the door in three more swings and hooked and poked the more stubborn stuff. She stopped when she had what she thought was a large enough opening. Then she sized up Gus's extra-stuffed frame, frowned, and immediately went back to work.

Gus didn't really appreciate that. "That's good," he said drily.

"Yeah?" Anna asked while catching her breath. "Think you can fit?"

"I'll suck in."

Anna smiled a tad sarcastically. When she finished beating out the glass, she handed the crowbar back to Nelson, and stooped as she entered the hole. Seeing nothing amiss, Anna moved past the clutter of bins and displays hauled inside the shop as the others followed her one at a time. Clothing, footwear, and sports equipment, Stanley's had it all. Gus wasn't one to shop there often, but he was impressed with the racks of hockey sticks, skates, sneakers, jogger wear and just about everything else one might be looking for if they were into an active lifestyle.

He immediately focused on a selection of baseball bats. "You think Stanley would mind if I took one of these?"

Rebecca stopped beside him. "Under the circumstances, no. I don't think so."

"What about some of these clothes?" Toby asked. "And I could use a new pair of sneakers."

She didn't appreciate that. "All right, listen," the Mollymart cashier said. "We don't have a free pass to loot the place, okay? So go easy on the stuff. Everything might be back to normal by the end of the week, so just take what you need, and nothing else."

His face partially hidden in shadow, a sheepish Toby placed his rolling pin on a small hill of boxed sneakers and picked up a hockey stick. He hefted it.

Gus pulled a wooden bat from a rack. "Get one of these. More weight to it. More smacking power."

"I'm more into hockey."

"Get a fuckin' bat, y'dummy," Gord said with impatience.

"Why don't you have a bat?" Toby asked with a note of petulance.

Gord held up the whammer.

Toby supposed that would do the trick too.

The rest of the shoppers swapped their rolling pins for their larger cousins. There were helmets, but no one went for any of those. There was hockey padding as well, but that was left behind. Gus thought about more protection, which a lack thereof always bothered him in the movies, especially when main characters were about to knowingly venture into hostile territory. But he decided not to get outfitted, as there was a sense of urgency amongst the people, and he doubted anyone would wait while he searched for sizes that would fit him. Besides, glancing at the assortment of chest, elbow and knee padding apparently available, nothing really offered any full coverage. Something was going to be exposed.

"Hey," Walt said, standing near the entrance wall. "Found out why the cage isn't lowered."

He flicked a switch repeatedly, to no effect.

Rebecca motioned for him to join her near the back, along with Nelson. And as the people geared up, the three Mollymart employees went deeper into Stanley's place and located the storage room.

Nelson returned a short time later. "Okay you guys, this way."

"You found the back door?" Mel Grant asked, carrying a bat.

"Yeah, it's back here and sounds all clear."

The paint crew and shoppers followed him into the storage area. Anna's bat looked positively miniscule in her hands, while the ones Rene (who still hadn't said much at all to anyone) and Carol the librarian held seemed much too big for them.

At the very end of a passage stacked with boxed goods, a fixed light beckoned. Walt and Rebecca stood before a red fire escape door.

"All right," Rebecca said, considering each of them in turn. "This is how it's going to go down."

She took a breath then, while Walt watched her.

"When you're outside, stay to the shadows and the walls," Rebecca advised. "Work your way around the mall to the parking lot. Make sure everything that's loose is tied down, make sure that your phones are turned off. You don't want a call while you're creeping around out there, got it?"

Gus held up his hand.

"What?" Rebecca asked.

"You said when *you're* outside," Gus said. "Where're you going to be?"

"I'm staying here."

Walt cleared his throat.

"*We're* staying here," she corrected herself. "We're staying. We were thinking that someone should stay back after all, and well, since we're Mollymart employees—"

"A company who doesn't give a fuck about you," Toby quickly pointed out.

"Which doesn't matter," Rebecca countered. "Despite what you might think. It's a job. My job. And I do what I can. And that includes accepting a certain level of responsibility for all the shit under Mollymart's roof, including all of you."

"That's ... a really noble thought there, Rebecca," Gus said cautiously, choosing his words carefully. "But I think management would understand you leaving with us. This situation."

But she shook her head. "Then we have to decide who stays back or who goes. No, I've already thought it through. If what you're about to do *fails* ..." she let that sink in. "Someone needs to be here to open the door. Leaving the door wedged open is too risky. A zombie could come around, get inside, and be here if we had to come back. Then, we'd be fucked. This way is best. We'll be fine. And really, if you guys do get to your cars, chances are the zombies will go after you when they hear the engines start up. You'll lure them away, so we'll be able to get out."

"In theory," Anna said quietly.

"In theory."

Gus looked to Walt. "You're going to do this?"

He nodded.

"Maybe we should rethink this, then," Gord said. "Change the plan a little. We don't all have to go out there. I can go alone. Head for my hatchback and do the same thing. Just watch out front. If you don't see me drive past the main doors, then I didn't make it. If I do, I'll lure them away. Then the rest of you go ... even you guys."

He directed that at Rebecca, who didn't say no.

"That makes sense," Anna said.

"Sounds good to me," Vlad Raymond added.

Rebecca exchanged looks with her co-workers. "All right. We're in."

"I'll go with you," Gus said. "I'll watch your back and take the truck. I'll lure them away while you ferry the others to their cars."

Gord approved. "All right then," he said, stepping up to the door. "The rest of you ready for this?"

They were. It was clear on their faces, and Gus didn't blame them. They had families or friends or significant others to reach, to make sure they were safe. He felt the same way.

"I'll head back to Mollymart," Walt announced, volunteering to watch the front to see if the coast cleared. Rebecca's expression tightened just a little as her co-worker left the group.

"I'll go with you," Toby said, hurrying after him.

Trying to focus her thoughts, Rebecca flicked off a switch set near the exit. "Just turned off the outside light."

"You ready for this?" Gord asked Gus.

"Yeah," he replied, limbs and heart already switching into high gear and buzzing with energy.

"Let's go."

Gord opened the door.

14

The back lot was clear.

Across the way, however, was another deserted-looking subdivision that rose above a line of evenly spaced street lights. Some of the houses' interior lights were on, but most were not. Gus believed the time to be after midnight, so he supposed people could have been asleep … but he doubted that. Even as he thought it, he detected movement between the distant houses, subtle flutters in the dark that attracted his eye.

Gord edged out onto the pavement and left the door to Gus. A concerned Rebecca watched them leave, mouthing the words *be careful* before the door closed.

Be careful. Yeah. Right.

But given the situation, Gus thought that the risk was worth the reward, and that the zombies were indeed distracted. The only thing that worried him weren't the zombies out front, but any zombies emerging from the subdivision just across the way. Those worried him, and oddly enough, it made him wonder about city zoning laws.

Gord crept ahead five feet, staying to the shadows, his shoulder nearly flush with the brick wall. Gus followed, hearing the primitive shouting from the front. The street and the lanes turning into the mall parking lot remained empty.

He bumped into Gord's back.

The collision was unexpected. Startling. Gord whirled and glared, his eyes twin lasers threatening to blast Gus's head from his shoulders. Gus drew back, winced an apology, knowing full well he'd fucked up.

Gord relaxed just a bit, and he turned away with one final, withering look.

Be careful, Gus scolded himself. *Be careful.*

They kept to the dark like a pair of cockroaches, making very little noise, certainly none to be heard over the commotion out front. A back door to another business approached, illuminated by a lamp fixture set just above the frame.

Well shit, Gus groaned as they approached the light. Rebecca had no control over those.

Hunched over and brandishing the whammer, Gord skittered through the first white cone and stopped in the patch of blackness in between. Gus followed in his version of a ninja-walk, holding onto his bat and feeling exceptionally exposed in the light.

Then he was on the other side.

Under that welcomed sheet of darkness, Gus leaned against the brick wall and released a sigh. Sweat ran off him in a boatload, and his painter clothes stuck to his skin.

Gord held up two fingers and pointed ahead.

Gus cringed at the lit doors.

The painters moved ahead, clinging to the dark, when Gord stopped in his tracks, looking to his feet. He glanced back, pointed to the ground, and stepped over what lay in his path.

A fist-crumpled pop can. Aluminium, just waiting to be kicked.

Gus stepped over the discarded trash as if it were a land mine.

Once past the can, they passed through the last two cones of light. Gus's blood pressure spiked each time. They got through without incident, and it was a clear twenty feet to the corner. Beyond that, the side appeared well-lit.

Again, Gord stopped, halting Gus not a foot away from his co-worker's back. Gus waited, eyeing his friend's profile before glancing in the same direction. Just across the distant road, and walking in a circle between a pair of street lamps, was a male zombie. The sight of the creature froze Gus in his tracks. Gord was likewise motionless, staring at the wandering figure, willing the thing to move off.

The thing didn't.

Dressed in shorts and a T-shirt, the zombie wandered about the street lamps, seemingly following a pattern, as weird as that seemed. The zombie had what appeared to be a leash in its hand, but with nothing attached to the end.

Gus watched the creature, wondering if it was looking for its dog—or was somehow hooked on a *memory* of walking its lost pet.

As the two men watched, the zombie stumbled to its knees. The thing righted itself, stood and stomped off down the sidewalk. It dragged the leash behind it, passing under street lamps.

Gus was breathing again. In fact, he couldn't seem to get enough air.

"You okay?" Gord asked.

Gus nodded.

"You sound like you're hyperventilating."

That got a violent head shake, but the truth was, being exposed as he was and seeing that zombie rattled his nerves more than just a little.

"This way," Gord said, cautiously moving to the corner, whammer clenched and ready. Gus followed.

Mollymart's west side was lit up like a school yard basketball court. Parking lanes, divided lines, and arrows glowed underneath four out-of-reach light fixtures. A broad loading bay door was closed, and the smaller work entrance was firmly shut and thankfully devoid of zombies. A parallel road ran north-south, and a small copse of trees and bushes lay beyond that. The Brush-It truck waited for them beyond the lights, shining in the darkness. Gord's hatchback was just on the other side.

At least two hundred feet away. From the corner they peeked out from to the other. Then there was the walk across a wide-open space, which was ripe for disaster. The sight of all that white-lined pavement seemed like a nowhere-to-hide kill zone. It unsettled Gus. The risk factor had suddenly spiked. Worse, there was another fifty feet or more between the far corner and the truck.

The zombies' morbid yowling was that much closer, daring the painters to take their shot.

Gord looked back at him, a worried question on his face. "What do you think?" he whispered.

Gus was about to honestly say *fuck this*, when all three lights along the superstore's side winked off in succession, dousing the entire wall in shadow.

Rebecca. Or one of the Mollymart staffers. Working the light and the switches.

"We're good," Gord spoke softly, his smile lighting up the dark.

Gus nodded in agreement, grateful for the night.

The two painters rounded the corner and snuck to the next, and as they approached, the widespread glow outside flicked on and off. Someone playing with the Mollymart's entrance lights, letting the two men know one of the staffers was in position.

Gus pressed himself against the wall while Gord peeked around the corner. He pulled back, swallowed, and seemed to think on things.

"What?" Gus asked.

Gord didn't answer. Instead, he shook his head and judged the distance from the corner to the Brush-It truck. Then, very carefully, he extracted his car keys from a pocket, and gripped them so that they didn't jingle.

"This is gonna be tight," he whispered to Gus. "There's a lot of them out there, and … and they're fucking *climbing* over each other to get inside. It's a pileup right in front of the store."

"So let's go then," Gus said, tempted by the proximity of the truck.

"Get your keys out," Gord ordered. "Carefully. Make sure your thumb's on the unlock button, because you'll need to get this right the first time, understand?"

Gus nodded.

"You'll need to be *on* this," Gord insisted, and that's when Gus saw a midnight flash of sweat racing down the side of his co-worker's profile. He knew right then that Gord was scared, perhaps even scared quite badly, but he was going for his car, anyway, because he had Mary to get to, and that was the kinda cowboy Gord Munn was. "When we go, we walk toward the truck, just like we're one of them, understand? We do *not* run. Unless they run for us then we go. Okay? You got that?"

Gus nodded that he did.

"Get to the car and truck, and when I unlock the doors, you unlock yours. They might hear the chirp and they might not. Regardless, five seconds minimum to get inside and lock the doors again. Then start up your machine and drive. We do a loop and draw them away from the front. You continue to draw them away and I'll circle around back and pick up our people. I'll get them to their rides and get whoever's next. Then we go our separate ways."

"What about Toby? He'll go with you?"

"I'll pick him up. You're heading to Tammy's?"

"Yeah."

"Hope she's okay, Gustopher."

"Hope Mary's good too, Gordo."

They shared a mutual second of uncertainty then, knowing they were on the precipice of danger but not knowing just how extreme.

"Here we go," Gord said, manning up. He stepped out and around the corner.

Gus was a second behind him.

And then slowed, as if suddenly stricken by a massive heart attack and gazing upon death itself. Everything decelerated, and a background of mewling and chewing filled his ears.

With the words *Holy Christ* on his mind but lacking the voice to give them sound, Gus saw the reason why Gord took the time to explain things. He saw why his friend and co-worker of eleven plus years looked scared. Then he realized just how goddamn *brave* Gord was to go for the cars anyway, even after seeing what lay around the corner.

It's a pileup right in front of the store, Gord had said.

He spoke the truth.

Sorta.

There was a *mob* mashed against Mollymart's face. A black rippling mass of heads and torsos and limbs all attempting to push itself through the glass by sheer weight and force combined. A savage amoebic *mound* that shoved and heaved against battered doors that could no longer be seen. The lights were on inside the vestibule, but it was fragmented, flickering, peeking through that human mudslide assault like a machine on the verge of breaking down. Zombies crawled over the shoulders of other zombies, actually reaching the upper frame of the brickwork. Those zombies on top struggled to breach the glass, but the ones behind wanted the same thing. Heads were yanked back. Shoulders pulled and shoved. Some of them staggered and fell off-balance, and those disappeared into the mob, perhaps sifting to the bottom, where the boots and sneakers thrashed and stomped and ultimately juiced those unfortunates. They squished their companions down, compacting them into a screaming, frothing ramp. A witch's tar of blood and fluid and ripe offal stemmed from that blob, pooling around hundreds of feet and causing some to lose traction. Dull rivulets issued from that manic press and spread across the pavement. There was no cohesion to the zombies' efforts. Certainly, no teamwork. Just a seething mass of meat and twisting limbs and clawing fingers, where a few shadowy figures pulled themselves forward before being hauled back.

And Gus was no more than a ten-second run from the scene.

No barriers were between him and the nearest night-cloaked zombie. His vision became a tunnel, and nothing existed beyond the edges of Mollymart's main doors.

Chirp-chirp!

The unlocking of a car jerked Gus back to reality.

A zombie, one clinging to the outer fringe, lifted its head upon hearing that mechanical note. It detached itself from the others and staggered around.

Dressed in pajama bottoms and an orange T-shirt, the zombie stood with a broken arm that trembled at its side. Blood ran from a gruesome spear point piercing the white skin, just below the elbow.

The thing lifted that broken arm, and everything below the compound break hung and swayed and shivered.

"RUN, GUS!" Gord barked from the other side of his hatchback.

That was all he needed. The hypnosis broken, Gus bolted for the truck.

The zombie charged after him, bare feet slapping asphalt the whole way.

Gord slammed the door to his hatchback as Gus reached the driver's side of the Brush-It pickup. Gus pawed at the handle much too fast and plied back two fingernails. That electric buzzer of pain only hurried him along, but he was very much aware of bare feet smacking the pavement. A sound that quickly grew louder.

The door opened. Gus got aboard. He locked the doors.

The zombie slammed into the truck's rear. A glance in the side mirror showed a pale figure turning the corner. A grimace of teeth flashed.

The hatchback flared to life, and Gord wasted no time in reversing away. Tires shrieked as the little car streaked across the parking lot, narrowly missing a few other vehicles.

Gus jammed the keys into the steering column, missing the ignition. He jammed them again and was denied. A face appeared in his side window. Gus jumped at the sight just as the zombie flapped a broken club of meat against the glass. Blood spattered. Bone scraped glass. The window trembled. Gus yelped and scrabbled at the ignition and again missed the slot. The zombie mashed its face flat against the glass. Split cheeks opened like multiple gills.

Teeth were visible through those cuts.

That nearly broke Gus right there.

But somehow, he shoved the key into the ignition damn near perfectly and started up the machine. The zombie shouted at him, a stream of gibberish demanding that he *stay STILL damn it!*

Instead, Gus put the truck into drive. The vehicle shot into a sharp turn that peeled rubber and shat smoke, veering away from the edge of the parking lot. The trees and streetlights sped by in a frightening blur. He checked his side mirror and gasped.

The zombie had its good arm draped over the metal protrusion, hanging on while attempting to batter the window with its other flopping limb. The thing briefly met Gus's terrified gaze just as it fell away from the truck's side.

Gus glimpsed a red-flared husk rolling across the asphalt before focusing on driving, but the fright left him speechless.

And entirely clueless as to what he was supposed to do next.

He drove around the other parked cars, seeing the hatchback race up the far end with a surge of power. Gus barked a laugh despite his fright, as Gord's little car shooting along the parking lot's edge looked like the head of one very pissed-off bionic duck. Parked cars sprinkled the lot, but they didn't block Gord's path.

The hatchback's headlights flared to life.

Good idea, Gus thought, so he switched on his as well. He slowed toward the lower corner of the parking lot, near the main road. Gord also slowed down and made a left turn back toward the Mollymart East main entrance. Toward the zombies still gathered there.

Light flickered and died as bodies moved. Some of the things turned at the speeding hatchback. Others broke away and charged, much to Gus's surprise. The hatchback's headlights whitened perhaps five or six zombies a second before Gord swerved around the attacking monsters. A nerve-twanging clap of bodies on bumper reached Gus and he glimpsed a figure performing a messy cartwheel up and over the speeding car.

Gus then remembered his own mission as a wet hand slapped the truck's passenger window. A hideous face with far too large a mouth peered inside with a raunchy grin, and it took Gus a second to realize the thing's mouth had been torn asunder, all the way its jaw hinge.

He stomped on the gas. The face in the window vanished with a lurch. Gripping the wheel two-handed, Gus turned left and headed back toward that skin-crawling pack of undead.

Or were they really undead?

Gord completed his turn and shot down the far side of the parking lot as Gus drifted right before swinging back left, bringing the truck not twenty feet away from the front of the mall and its sidewalk. Glowing signs flashed by, still suckling off a live grid. The handful of zombies Gord had blown through came into sight. The ones standing turned in the direction of the charging pickup.

But Gus only glimpsed them, because his attention fixed on the zombie his co-worker had hit. The thing appeared dead from the collision. Half its head was squished flat.

Zombies flung themselves at the pickup as he sped by. A multitude of hands slapped the vehicle's sides.

He drove on.

White beams flashed over the pileup choking the Mollymart entrance. Glowing faces and eyes snarled in his headlights. A few figures peeled away from that congealed mess clinging to the store front.

Positioned as high as he was, the pickup effortlessly slammed into three bodies and carried them along for a split second before gravity sucked them down and shat them out the back. Amazingly, none of the three hit the windshield. Gus realized charging them headlong while only doing forty could have been disastrous. The truck bucked and jumped then, running over bodies, and he quickly decelerated before he lost control. He stopped not far from where he'd parked the truck earlier that evening. He slapped the truck in reverse and watched the rear camera wink to life.

A dozen or so zombies were rushing him.

More were detaching themselves from the storefront.

He shifted gears, hit the accelerator, and drove away, taking the same path as before, forming a route that might've looked like a squished box.

The hatchback's tail lights flashed red before they disappeared behind the distant corner of the mall. But that didn't really interest Gus.

The zombies coming from the surrounding suburbs did.

As if the revving engines had somehow disturbed a veritable undead empire, drawing shadows out from the deepest night, figures trailing streamers ran down lawns and hills. They emerged from between houses and out from around trees. They crossed the roads and stumbled into ditches. Outlines clambered across asphalt strips without hesitation and zeroed in on Gus and his truck. Some were dressed in summer clothing, some in pajamas. Some clothes were in tatters, for reasons unknown.

The action in the parking lot attracted them.

Gus pulled away and concentrated on driving. He pumped the gas, revved the engine, and again ringed the parking lot. More zombies became less interested in Mollymart's dark main doors and more interested in that huge metallic turkey flashing by them. Gus stayed away from the other cars, and as he turned back to the superstore's front, his headlights showed him the earlier victims of his truck.

Men and women crawled toward the oncoming vehicle. Their clothes hid their injuries, but their arms worked well enough. Some hands hung off broken wrists, some forearms dangled, creating fleshly pinchers. All slunk along the ground like energetic caterpillars.

Gus tried to avoid them. Something about those broken people inch-worming their way toward his headlights stopped him from running over them. So, he steered clear.

Unfortunately, he had to slow down. Even worse, his deviated path took him into the area where most of the cars were parked.

Gus braked.

And jumped in his seat when something slammed into the side of the Brush-It truck. He hit the gas and powered forward, bashing the front of a family-sized sedan in a flurry of glass. The impact was ear-popping. He rattled forward, then bounced back, realizing the hard way he wasn't wearing his seatbelt. A figure fell away from the truck's side. Others charged around an SUV and rushed the passenger door. More figures raced in from behind. Hands slapped the pickup's shell. Fists bounced off the side windows. Gus turned left, then right, knowing he was running over feet. The company truck bashed through a series of torsos. A zombie reached out for the driver's side mirror and missed, falling in the attempt.

Then the way was clear, and Gus accelerated toward the south end of the parking lot, toward the main drag.

And saw the line of shadows running at him.

A determined Gus turned left, cutting across the lot and avoiding the other parked cars. The zombies from the superstore's doorstep were pursuing— those that could, anyway—which was when Gus realized something.

He was going to have to leave the people trapped inside the mall.

An odd knot of self-preservation, duty, and guilt pulled tight in his chest. Gus slowed down to thirty kilometers an hour and made for the parking lot exit. Figures darted underneath street lamps, running toward him. More outlines streamed across the parking lot, away from the supermarket's wrecked doors. Some of those limped or weren't running at all, but Gus didn't linger on those.

There were plenty to be worried about filling the street.

And with the slower speed, the engine wasn't working as hard, and Gus picked up on a low buzz of static. A stadium's worth of wild cheer came from outside, a sound which made his lower extremities go cold.

Screams. Howls. Cries of pure insanity and uncorked rage.

Hands whacked at the pickup's ass as zombies from the subdivisions charged across the road. Gus increased speed. Bodies whipped by the windows. He turned into the exit as fingers scrabbled at the glass and metallic sides. A set of lights were green, and Gus swung right and accelerated a little more. Figures rushed the driver's and passenger's side, the faces lit up with a maniacal glee. Blood streamed from their mouths. Hooked fingers reached for Gus's side mirror and missed. And like hounds on the flanks of a deer, the zombies kept up with the truck, swatting the body as he completed his turn.

"*Jesus Christ!*" Gus winced and sped up, leaving the mall behind.

In his side mirror, however, the mob sprinted after him.

He shot down an inner town road, one that, in the daytime, would appear quite neighbourly with its assortment of old and new homes, carefully measured lots, wide driveways, and cut lawns with the occasional bicycle or children's toys left outside. Even at night, it was a nice street to drive along.

Now, however, heads rose at the truck's approach. Shadowy figures, at a loss about what to do with themselves, turned in their driveways. Cars were stopped on the road, their doors opened. In some cases, the doors *weren't* open, and the occupants contained within became frighteningly animated when Gus drove by. An SUV had rammed itself against the base of a mighty elm, and the driver, a woman in a summer dress, scuttled over the grass, toward the approaching pickup. Her hand skittered over the curb while her torso seemed to push-steer her head upon an obvious broken neck.

Gus zipped past the thing.

More stopped cars appeared on the road, either empty or deserted, forcing him to slow and move around or between vehicles. Gus didn't come this way earlier in the day, but he wondered what the roads would have been like, and then he thought more about Rebecca's zombie theory and the flu bug visiting the city. He'd seen enough zombie movies in his life. George Romero was the grandfather of the genre, in his opinion.

But an actual, honest-to-fuck zombie outbreak?

In *Annapolis?*

Two trucks stopped in the middle of the road, creating a bottle neck. Gus threaded the white line straight through the opening, clearing the gap by a finger on each side. The shock of not colliding with the vehicles left him bug-eyed and breathless. He slowed down and glanced in his side mirror. His pursuers were nowhere in sight.

That made him think again.

He'd have to go back to Mollymart. A twinge of guilt overcame him. He *had* to go back. Just to make sure that the others got away. His conscience wouldn't allow anything less. Check on them, make sure they were gone, then go for Tammy.

Gus ran a hand over his face, found it coated in sweat, and wiped it clean on his painter duds. *Zombie outbreak*. There had been a flu bug in the valley, yes, but how the hell did it decide to *activate* itself tonight? Then again perhaps it had already activated itself. He remembered the professor in the skimpy cutoffs earlier that day, remembered the guy's wife arriving home. He even remembered her hacking cough through the walls. All through the week he'd heard of people getting sick, heard Toby and Gord talking about friends and family coming down with some wicked virus that took the very life out of them and rendered them bedridden.

Hell, he even remembered the outbreak being reported on the news.

But it was the *flu*. Some weird strain of influenza.

He just hadn't seen it … until tonight.

And in a timeframe of about four or five hours, things that were just out of sight and rapidly becoming out of control, finally bubbled over, like a pot of soup left cooking on a stove.

A side road popped into view, and there were people out walking just beyond streetlight's warm glow. They didn't walk like regular people, however. Their hands hung at their sides. Their posture was poor, their shoulders slumped. And when Gus took the turn, looking to get back to the mall, they started walking for him.

When he sped away, they *ran* after him.

The sick cries of outrage sealed the deal. They weren't calling out to him. They were wailing.

The road took a left turn, then a right.

And that last right hit Gus the hardest.

There, out front of a dark bungalow was a group of people poised over one section of the lawn, as if searching for a lost set of car keys. A motorcycle was parked in the driveway, and Gus could see them moving just past the edges of the bike.

Legs and arms came into view, but when the headlights' glow washed over them …

Gus was speechless. He stopped thinking, stopped breathing, and just let his hands do the driving for the next few seconds (that felt like a year), while his brain struggled to process that scene on the lawn.

Five. There were five people eating a body. Whether it was a man or a woman, Gus couldn't see enough to say, but when the lights flowed over them, saw the faces of the feeders jerk up and snarled.

Red faces. Red fists. Everything dripped matter.

Gus squeaked a horrified note as the truck rolled by that terrible feast. The feeders rose as well, but then he was too far gone to see if they were coming after him. Then he remembered he was still driving and pushed the machine to greater speeds.

As the engine worked and hummed in his ears, shadows chased the truck. *Eating. They were* eating *that poor bastard* ...

His gullet lurched, but nothing came up. He held onto the steering wheel, staying in control, yet knowing everything was suddenly beyond any semblance of control. Those people were feeding on a dead person, and he couldn't shake the image from his memory, couldn't unsee the feral working of jaws and twinkling eyes. His doubts about a zombie outbreak, however, were no more.

Those silhouettes disappeared as Gus linked up with a smaller two-lane street and turned back toward Mollymart. It was a straight strip of pavement collared by thick bushes on the left. He accelerated for seconds before shifting his foot to the brake.

A huge transport trailer had stopped not a kilometer ahead. Red tail lights and white warning lights flashed in the distance, outlining the rectangular shape. The tailpipe smoked.

What the hell? Gus wondered and slowed down, just in case. There was no real choice in the matter, anyway. The big rig had stopped in the middle of the road, and the driver stood at the front.

Then Gus saw the body lying on the pavement, his head and chest crushed.

As soon as he saw the corpse, Gus's foot shifted from brake to gas pedal.

But then the driver's arms started to wave in a very unzombie-like fashion.

Gus steered around the body and the transport's rear. The Brush-It truck lifted on the right as the tires went up and over a nearby curb.

"Hey!" the trucker guy shouted as Gus stopped and lowered the passenger window just a crack.

"What's wrong?" Gus demanded, a little harsher than necessary.

The trucker was tall, lanky, and red-eyed from crying. "I hit some poor bastard."

The words didn't quite register with the house painter. "What?"

"I didn't mean to hit him," the trucker quickly explained. "I didn't see him. I mean, the stupid dingbat jumped right out in front of me. I didn't have a chance to do anything. He just—just jumped right at the goddamn grill. Most fucked up thing I ever saw. He was like a trout going after a fly-hook ..."

"You okay?" Gus asked, studying the guy's distressed features.

"Huh? Yeah, sure I'm okay. I mean ... but the guy is ..."

"Where? Where is he?"

The trucker, unshaven and sporting a mustache a bear would've wanted, said, "He's under the rig. I must've dragged him forty feet or so. I didn't mean to—but these things don't stop on a dime. I felt him go under, man. Under the tires."

"Is it dead?"

The question caught the trucker off guard. "What?"

"Is it *dead?*"

"Yeah," the trucker replied with grim confirmation. "He's dead. Tires flattened his skull. It's not pretty near the back. Listen ... you got a phone? I can't get anyone on mine. Not even the cops."

"Get aboard your truck and drive."

He gave Gus a questioning look. "What?"

"Get aboard your rig and get moving! Get *outta* here! You know what's going on?"

The trucker clearly didn't. Gus faltered, wondering, *knowing* what he was about say would sound utterly fucked up.

But then the trucker glanced back at the road behind the trucks. His face crunched into a question, and even before he spoke the words, Gus heard.

Voices. Angry voices. Several of them. Screaming gibberish.

"The hell is that?" the trucker asked, taking a step back.

"*Get out of here right fucking now!*" Gus yelled.

The trucker retreated from the pickup's window and nodded fearfully, focusing on a section of darkened road where figures were only just appearing. Figures that were running. Charging.

The trucker climbed into his machine.

Gus rolled up his window and drove off, taking the lead ahead of the big rig. The transport huffed and roared and started moving.

Far too slow.

The zombies caught the vehicle.

They groped and clung onto the transport, covering the grill with their torsos and seeking handholds. They scaled the sides. A couple quickly advanced to the windshield, obscuring it. The trucker rolled ahead a few meters, veering left then right as if attempting to shake the boarders loose. The engines revved. Zombies held onto parts, but some lost their grip as they tried to advance. Some were pulled under the merciless crush of the rig's tires.

Others fell flat, unable to regain their handholds on the moving machine. Those that avoided the crushing tires scrambled to their feet and resumed the chase, racing at an astounding pace, their faces hidden in shadow.

They were relentless. Fearless. And without any concern for their lives, just like those at the superstore.

The road curved then, and the last Gus saw of the transport before it disappeared was the headlights veering sharply to the right and up the side of a hillside.

Then it was gone.

Sickness and grief swelled through Gus, and he reprimanded himself for not attempting to help more. He should've told the guy to get aboard with him. He should've *ordered* the guy to get aboard the painter truck. Too late now, and chances were the driver was already dead, and Gus was *still* moving in the other direction.

Too many people to save, his mind waved at him.

No, he thought back, *I just need to get things in order. Focus. Prioritize. Be more proactive.*

His mind didn't comment. That was fine by him.

He couldn't help the trucker, but he'd get back to Mollymart. Make sure that everyone trapped there had gotten away.

Then he'd head for Tammy.

Plan set and mind determined, he drove for the mall.

15

Gord slammed on the brakes when his door was directly alongside Stanley's rear exit. The skid jerked him out of the hatchback's seat. Upon settling back, he jammed a palm heel into the horn.

"Come on!" he shouted.

The door opened. Rebecca scanned for attackers.

Undead attackers, as cliché as that might sound. They were undead, or dying anyway. Gord had hit and run over enough of them to see it for himself. Zombies. As much as he hated the overused word, the things attacking the mall fit the profile. The ones he'd struck and left behind in a cloud of exhaust still moved, and even worse, on a second pass, they still crawled toward the car with that same mindless, pissed-off ferocity, despite broken backs and limbs.

The sight only heightened his resolve to get home. To get back to his wife. She'd been okay when he left the house that evening, but their neighbours, Burt and Sally Tuttle, not twenty feet away from them, had both come down with the same flu bug and quarantined themselves inside their split-level home. Then there were the Sampsons across the street. May was fine, but Clark had been suffering for three days. And, once he got thinking about it, Gord hadn't seen the Dales either—or any of their kids.

Gord and Mary Munn lived on a quiet street of about fifteen families, in an area festooned with about a hundred more households, one of which were the Keeves. The *Keeves*. Gord's knuckles tightened on the steering wheel. The Keeves had ten members under the one roof, including grandparents. A virtual zombie mob ripe for infection.

A hand slapped the glass, jerking Gord back to the present.

A fearful Carol Freeman, her eyes huge behind those librarian rims.

"Other side," Gord yelled through the glass. "I can take two more."

"Can we run?" Anna shouted back, stepping out of the doorway like a huge bouncer.

"It's not safe. I'll come back."

And he would. Mary was on his mind, but these folks had families too. He'd get them to their cars.

Carol yanked open the passenger door. She climbed in as Rene entered the back seat. John Maple urged her to hurry.

Mel Grant pushed her way around Anna and bolted for the other side of the hatchback.

"Where you going?" Anna yelled after her.

But Mel didn't answer. She crammed into the back seat, pushing Rene into John.

Gord gave her a *the-fuck-you-doing?* look but kept his mouth shut once he saw they all fit back there, though it looked tighter than a mosquito's bag stretched over an elephant's ass.

"Just drive, dickhead," Mel blasted him, glaring red-eyed heat.

Gord left her alone. "I'll come back!" he shouted at the others standing in the doorway.

A watchful Anna withdrew, closing the door while pushing Rebecca back.

Gord stomped on the gas.

Only to quickly brake, realizing that Gus was still out front, that the zombie siege was out front. Gus would lure the zombies away, or at least try to lead the bastards away.

He killed the headlights and drove to the first corner.

"You're driving too slow," Mel Grant whined impatiently from the back seat.

Gord ignored her. He ignored Carol Freeman's stare. He braked at the corner and eased around it, entering the dark side of Mollymart. Far ahead, figures emerged from the night and raced past street lights, charging into the parking lot.

"Where'd they come from?" Rene asked from the rear, breaking her silence.

"All around," Gord said. "This place is dead center in a residential area. I'd like to meet whoever planned the city grid."

"Why are you driving so slow?" a frustrated Mel repeated.

"Giving Gus a chance to draw the ones away in the parking lot. So you have a chance to get to your cars. You all got your keys ready?"

"Course I do," Mel replied in a snotty tone. "Just drive past the main entrance. My Mustang's parked closest."

"I'm ready," John replied.

"Me too," said Rene, breaking her silence yet again.

Carol dug around in her handbag, searching. "Got them," she finally said, holding up her car keys.

"All right, I'll let her out first then work my way back," Gord told them all. "Sound good?"

"Sounds good," Mel answered for them all.

Figures, Gord thought.

He released the brake. "Here we go."

The hatchback eased forward, hidden under the protective dark. When they reached the corner, Gord leaned over his steering wheel, straining to see.

Four figures.

They were standing idly about, as if determining where to go, what to do, their features only partially seen by the glow from the parking lot lights. Only a handful of what had been before.

The car's engine got their attention.

And one after the other, the foursome charged.

Gord accelerated.

The bumper clipped the first zombie across the hip, skidding him up the hood where his arm and part of his head hit the outer windshield frame with a clatter. He tumbled to one side as Gord turned the car into the second zombie and caught him across the waist. The thing's arms crashed across the hood before the car yanked the body underneath.

The hatchback lifted.

Carol screamed. John Maple screamed.

Gord held onto the steering wheel and rammed the last two.

One bodysurfed off the hood and crashed into the windshield, transforming the glass into a gummy spider web. The second zombie landed behind the first, and both trembled on the moving car before falling off.

"Fuck," Gord said, scooching down to see through a clear spot in the ruined windshield.

"That's my car!" Mel screamed. "That's my car right there! Right there!"

A black Mustang. Parked in a designated blue zone for the disabled.

"I can't stop here—" Gord told her.

"Stop here!"

"There's zombies still in the lot!"

"Stop this fucking car right here!"

Gord did not.

And Mel saw that he wasn't.

So, as he drove by her vehicle, she opened her door and threw herself out.

16

Toby caught up to Walt as the cashier passed through the wrecked hole in Stanley's Sporting Goods shop.

"Stan's gonna be pissed," Toby said.

"Stan's a nice guy," Walt said. "And his name's really Vidur."

"Stanley's real name is Vidur?"

"Yeah."

"Stanley Vidur?"

"Just Vidur," Walt huffed as they raced through the mall's corridors. "Don't know his last name. Very nice guy, though."

They reached the inside entrance to Mollymart. Toby peered out onto the parking lot. Forms hurried across the lot in the direction of the breached doors. Walt tapped him on the shoulder, breaking his horrified stare. The pair went inside the grocery store and heard the zombies wedged inside the vestibule, still hammering away at the glass. In seconds, the two men saw that trapped mass and kept low amongst the many bins inside the entryway.

The dead didn't notice them.

Walt stopped behind a shelving unit filled with apples

"Okay, listen," Walt said. "The lights are just over there. I'll flick the lights on and off until I hear your buddies outside."

"Gus and Gord."

"Gus and Gord," Walt clarified.

"And what do I do?"

"Ahh … let them see you. Until you can hear the cars. Then get out of sight."

"Hey!" a voice called out.

Both men turned around to see Nelson and his crowbar running past the deli counter. Nelson scooted down and bobbed his way toward the two men.

"Rebecca sent me," the stock guy said. "And I remembered something on the way over here. We need to kill the lights over the loading bay area for those guys. It's all lit up over there. I can do that."

"Go with him," Walt ordered. "Just in case."

Toby pointed to the weakening doors. "But—"

"Turn off those lights and get back here." Walt wasn't in the mood to talk things out.

Toby looked to Nelson and gestured for him to lead on. They left Walt circling fruit and produce bins in the dark, moving toward the light switches. Toby glanced over his shoulder once as they neared the double doors leading out back. The distant front was dark, with shadows jumping behind the vestibule's glass.

The sight left Toby in a rare moment of speechlessness.

Nelson pushed through the swinging doors, bringing Toby back to the present. They hurried inside, past the aisles brimming with boxed foodstuffs.

Toby slowed, very much aware of the freezer unit and the zombie imprisoned some thirty feet away back there.

He listened.

Realizing he wasn't being followed, Nelson stopped and looked back. Toby held up a hand, asking for quiet.

Boom.

The prisoner hit the door. He was still in the box. All was good.

Toby caught up to Nelson. "He's still in there."

"He's not going anywhere. The guy's gotta be super strong to push that pallet of water away. And then there's the door lock."

"Thought you said it was a push lock? A safety release?"

"Yeah, but it's a zombie, man. He can't figure that thing out. They're brainless."

Toby reluctantly nodded, but there was something in that reasoning that seemed off to him.

The pounding on the freezer door receded as they ran past the aisle mouths. The unloading zone lay just ahead, and the huge area shone under florescent starlight. Boxes of foodstuffs were stacked and cluttered the area. A forklift was parked on the other side of the doors, a good sixty feet away. Nelson ran to a large panel at the top of a small platform to the left of the doors. He opened the box cover, revealing a lever and two columns of switches.

Nelson started fanning switches.

Lights snapped off overhead, and Toby voiced his alarm by grunting and pointing.

"I got it," the stock guy assured him and started turning things back on. Light reappeared. Nelson took a better look at the controls and became a little more selective. This time, the interior lights stayed on, much to Toby's relief.

"That's it," Nelson announced, stepping back from the panel.

"All off?"

"All off. Darker 'n hell out there right now."

"All right." Toby nodded at the levers. "Those for the doors?"

"Yeah. Raising and lowering. Let's get back to the front. Walt's waiting for us."

They started jogging, and Toby had the presence of mind to think about how out of shape he'd become. Work was non-stop this year, and as a result, if it was sunny, you painted outside, rainy meant inside. They were split over two jobs as a result, and run ragged. Though he didn't *look* out of shape, he felt it.

A scraping stopped him cold.

Nelson halted in his tracks, and the two men exchanged fearful looks.

"The hell is that?" Toby quietly asked, but he knew. He knew Nelson knew.

They ran for the freezer.

Zeroing in on the row of stainless steel units, they both saw that the makeshift prison with the pallet of bottled water upon it had moved. Not much, but enough to see the freezer door ajar.

"Oh my fuck," a bewildered Toby realised.

The door moved, as if vibrating, producing a metallic grunt that neither man could identify. A forceful release of air spiked the air, a groan of absolute effort, and a flicker of movement along the door's edge. A second wheeze of breath.

The door jerked open less than a finger, but it opened.

Another intake of air, and another strongman's groan of exertion.

Toby looked to Nelson, who was shaking his head in disbelief.

"That's not quite a ton of water, but fuck me," the storage guy whispered. "Those wheels are locked."

Locked didn't mean immovable.

Nelson edged toward the door. Toby did not want to follow, but he did anyway, holding his bat like a protective talisman. The door shivered yet again, moving the water pallet resting against its base. The thing inside refilled its lungs and doubled down, exerting an impossible force considering its injuries. But it was obviously free of its bindings, and somehow, Toby realized, it had figured out the safety release. Or perhaps the creature had simply pressed itself up against the door, shifting across the surface until it felt the mechanism that would unknowingly grant freedom and blindly shoved against it. The release pressed inward, and that sensation of give, of weakness, was enough for an instinctive spark of understanding in the zombie.

And so, the creature applied itself, pushing against the door, mashing its upper body against the metal and utilizing whatever strength it possessed.

Locked wheels protested, giving up ground by the steady millimeter.

Nelson hefted his crowbar just as the top of a very bloody head appeared from behind the opening door.

Nelson yelped.

Toby didn't make a sound, but the sight of that gore-spattered skull issuing from the freezer jolted his entire system, leaving him stunned on the spot.

The head pushed forward, straining, the profile leering. Blood coated the enamel shards where the thing had smashed its face against unforgiving walls. Blackness spurted from the zombie's crushed nose as it continued forcing its way through the narrow gap. The point where its jaw hinged to its head appeared, then the ear, stretching to a point where Toby thought that clover of skin and cartilage might be ripped from the side of the zombie's face. Wet and dismal craters covered the thing's forehead, and it took the men a few precious seconds to realize the craters had once been egg-sized contusions, ruptured and flattened against the door.

"Oh my God," Nelson was whispering. "Oh my God."

The zombie heard him.

The head snapped up at the words. It turned as much as it could, with a feral look of *ahaaa!* And then it really started working on the door.

Nelson moved forward.

"What're you gonna do?" the painter asked.

"Gonna bash its skull in."

"*What?*"

"We can't let it get out," Nelson explained.

"You're gonna kill it?"

"Fuck yeah, I'm gonna kill it."

"Oh, Jesus Christ."

"Stand back if you think you're gonna see something you're not gonna like," Nelson announced before strapping on one of the disposable masks he'd taken from the meat cutter's facility. Once ready, he moved around the pallet.

An arm that ended in a destroyed hand flailed from the gap. The zombie waved that wrecked appendage up and down in a very unsettling way, as if it were controlled by a puppeteer who'd choked down a pint of whiskey in a very short time. The arm flailed at Nelson as he approached. Toby rounded the pallet's corner, positioning himself as a reluctant backup, dreading what the Mollymart employee was about to do.

The zombie's mouth hung open, the jawline a frightening purple-blue and red. Its tongue darted out as it released a stream of angry nonsense, and both men realized the thing had broken its jaw.

Remembering his own mask, Toby dug it out of a pocket and hooked it over his ears.

Nelson darted in and struck the zombie's head.

The blow knocked the skull down, but the zombie righted itself and snarled. Fluids flew from its mouth. Nelson flinched and retreated, only to rush in and strike the zombie a second time. Then a quick third and fourth, batting the head as if it were a boney piñata.

But the thing didn't go down.

"You're not doing it right," Toby yelled. "Break open the head!"

Instead, Nelson turned the crowbar around and stabbed. Two-handed, swinging that blunt steel tip out and up as if he were forcefully tossing out a bale of hay. The crowbar punctured the thing just below the sternum, and continued up into neighbourhood of the heart.

The effect was immediate. A berry-red stream jetted from around the puncture point, spraying walls. The thing's cries stopped, and it collapsed in that stainless-steel gap, crumpling upon the freezer's threshold.

"Oh shit," a horror-stricken Nelson said as he fell back, slamming his back up against the end of the aisle.

"You got him," Toby said, creeping in and inspecting the kill.

"I got him."

"Holy fuck," the painter whispered. "Right through the heart."

"That didn't feel good. At all."

"Felt worse for that guy." Toby pointed and smiled weakly.

No sooner did he say the words, the thing with the crowbar still stuck in its chest rolled over.

Both men jerked back from the sight of seeing that bleeding body try to pull itself back into the freezer only to be stopped by the length of metal protruding from its body. It moaned, twisted one way, then the other, and looked around. The crowbar clattered against the framework. The zombie got to its knees with the help of the surrounding walls, making no effort to remove the tool from its chest.

Somehow, it stood.

And lifted its face.

Nelson and Toby were already running.

They crashed through the swinging doors and made smoke through the household aisle. Up ahead, all the lights were off, yet figures thrashed against the glass of the vestibule. A shadow detached itself from the side and charged the two men.

"Run!" Walt shouted.

The three men ran and joined up at the side doors to the mall. Nelson yanked them open and ushered the others through. When he left the grocery superstore, a zombie slammed into the glass.

Toby and the Mollymart men backed away from the portal, thankful that the door opened inward to the supermarket. The zombie slapped a hand against the transparent glass, fouling it. A face pressed against the surface.

"They got through?" Toby huffed.

"Yeah."

Another zombie joined the first. They hammered the door.

"We gotta get going," Toby said.

So they ran.

17

"Stupid bitch!" John Maple exclaimed as the hatchback door swung shut on its own.

"Is she alive?" Carol asked, searching first her side mirror then glancing over her shoulder.

"Doesn't matter," Gord said, turning the wheel, attempting to see through one little patch of windshield not ruined by body-slamming zombies. "Where'd you park?"

Carol peered ahead, barely able to see anything through the broken glass. "Ah ..."

"That's my car right there," John said, pointing to a green or blue family car just ahead.

"Get ready," Gord said while hunched over the wheel. He slowed to a stop.

"She's alive!" Rene said, looking out the rear windshield.

Gord didn't bother with Mel. She'd made her choice. "Go!" he yelled at John, but the guy was already out the door. John quickly unlocked his car and slipped inside.

When John Maple shut the door, Gord accelerated.

That was one.

Two, he supposed, if he counted Mel.

"Where's your car?"

"Just over there," Carol pointed a few empty slots away on the near-barren parking lot.

"That's my car two spots over!" Rene said, becoming more of a chatterbox.

Convenient, Gord thought and drove between the vehicles, not happy in the least about his level of visibility. The windshield remained unbroken around the edges, but a crash print resembling a wet spider web otherwise ruined the glass. It would have to do as he wasn't about to roll down the window. He braked as John Maple sped away. Seeing those red tail lights flare as the car cut across the parking lot did his heart good.

Another car whizzed by in his side mirror. Mel Grant got away.

"You guys anywhere near Wilson Park?" he asked the others.

Carol shook her head. "I'm up by the university."

"I'm in Port Williams," replied Rene.

Nowhere near where he lived. "Go ladies, I'll wait here 'til you're inside."

"Good luck," Carol said as she slammed the door.

"Thank you, and good luck," Rene said, leaving him as well.

Gord watched them. Watched the parking lot. Then froze.

From the right side, illuminated by the parking lot lights, a figure shuffled into view, dragging his foot behind him. Gord wasn't sure if it was one of the two he hit or fresher zombies, not that it mattered. The person took a step, and for a moment, the foot dangled on a broken joint, and when the zombie put weight down upon it, it limped forward on the awkward point of its leg.

Arms swinging, the thing came for the cars.

Then Rene's headlights flared to life, and she turned into a wide arc, steering toward the side exit of the parking lot. Carol's car started up a second later, and she zipped for the south exit.

With the first part of the mission complete, the nagging feeling to get away grew even stronger. Gord aimed his car for the mall's corner, intent upon driving back into the dark side of the loading area and returning for the others. Help them get away and then he was out of there.

But not yet.

Gord drove toward the shambling zombie. The figure—a woman—reached for him as if saying *HALT!* just as he clipped her hip and sent her twirling.

"Take that," he whispered, bent low to see through the one clear patch available to him.

He glanced into his side mirror to confirmed his kill, taking his eyes off the road just for a second, but that was all it took.

He didn't see the second dark mass rising unsteadily from the pavement.

That two-legged chunk of meat crashed over the front of Gord's car and planted its ass squarely through his already weakened windshield. The impact frightened the shit out of the house painter, and he stomped on the gas out of pure reflex. The car blasted forward and smashed into Mollymart's unyielding corner, whipping the vehicle around in a violent arc.

The zombie boomeranged into the night.

Gord flew ahead and mashed his face against the dashboard, breaking things like his nose, teeth, and skin. His world became a spinning vortex before darkness enveloped him. He crumpled back into his seat, a hand flopping to his face. There was a hissing from the engine block.

The car was dead.

Gord's consciousness sputtered in and out, the shock flooding his system, just enough to cope with the pain of his face and chest from where the steering column caught him square in the sternum. A warm, moist drizzle covered him. It must've rained, because Gord felt it on his face, thick and dewy. He couldn't see, but that was fine. That was okay. Mary was nearby. He sensed her. Reached for her.

Someone shook him.

Forced his head back.

He cracked open an eye and glimpsed an out-of-focus rack of teeth. *Smiling* teeth.

"Mary," he whispered weakly, or he meant to say, but all that came out was *muh*.

He still didn't know what exactly was going on, even when the zombie bit into his cheek.

18

The Mustang bounced over a speed bump, and Mel Grant's head connected with the ceiling.

"God*damn it*," she swore, reaching over her shoulder. She struggled with attempting to fasten her seatbelt and driving, but she was away from that fucking mall. Away from those fucking wastes of skin and town hicks, and by that she meant the living. They deserved whatever they got, in her opinion. Ethan had been right, as he lay on their bed, coughing and writhing in misery. She should never have gone to Mollymart this evening. God how she hated it when he was right, but the supermarket was closer than Sobey's, and even though she despised the idea of venturing inside Mollymart's doors (she despised the company), she needed to pick up a few things, and it was the closest.

Disposable masks were on her list, which she would've gotten around to picking up if that screaming lunatic hadn't chased her. Mel had seen enough people with mental issues and watched enough television to recognize someone off their meds. She'd even planned on asking Ethan for the contact information of his lawyer friend specializing in personal injury when the mob (as she mentally labelled the dozen or so people inside Mollymart) decided to throw the poor sap into a *freezer*, of all things. She could've ranted. She certainly could've raved, but in the end, she chose to take names and pictures.

A bad movie. That's what the evening—hell, the *week*—had been. A bad horror movie.

But now she was away and aboard her machine, the pet name for her car. She didn't have her items with her, the ones she picked up at Mollymart, but she'd get them later, after she connected with a few police departments and other practitioners of the law. That super-sized cave-bitch wasn't about to get away with threatening Mel *Grant*. No sir. Mel intended to make Anna bo butch regret ever laying eyes on her, let alone opening her mouth to give orders. The very idea of some farmer hillbilly momma telling her what to do irritated her beyond belief. Mel very much knew what to do, with managing a boutique downtown and overseeing the operations of a staff of five in addition to raising three kids and a husband. She knew how to survive and adapt.

Traffic lights were red up ahead and, out of habit, Mel slowed to a stop. She looked around, finally seeing her surroundings for the first time since jumping out of that painter's car. He was only moving at thirty klicks but her knees still ached from the impact. She'd probably skinned them both, but otherwise, she got away with minimal damage. She was tough that way.

The cars stopped alongside the road got her attention.

Some had their doors open, while others did not. There were people inside the vehicles that weren't opened, and there were a few people wandering around the road, plodding along, looking like a mind-erasing bomb had been dropped on the city. Worse, they ambled toward her Mustang in a gaining-speed sort of gait, where their arms swung loosely at their sides. Some appeared disheveled, while others were staring and had their mouths locked in a cough.

The light turned green.

Horrified that she'd stopped at all, Mel floored it, racing past the enclosing circle of slack-jawed individuals. Had the entire city gone crazy? And where were the police? If they were all out on calls, where the hell were they? You'd think she'd be able to see a cruiser on patrol somewhere. She'd bring this up at the next public meeting on city services.

Houses perched atop a low hill streaked by her windows. Lights were on, which suggested all was well, but the people wandering the property made her think otherwise. Some stopped and stared at her, while others pursued, waving their arms as if they'd missed a bus.

Fifteen minutes out from home. On the other side of the city. She'd be there in no—

Time.

People filled the road ahead in such droves that Mel thought there was some mass demonstration happening, or perhaps even a house party that had grown out of control. When her headlights hit the masses, however, she saw differently.

Mel hit the brakes, tires screeching to a stop.

Faces turned, mouths opened, eyes half-rolled back into skulls. People dressed in summer wear. Some looked as if they'd been sprayed with tar while others leered and grinned in a collection of diseased insanity. Mel saw bare feet, saw children, and even saw a few crawling amongst the legs, and they all took notice of her stopped vehicle. In fact, the instant that she stopped, the crowd streamed for her like water slowly leaking from a collapsing embankment.

She scrabbled for the gearstick. Seeing no way to drive through the crowd or even around it, Mel shifted into reverse and jumped with fright when a line of runners flashed across her rearview screen.

Just before they slammed into the back of the Mustang.

The screen went black. Mel screamed. She hit the gas pedal and bulldozed through her attackers, the ride suddenly becoming jumpy. Hands and arms clattered off the Mustang's shell in a disturbing flurry. Mel cleared the handful of attackers and crashed into a parked car, mashing its front demolition derby style. The impact bounced her off her seat and flung her forward, cracking her neck like a buggy whip despite her seatbelt. Dazed, she glimpsed that town square gathering of locals rushing the front of her car, and for an instant, she thought they were going to help.

Then someone peered in at her from the driver's side.

When she looked, she gawked at a sleepy face with only one eye and a bloody socket, and a mouth without any teeth.

Mel found the gearstick. She shifted into drive.

But the crowds were upon her, blinding her. The Mustang turned, making a half-moon across the street. She clipped the foremost runners, buckling them over the hood as if she were driving through a violent corn field. The sleepy face on her driver's side kept pace, watching her with that semi-conscious expression, oblivious about where either of them was going.

The Mustang bounced over a sidewalk. Concrete slammed and stroked the chassis. The impact launched Mel to the left. She kept hold of the wheel before she smashed into the rear of a parked minivan. The jolt of impact stunned her, left her rubbery in her seat. She rubbed her face and found her hand slick with ink, not knowing how she'd gotten that in the least. Bare palms and fists swatted the windows. People clambered over the hood, filling the windshield, blotting out the nearby streetlights. The interior became even darker. Faces pressed up against the glass, spying her.

Gritting teeth and moaning, Mel shifted into reverse. The rearview camera showed a black screen between a pair of red lines. The sight frightened Mel even more. She accelerated, and the Mustang's rear split apart the masses with one powerful, fuel-injected rocket blast …

Before colliding with a streetlight across the street.

Sparks frizzled the air. The streetlight went dark and karate-chopped the car's roof.

Not that Mel had noticed. The sudden stop had stunned her again.

Zombies swarmed the unmoving vehicle. They hammered the windows repeatedly, with a collective might. Glass broke and crumpled. Shards were peeled back. Pebbles rained down upon the glass.

The sound brought Mel back to consciousness, and she weakly reached for the gearstick.

Hands pushed through holes. They reached in and grabbed Mel's face, her hair, her shoulders, her neck. They grabbed her and held on, drawing her in separate directions. She gasped at the strong grips but refused to scream. Her eyes rolled wildly in her head, peeking out through splayed fingers that were not hers, smelling that metallic tang she'd remembered from childbirth.

Her fingers tickled the gearstick's head.

That was as far as she got.

The mob pulled her through the driver's window and into the street.

19

"How long's it been?" Anna asked, her face pressed against the surface of the back door.

"Over almost ten minutes," Rebecca answered her. "Maybe fifteen."

"That's a long time," the big woman said, fidgeting uneasily. "Too goddamn long."

"You think they maybe all just drove off?" Vlad asked, glancing around at everyone waiting.

That didn't sell with Anna, and she could tell with a look that Rebecca thought the same. It made no sense for the painters to abandon them.

"No," Anna said. "I don't think so. But something's—"

The sound of a door opening out front distracted them. Anna readied her bat, prepared to investigate, just as the three men returned from the mall, out of breath and white-faced.

"They're inside," Walt gasped. "They're at the mall's side entrance. The door won't hold long."

"How many?" Rebecca asked.

"Hard to say," he managed. "But there was maybe three or four dozen inside Mollymart. All mashed together."

"They couldn't lead them away?" Anna asked.

"They did," Walt said, "but these are the ones who were already inside."

"Shit," Anna shook her head.

"Barricade that front door," Rebecca ordered the guys. "Anything and everything you can find. Against the door."

The Mollymart men got to work. The painter didn't seem to know what to do for a split second, then joined them.

"They might not find us here," Vlad said hopefully.

"They'll find us eventually," Anna spoke up. "No doubt. If that Gord guy doesn't get back soon, we'll have to head outside ourselves."

A stressed-out Vlad couldn't believe what he was hearing.

"Oh, you heard me right," Anna stated, brandishing her bat. "I don't care who they are, zombie people, hicks, or plain dumb asses. Anyone takes a run at me, and I'll send them over the left-field wall."

Perry dug at a pocket.

"Leave the camera, dickhead," Anna warned him. "I see that cell phone now and I'll knock you the fuck out."

Perry's cheeks flushed red.

Wheels screeched outside of the door, distracting them all. A horn sounded.

"That's him," Rebecca said.

"We go," Anna said. "Get the others, pudge."

Not yet recovered from the threat or being called a dickhead, Perry didn't like being called pudge either. Anna caught the venomous yet sullen look from the guy as he turned to carry out the order. She'd watch him in the next few minutes, just in case. She'd encountered enough poison dicks in her bouncer days, and she had to remind herself that he was the first one to side with that righteous muffhole Mel Grant. The ringleader wasn't around, but Anna knew from experience that didn't mean squat. Sometimes when the top dog was absent, the pack members had to be watched even more carefully.

Rebecca opened the door and saw the painter's truck ready to roll.

"Where's Gord?" she asked, at a loss.

"Dunno," Gus replied, his window lowered just a crack. "I was about to drive off. Didn't think you guys were still here."

"We're waiting for him to come back."

Gus peered ahead.

Anna was already getting impatient when something crashed behind her. A flurry of movement in the aisle became the men sent to barricade the door.

"They're at the door!" Nelson yelled. "Go! There's no time!"

Anna hurried outside, holding the door's edge, and motioned Rebecca to hoof it to the truck. "Go! *Go!*"

Rebecca opened the rear door of the Brush-It pickup's crew cab and lunged inside. The three guys stormed pass Anna, just as a glut of people entered the back room. Shadows tripped and stumbled through the aisles of stored merchandise, sending boxes of footwear flying.

One head popped into view, the face livid.

Anna released the door and ran for the truck. She rounded the grill when the invaders slammed into the Stanley's back door. That didn't concern her. What was behind her was behind her, and the way ahead was all that mattered.

Toby already had one leg into the front passenger side when she stopped him. "Get in the back!"

"Huh?"

"In the back! *Now!* You'll fit better!"

They boarded the truck, cramming into the rear and sitting on laps while Anna and Gus rode up front. Perry was the last to climb in when the rear door burst outward and a mass of bodies and contorted faces charged the truck.

For an instant, Gus glimpsed a figure—with a crowbar sticking out of its guts— rushing toward the window. It should've surprised him more than it did, but given the situation, Gus stomped on the gas and let the mob flail at exhaust.

The truck peeled away from the store exit.

"Holy shit, you see that?" Nelson exclaimed. "I just saw the one we put in the freezer, man!"

"You sure?" Anna asked.

"Oh yeah, it's him. I shoved a crowbar up his ass and left it there!"

That caused Gus to squirm.

"Nice to see you," Anna said to him, holding onto the overhead grip.

Gus did a double-take before smiling. He overshot the first corner, turned, and felt his guts go ice cold when the headlights washed over the smoking wreckage of Gord Munn's hatchback.

Three shapes stood over the car.

Two of those figures flinched and straightened with the indignant expressions of being interrupted at mealtime. The third, with its head partially inside the windshield, or where the windshield should've been, didn't react as quickly, being so immersed in its feeding. Their lower faces were coated in black.

The Brush-It truck rolled by the car wreck, where the zombies—as those things clearly *were* zombies—were chowing down on Gord's face.

Gus looked away, but the afterimage of his dead friend and co-worker had already burned itself into his brain.

Anna felt a pang of sympathy for the guy, but that was all. There was no time for anything else. "Turn here," she said, breaking the moment.

Gus steered the truck onto the main parking lot, where things flopped around or crawled on their bellies.

One of the zombies was sitting, as if just completing a stomach crunch. Gus ran him over, the crushing bump startling his passengers into silence. Anna decided not to comment. "Who's first?" she asked the others.

"That's my car right there," Nelson said, indicating a black family car on the lot.

"Gus?" Anna asked and pointed.

"I see it."

The truck slowed to a stop, attracting the few zombies. There were a few others still trapped in Mollymart's vestibule, and they slapped glass and waved at the vehicle, ignoring the ragged entry hole to get back out into the lot.

Nelson shared a look with his two co-workers. "Good luck you guys," he said. "Thanks for the lift."

He jumped out. Perry followed him.

"Where you going, pudge?" Anna asked him.

"That's my car two spots over," the camera man whined.

"Think you can make it?"

Perry slammed the door as an answer.

"I think you pissed him off," Gus said.

"He pissed me off with all that camera shit. Fuck him. If you haven't noticed, I don't like assholes."

"I noticed."

Anna studied him for sass and detected none. "All right then, who's next?"

"That sedan's mine," Walt said, pointing ahead.

"Rebecca?"

"I'm with him," the cashier said, tilting her head toward Walt. Anna looked back and realized the two Mollymart workers were practically squished together, but unlike the others, they didn't seem to mind too much.

"I got a lift into work today with him," Rebecca said.

"You saved us back there," Anna told her. "All you guys did."

"How?"

"Locking those doors, keeping a level head. You got us out of Mollymart."

Walt looked to Rebecca. "Thanks," she said. "But I don't know if we saved anyone or not. Anyways, thanks for the lift."

"Yeah, thanks," Walt said.

Gus stopped the truck beside the smaller car. The zombies crawling around on the lot adjusted accordingly and dragged themselves toward their quarry.

"Good luck," Rebecca said as the pair exited the truck.

"Jeeeeezus," Toby breathed. "Thank Christ. I think I crushed my nuts back here. And I'm pretty sure that Perry guy tried to goose me."

"Why didn't you slap him, then?" Gus asked.

"Slap him? You see how we were packed in back here? It's a crew cab, not a fucking hotel."

When Walt and Rebecca were in their car and starting it up, Gus rolled away.

Anna looked to Vlad and Toby in back. "Just us left."

"Just you," Toby corrected and nodded at Gus. "I'm riding with him."

"I parked over there," Vlad said and indicated the furthest cars away from the main entrance.

"And I'm one lane over," Anna said. "Great minds and all that, eh?"

A fleeting, uncomfortable smile appeared and vanished on Vlad's face.

"Hang on then," Gus said and turned south, toward an SUV and a mid-sized car. "Why'd you park all the way back here?"

"Exercise," Anna told him.

"I don't want my doors getting dinged," Vlad said.

Ahead, the whirly lights of an unseen police cruiser lit up the nights just over the nearby housetops. Gus stopped the truck between the two vehicles and watched those swirling beams.

"Thanks guys," Vlad said and jumped out, slamming the door behind him. He went for the mid-sized.

To Gus's right, a pair of cars left the parking lot and drove off in different directions.

"Think they're alive?" Anna asked, her hand on the door handle.

"Huh?"

"The cops."

"I dunno. You should get moving."

Anna hefted her bat. "You live around here?"

"Further up the valley."

"Be careful, man."

"Where you headed?" Toby asked her.

"Falmouth."

Gus became concerned. "That's a long drive at night."

"At any time," Anna said. "I'm used to it. Or I was, until this all happened. Anyway, be safe."

She got out of the truck.

Toby quickly jumped out and went for her vacated seat up front.

Then he saw her ride.

"Pink, eh?"

"Yep," she replied. "Pinkest SUV in the valley."

He believed that. "Watch your ass out there," he said before climbing aboard.

Anna held up her bat. She barely heard the guy because a zombie was crawling energetically behind the vehicle. Its legs were broken, but its arms worked fine. Part of a cheek hung off its right cheek, creating a skeletal smirk. Anna screwed up her face at the sight and brought up the bat. She walked over to the approaching body and clubbed its head until it stopped moving. When she was done, she retreated a step, inspected the kill, and nodded with grim satisfaction.

Goddamn zombies.

As if the world didn't have enough problems.

She got aboard her SUV, waved one last time, and disappeared inside. Seconds later, the machine fired up, casting a cone of light across a slick pavement awash in bodily fluids and crushed carcasses.

Anna tooted her horn as she left.

That was the last time Gus ever laid eyes on her.

20

Toby settled in, adjusting his painter clothes around the crotch. Gus waited until both Vlad and Anna were away. He saw her bash in a zombie's head in the parking lot, or at least he saw her swinging her bat and assumed it was a zombie. She was a tough one, no doubt. The display took his mind off Gord, and for that, he was thankful.

Vlad sped away from the lot.

Gus looked to the subdivision across the street. The cruiser lights continued to spin, a worrying beacon in a weird and unsettling suburbia.

"Where to?" Toby asked.

"Tammy's place. Then I'll drop you off."

"Drop me off where? Fuck that. I'll stay with you."

That was fine with Gus. He picked up the company phone as he drove and called Tammy's number.

No answer.

"Can't believe Gordo's gone," Toby said, holding onto the overhead grip. "I can't ... just can't ..."

Gus didn't comment. He hung up as the truck exited the parking lot. The lights got his attention again.

"You wanna check it out?" Toby asked quietly.

As a reply, Gus hit the gas, shooting up the roadway.

Streetlights flashed by with ghostly luminance. Shapes straightened and scuttled toward the truck as it passed by, only to be left behind. There was no traffic, so Gus drove straight down the middle lane, passing the same collection of vehicles both abandoned and still occupied.

The driver of an SUV parked before a small house became disturbingly animated when the Brush-It truck rolled past.

"Holy shit," Toby whispered. "Someone was in that rig."

Gus stopped, reversed, and watched for zombies. The truck halted before the SUV window. By the glow of the SUV's dashboard, a man stared out at the painters, pressing both hands against the glass. His expression was vacant, vapid, clearly not understanding what he was seeing.

But then, with all the malice of a spider sensing prey within its web, the man's fingers scrabbled against the glass. He moaned. Loudly. And attempted to chew his way through.

That was a sight neither painter needed to see.

Toby shrank back into his seat.

"Satisfied?" Gus asked.

The painter nodded.

They drove away.

"The hell is happening …" Toby muttered.

"We already know what's happening," Gus said. "We just don't know the extent. Or what's being done about it."

"You mean the whole city is like this?"

"City? Yeah. If we're lucky. If we're unlucky, the whole country."

"How?" Toby stressed. "I mean, I didn't hear anything about this going on until tonight."

"We did hear shit," Gus said. "And saw it. People sick all over. We just thought it was a flu bug or some other shitty-ass virus. Sure as hell didn't think it was *this* shit. Been going on all week like Rebecca said. And tonight, it's breaking out. Reaching its boiling point. And by that, I mean the virus is changing people. Whatever that word is. Becoming, I dunno, active. Or whatever."

Gus passed the side road he took before, which eventually led to the trucker. He pressed that memory away and focused on driving.

"Or what?" Toby asked.

"I dunno, Toby," Gus said, his nerves very close to ungluing. "I'm not a doctor. Or a scientist. Or anyone with a degree in fuckin' zombieology. I'm just … I'm just trying to get back to my girlfriend's place to make sure she's okay."

"Gus." Toby pointed.

He saw it. A zombie appeared up ahead, popping up between a pair of cars dead in the street. It stepped into the road and charged the Brush-It truck's headlights in a flash of bleached rage. Gus was driving too fast to change course. The zombie baseball-pitched its arm across the hood as the pickup flashed by. The limb bounced and whipped into the windshield as the zombie violently rolled along Gus's side before falling to the pavement.

"Christ, I'm not going to get used to that," Toby barked, looking into his side mirror.

"I'd be scared worse if I did get used to it," Gus said.

"Maybe we should've stayed in Mollymart," Toby said quietly, holding his chest as if warding off a heart attack.

"Maybe."

He turned at a set of lights, ignoring the red. A second transport trailer had rumbled across a small wooded park and splashed down in a duck pond, demolishing a fountain situated in the center. White arcs sprayed over the monster truck's engine and cab.

"Shortcut," Gus announced.

Zombies wandered into the headlights, forcing Gus to slow until he was sure they weren't people at all. Then he blew by them, the truck absorbing a few hard knocks.

"The fuck are the cops?" Toby asked.

Gus didn't have an answer. He shot past a familiar street that would've taken him home, but that wasn't his goal.

Toby switched on the radio. Most were silent. One was playing adult alternative.

Then, "—side your houses and lock your doors. Stay back from windows and points of entry. Best keep your lights off. Do not attempt to wave for help from those in the streets. When police have the situation in control, the chief informs me that they'll initiate a door-to-door check. He's assured me that the force is doing all that they can right now and asks the public to stay inside their homes and out of the streets until further notice. Stay inside and wait this out. Defend yourselves if necessary, especially if the intruder attempts to force their way inside your home. Gunshots have been reported in the valley. If anyone can confirm these shootings, give me a call. And if you have firearms, remember, Sheila and Bill from Kentville say that these things do *not* die from body shots, that it takes a shot to the *head* to put one down and keep them down. Keep that in mind."

"Keep it on there," Gus said.

"We already figured on the head shots. Sorta."

"Yeah." Gus hoped Anna and Rebecca and Walt and the others made it to wherever they were going. "Now it's official."

"You think Gord will become one of them?" Toby asked.

"Huh?"

"You think Gord will become one of them."

"I dunno."

"They were eating him," Toby said, unusually somber. "I mean, in the movies, that means he'll change."

"Yeah."

"How long, I wonder?"

Gus shook his head, not knowing that either, and not really wanting to think about the matter.

"I mean," Toby continued, "in the movies they never really go into that. Well, some do, I guess. And most folks who were initially infected, well, they were laid low for most of the week. They weren't fucking insane like they are now. And that one guy in the freezer, the one we put a crowbar into—"

"You did that?"

"No, that Nelson guy did. I just watched."

"Jesus, Toby."

"Had to be done, not like it did anything to that undead ass. You saw the thing coming out the door."

Gus did.

"Anyway, what I was saying … now that the bug is fully, uh, active, will it be *more* contagious? I mean, should we be wearing the masks Nelson gave us?"

"Probably a good idea."

"So, okay, that would protect us from the coughing, but what about the ones not coughing? Are they about to become more contagious or less? Are they, like, peaking? Or leveling off? I'm trying to figure out the danger level."

A set of headlights flashed, distracting them. The vehicle buzzed through an intersection up ahead, hauling ass and ignoring the speed limit.

"Someone else on the run," Toby muttered.

"Yeah," Gus said, turning at the intersection and going in the other direction.

"Wonder why there aren't more."

"It's almost ten minutes to one." Gus nodded at the dashboard clock. "It's late. Maybe most people are already gone. Or changed. Or eaten. Or just dead. Maybe they're still sleeping. My thinking? Best stay the fuck away from anyone walkin' the funky chicken. Howzat sound?"

"Good to me."

The truck moved along a curvy road with houses on either side. A few unmoving corpses lay around the front lawns and steps. The bodies had sustained what looked to be gunshots to the head.

"But," Toby resumed, "getting back to what I was saying, if they are zombies, can they change us into zombies? Or just eat us? And if they can change us, how do they do it? I mean is it just a bite? Scratch? Or just breathing in the same air?"

"Assuming they breathe."

"Exactly. And if any of that happens to us, well then, how fast is the change? Seconds? Hours?"

All good points.

"And if they *are* eating people," Toby continued, trying to figure matters out, "how much do they eat before they stop eating? I mean, if a shitload of them are eating someone and infect that person, how much do they keep eating before the person changes? Or do they just keep on stuffing themselves until they get full?"

Gus thought about it. "Maybe whatever's in the zombie gets passed on to the victim within the first few bites? And that changes the taste after a short time? Making the feeders move on?"

"Onto fresh meat, y'mean?"

"Yeah."

Toby glanced over at him. "That's fucking it, man. Or damn close."

"Maybe," Gus said, hunkering low over the steering wheel. Beyond some of the lower houses, a fat, six-story monolith rose into the sky, replacing the stars with manufactured ones. Streetlights lined the road, so he switched off his high beams.

"We're here," he said, turning into a parking lot half-filled with cars—a lot less than what was usually parked outside the building.

Drawn to the sound of the approaching truck, three figures stumbled out from between the cars. Two men and a woman, their summer clothes splashed with blood.

"Oh man," Toby moaned, beholding the trio's assorted wounds.

Gus drove by them, avoiding confrontation, but his attention remained on the apartment building's main doors. They were open about a foot or so, as if something was preventing them from closing. Gus steered through the lot, knowing the layout. There were two emergency stairwells on either end of the L-shaped building, and a central stairwell. There were four elevators as well.

"How many people live here?" Toby asked.

"Six floors, about fifteen to twenty units a floor." Gus checked his mirrors for pursuers. "Some families. Some couples and singles. Maybe a hundred fifty people? At least."

"Oh *man*," Toby moaned again.

"I gotta go get her."

"Where does she live again?"

Gus became silent.

"Hey you hear me?"

"Fifth floor," he said, turning around the building's corner.

Toby cranked his neck in disbelief. "And you're going up there?"

He didn't hesitate. "Yeah."

Toby was impressed.

"If Tammy's alive," he said to Gus, "she's gonna give you the sloppiest blow job ..."

21

The first emergency exit was closed, so Gus drove around back, over reclaimed dyke land. The Bay of Fundy lay to the west, and Tammy's building had an unrestricted view of the water. They often watched the evening sun from her balcony.

Gus slowed down and looked up, locating her apartment, knowing exactly where it was.

The lights were on.

Which didn't mean anything.

"Lights are on," he said, but Toby didn't comment. He scanned the shadows for zombies.

"What's that shit on the pavement?" Toby asked.

"Huh?"

"There," Toby pointed. "Like …," his hand went to his mouth. "Oh, my fuck. Don't tell me …"

A warm blast of horror overloaded Gus's system then, as he realized what he was looking at, splayed out along the asphalt like overfilled garbage bags tossed over a railing somewhere high above. Except the people who had jumped from the building's height had much more stuffing in them, much more fluid. And more than a few must've done somersaults on the way down, according to how they landed—teeth first. Their gruesome remains covered the asphalt in chunky spatters.

As the two painters gazed upon the clearly dead, the busted corpses twitched and moved, coming to life with broken wire connections, or slow, ruined rustlings. Their weak but determined movements mesmerized Gus. His hand wavered, actually thinking about switching on the headlights, but in the end, he did not. For fear of seeing those destroyed white faces lifting toward him. And for fear of seeing Tammy amongst that thick stew of broken torsos and limbs.

He realized there was no way around that soupy mess. The incline at the parking lot's edge was steep and ended in a path a few feet below. Tearing his attention away from the crawlers, he turned the truck around.

A rear tire went over something. Gus hoped it was a curb.

He drove back to the front, passing the three zombies again. They followed his rear bumper for a bit, not quite fast enough to keep up, and Gus quickly left them behind as he made the next turn.

Thankfully, there were no balconies on this side of the apartment building, and no undead jumpers. The second emergency exit was also closed. Gus wished he had a crowbar. He remembered where he could get one and told his brain to fuck off for even thinking of it. Keeping those thoughts to himself, he turned the truck around again.

Two more zombies had joined the others standing in the parking lot, closely grouped like a regular frame of five-pin bowling.

Tammy might be one of them.

Tension contorting his face, Gus switched on the high beams.

The pack of zombies flinched at the unexpected blast of light, drawing back and growling gibberish. Two charged the truck, one pasty guy in a pair of silk boxer shorts and a woman in a nighty with a sleepy duck on the front. They rushed forward with their mouths open, as if looking to bite the front bumper.

Gus ran them down and continued on through until he nailed the other three.

The higher hood and grill caught them all around shoulder level, though one had his head rudely shoved to one side upon mating with the greater moving mass. There was a flurry of bangs and a jumble of arms, but the unsettling thing, the thing that truly disturbed Gus, wasn't the feral surprise on the faces when the truck hit them.

It was his sudden determination.

He stopped the truck fifteen feet from the building and saw that an overturned wastebasket was wedged between the front doors and kept it open.

Gus grabbed his bat and covered his mouth with the flimsy disposable mask Nelson had given him a lifetime ago. "You don't have to go in," he said to Toby.

"Good."

Gus did a double-take at his co-worker, frowned, and cracked open the door.

"You're really not dressed to go up there," Toby said. "I mean, you should be in body armor or something."

"I don't have body armor or something."

"How long will you be?"

"If I'm not back in fifteen minutes, you're good to go."

That sobered Toby. He nodded.

Gus slid out of the truck and closed the door, wincing at the noise.

Then he smelled the blood.

A veritable lake covered the lobby floor, already congealing under the ceiling lights. The sight of all that bright body juice halted Gus on the threshold and gripped him in a moment of surreal disbelief. He should've expected it after the gruesome landing pad he'd just seen. His newfound determination faltered just a bit when he suspected he was going to see even worse things on his way to Tammy's place.

Maybe even the worst possible thing of all.

Breathing hard through the mask and loathing the way it heated his face, he regained control of himself, and proceeded into the lobby. Blood stuck to his sneakers, and he left a white trail of prints that slowly filled in. That sight alone slowly twisted his guts. His eyes watered, and the mask wasn't doing shit to stop that cold metal smell. He passed a billboard festooned with notices. A sign for babysitting services had a bloody palm print right in the middle. A wall of mailboxes had been hosed down in red, so much red and yet not a body to be seen.

The elevators were closed.

Not ten feet away was the door to the stairwell. Gus hesitated, wondering which would be the safer route. Then he realized he was in no shape to go up five flights of stairs. He'd be just as fucking dead as the five gimp things he'd only just ran down, and certainly in no condition to run, fight, or shit if he met anything along the way. Swearing at his ample self, he gingerly stepped through the blood, hating that clingy, dewy touch of it all, and called the elevator. Gears clacked into motion from somewhere above, and the number five lit up. *Number five.* Maybe Tammy was about to leave. That thought stayed with Gus until the number three flared to life.

He realized he was standing right before the elevator.

Gus went to the side and, as an afterthought, cocked the bat as if expecting a fast ball to come through the elevator doors.

The lift settled onto the ground floor. The doors opened with a ding.

Nothing came out.

Gus leaned around the corner and peered inside, seeing only a beige box with a golden railing. He looked up, then down, sighing at the soaked carpet. He hoped his feet stayed dry even though he knew his sneakers would look like shit after this. He went inside the elevator, his innards turning even further at the squishy, oversaturated sound of each footfall. It was just like someone's hot water tank had rusted through. Oh, how he wished it was just a busted hot water tank.

He thumbed the number five. The doors closed, and the elevator lifted him into the soon-to-be-known. He leaned heavily on the railing, waiting, wondering, hoping that Tammy was fine, that maybe she wasn't changed, that maybe she had some kind of natural resistance. One that a government taskforce would need to sample to concoct an antidote for all the shit going on. That happened in the movies. All the time.

The doors opened with a ding and Gus jerked into a batter's pose. His temples throbbed, coping with the rising tension, and his body pleaded for action, to bleed off some of the adrenaline seeping into his system.

Oh, my nerves. He shuddered at the sight of a huge blotch staining the beige carpet of the corridor beyond. A thin thread of scarlet ran back to an open door that wasn't Tammy's apartment. Gus listened, forced himself to remain still, and then the elevator doors started closing on him.

Cocksucking sonsa— He jammed a hand into the gap, causing the doors to reopen with a mechanical lurch. The doors receded, stopping with a bang as loud as a goddamn dinner gong, or so it seemed when he was trying to be a ninja. Gus got off the elevator, supremely pissed at his lack of stealth mode, and waited for any zombies to come after him.

None did, however, as much as he deserved it.

Vowing to never fuck up like that again, Gus checked the open corridor both ways before backing away from the blood trail leading to the open door. He walked the other way, where the carpet wasn't a gory sponge. The red tracks he left behind didn't make him happy, however. Not in the least. He even stopped at one point and fumed at what he was doing, or at least attempting to do, and how totally slap-ass unprepared he looked. There he was, dressed in his painter duds, with nothing more protective than the clothes covering his fat ass, a Louisville Slugger bat, and a bargain-bin face mask. Then there was him leaving bloody prints with every step.

All he needed was a sign around his neck saying *Just Fuckin' Eat Me,* then the picture would be complete.

He passed the first two doors without incident. No sounds issued from those apartments. The next door was open, and Gus paused at the frame's edge. He listened, even snuck a quick peek inside before withdrawing. Then he got serious, psyched himself up for the next move, and quickly stepped past the open doorway.

Nothing stirred.

The smell of blood wasn't so bad on the fifth, but considering what he'd just walked through, that wasn't saying much. There was still enough of it to make a regular person yark or just outright puke.

Two doors to Tammy's place.

The next one was open.

Gus remembered this place, remembered a couple's heated argument over credit card bills. He stopped at the doorframe, left shoulder almost touching, and cocked the bat. One quick breath to fill his lungs and he peeked inside.

An inner light way back in the living room was on, so when the shirtless man stepped into view, the shock cost Gus a second. Bushy-haired, pale, and sullen-looking, the man hissed, revealing a mouthful of bloody fragments.

But that wasn't what really frightened Gus.

What really frightened him were the things sticking out around the guy's mouth.

A collection of raw sores and angry goose bumps freckled the guy's skin, as if he'd had an extreme reaction to some shaving gel.

Gus bashed him in the face.

The blow staggered the zombie back, but didn't put him down. Gus struck him again, more frantic that time, and only clipped the shoulder. The thing crashed into a wall and flailed an arm. Gus darted back, reset, and whipped the bat into a knee.

The zombie dropped.

And in one of those instances where mind and limbs are connected and in perfect sync, Gus whipped the bat overhead and crushed the zombie's skull with three quick, decisive blows.

Chest heaving, Gus slumped against a wall and upended a painting there. The thing crashed down over his head, and he thrashed back with a livid squawk, thinking another dead bastard had snuck up on him. The painting— an oil rendition of a sunset beach—flopped to the carpet. Realizing what it was, Gus scowled at the piece of art, and stomped on the frame in the afterburn of his fright.

Then he glanced at the destruction he'd done. He looked to the living room and the hallway, waiting for more. Nothing investigated the short but violent confrontation, so he stood there, composing himself as best as he could. He glanced at the body and told himself he didn't just beat a man to death, but a thing that would've eaten his face off. Just like Gord. He looked up and whimpered, thinking he was going to be sick.

It was one thing to run them down in a pickup truck.

Totally another to bash in a head.

And he didn't like the very personal effort it took to connect wood to bone. Not at all.

Feeling his stomach snake into a queasy knot, Gus staggered into a nearby washroom and flicked on a light. His masked reflection stared at him, and he saw blood speckles covering the lower part of his mask. Gus ripped it away and chucked it, saw the soap, and scrubbed his hands and face. The cold water helped settle his guts, until he realized he was standing at the porcelain wash basin of an infected person.

Worse, he had no mask anymore.

Oh my God, his mind rambled. *Oh, Christ.* Gus left the bathroom, stepped over the unmoving corpse in the hall, and left the apartment. His eyes were on high beam, scanning everything. He walked quickly, not so concerned with stealth, only knowing he had to get out of this apartment building as soon as possible. Just being inside the place exposed him to God only knew what, and that realization strummed his nerves like a heavy-metal power chord.

The main corridor remained empty, so he marched past the next door, which was closed.

Then it was Tammy's place.

Gus stood in the open doorway, gazing inside, very much scared about what he might see. Or become. Or be exposed to.

But he had to find out where she was.

"Tammy," he said in not quite a whisper. Then he listened.

Nothing.

"Tammy?"

No lights were on, so Gus reached in with the heel of his bat and flicked on one. The hall light came on, and when it did, he noticed something clinging to the bat. Blood, and a few hairs coated the top part.

"Oh, Jesus Christ," he squeaked, near breathless. The sight sickened him. He immediately proceeded to scrub the bat clean on the corridor carpet.

When he finished, he took in another deep shot of air (which did nothing for his nerves) and peered inside the apartment. "It's Gus, babe."

He entered.

The kitchen was empty. As was the bathroom. He didn't go near either, fearful of inhaling germs from the very air. With his elbow, he turned on the living room lights. Drapes swayed across the room. A quick investigation revealed Tammy had left the sliding door to the balcony open just a few fingers. The barest breeze rustled the hanging fabric.

She hadn't jumped, however. That was a relief.

Gus eyed the short hallway to the two bedrooms. He went around the living room and stopped in the hallway.

"Tammy?"

He waited for a dozen heartbeats and went to her bedroom door.

And looked inside.

Darkness.

"Tammy?" he whispered.

Something lay on the bed.

"That ..." his voice faltered, suddenly dusty dry. He swallowed, fearful of what he was about to see. "That you ... babe?"

No reaction. Not yet.

He knew where the lights were, so he flicked them on with an elbow.

And saw the teddy bear lying on what was his side of the bed.

"Oh, goddamn this shit," he moaned and shook his head. He wasn't built for this kind of tension. The good news was that Tammy wasn't there. The bear stared at the ceiling, button eyes and mouth indifferent. Her bed was unmade and slept in, but the summer sheets were pulled back as if she'd gotten up to take a leak. A cell phone lay on the bedside table, and Gus's heart sank. The adjoining bathroom was empty, as was the spare.

Tammy was gone.

Shoes.

He went to the front door, to the coat closet.

All the shoes were in place.

"Oh no," Gus sighed miserably. His eyes moistened. His throat tightened. "Oh no," he repeated in despair and exited the apartment, looking both ways before heading to the stairwell at the end of the corridor. He ignored the red EMERGENCIES ONLY sign and pumped the steel bar.

He heard them when he opened the door.

People.

A *lot* of people. Voices of men, women, and children issuing from below. Some of the plastic shells protecting the light bulbs had been smashed, creating a shadowy white pit. Gus stood there, his shoulder keeping the door open, and peered down the beige-painted stairwell, where the steps disappeared at the first landing. He couldn't tell if there was anyone above him, but there were certainly folks below.

There was a landing just below the fifth, and stairs descended into that dark pool. Gus leaned out, gasping, not wanting the door to close behind him. Below, he could just see the next flight of stairs, revealed by light a little farther down. He teetered for a second, tightened his grip on the bat and stretched his neck out, trying to see more.

A shadow fluttered across the stairs. Angry groaning grew louder. The back of a head came into view and turned.

Gus pulled himself back, letting the door close by itself.

And ran for the elevator.

22

Gus scared the shit out of Toby when he ran out of the main entrance. When he pulled open the door, Toby was about to jump out on his side.

"Say something!" Toby barked at him.

"She's not there."

Toby relaxed, but he wasn't relieved.

"She's gone," Gus said and got aboard. "Without her shoes, her phone, everything. Just an empty apartment and a fuckin' open door."

"She opened her door?"

"Who knows. Maybe she wasn't changed then. Maybe she heard shit in the corridor and went to check it out. I dunno. She's not there."

Gus leaned over the steering wheel and found the keys in the ignition. "I smashed a guy's head in."

Toby made a face at the news.

"Yeah, it was like that," Gus said. "I lost the mask."

"When did you lose the mask?"

"After I killed that guy."

"After you killed that *zombie* guy," Toby clarified.

Gus swallowed that. "Yeah."

"Jesus, Gus you could be infected now!"

He didn't say anything to that.

"Jesus Christ," Toby blurted and fixed his mask into place, glaring at his co-worker. "You better not infect me, man. I'll put boots to your ass."

"I feel fine," Gus released. "I mean, shitty, but fine. I gotta find her."

Silence for a moment. "She's gone, Gus," Toby said, a tad calmer. "No shoes and no phone? Chances are she's ... you know."

"I know. I know. I just gotta ... know. For certain. Just gotta know what

151

happened to her, because not knowing will kill me. Closure, right?"

"Yeah."

In the silence that followed, Gus started up the truck.

"So, what do you wanna do?" Toby asked.

"Look for her."

"Out there?"

"Yeah."

"She could be anywhere, Gus."

"I know. I'll drop you off wherever you like, if you want. There's plenty of rides around. Some of them might have keys still in the ignition."

Toby sighed, clearly not impressed with the situation. "You're sure you're okay?"

"I'm okay." *I think*, Gus thought, but there was residual tension in his calves and in his hands. His forearms even. Thrumming, like overloaded power lines. He didn't know if that was from the frights of the apartment building or something more sinister.

"Think of it this way, if I *am* infected, you get to see firsthand how long it takes for someone to change."

Toby made a face. "I don't wanna see that."

"You just might."

"You're freaking me out here."

The sounds of the stairwell revisited Gus's mind, and the sight of that head appearing, turning, made him wonder if that hadn't been Tammy. It wasn't of course, the hair had been much too short, but that didn't stop the evil part of his brain from tormenting him.

He put the truck in gear and kept the headlights off. "Last chance," Gus informed him.

"I'll stay. Fuck it."

But all the same, Toby cracked the window on his side of the truck.

Five minutes later, they were driving along a few back streets of Annapolis, over what was once dyke land. Zombies roamed the streets, dressed in summer or night wear. With the headlights off, most of the creatures didn't seem to care about them. Or perhaps the newly dead (or undead) were coming to terms with their condition.

"We're not going to find her," Toby muttered behind his face mask.

"Listen," Gus said, studying the faces of the freshly converted before driving on. "I don't need to keep hearing that. I don't need to hear anything negative right now. I haveta try. You don't. So, whenever you get tired of this, just let me know and I'll drop you off in a safe place."

The truck passed a front lawn with a person in the middle of it, stargazing. The night concealed the figure's identity, but whoever it was, was tall. Too tall to be Tammy.

"Better be a real safe place," Toby said, taking his eyes off the individual.

Gus looked for the next zombie. "As safe as you want."

"How safe? Like, bank safe? Cop safe?"

A hand crashed into the glass, causing it to vibrate. A flash of vacant eyes and a snarl of teeth and Gus was already hitting the gas. The truck shot forward, leaving the zombie behind.

"The hell he come from?" Gus gasped, eyes on the road.

"The lawn back there."

"Well, then, keep your fuckin' eyes peeled and let me know. All I need is to shit myself."

"All I need is for you to shit yourself," Toby agreed. "Which is me saying don't shit yourself."

More zombies flashed by the speeding truck, and a few more derelict cars cluttered the streets.

"They're just walking around," Gus observed. "Just walking around."

"Looking for something to eat," Toby added. "A late-night snack."

"That one there," Gus said, pointing to a pajama-clad woman standing near a sidewalk bench. "That could be her."

Before Toby could say anything, Gus turned the wheel and flicked on the high beams, lighting up the person thirty feet out. The woman didn't react to the sudden flash.

Nor was it Tammy.

Gus's initial surge of hope faded when the zombie rushed the truck head-on, snarling face lined up with the grill. The Brush-It truck smacked her down, easily winning the battle of masses.

Neither man said anything when she went under the wheels. Gus flicked off the headlights.

Two twenty-seven glowed on the dashboard clock.

Gus looked at the time and frowned. "No radio?"

"That guy stopped broadcasting just after you went inside. The other stations are just playing music. There's nothing. Not even anything from Halifax or New Brunswick. Listen." Toby pressed the SCAN button and got two snippets of music in between bouts of silence.

A convenience store appeared on the right, the lights on, two bodies lying in the threshold, preventing the doors from closing. There were people inside the building, walking the aisles.

"This is bad," Toby said.

"I know it's bad," Gus said.

"I mean really bad."

Gus knew that too.

"Look, maybe we should head for the cop station," Toby suggested. "They're the ones trained to handle this shit."

"Not sure they can handle this level of shit," Gus remarked.

"What are you gonna do if you do find her, man?" Toby said. "I mean chances are she's one of them now. You already said she left her shoes and her phone in her place. So, what if you do find Tammy and see for sure she's gone over to that? Huh?"

The reasoning was sound, and Gus couldn't comment. "I don't know," he muttered in the end. "Like I said, I just … I just need the closure."

Toby saw the look on his co-worker's face. He didn't press the matter. He looked ahead and suddenly pointed. "Them cop lights?"

Gus saw that hyperspace light show whirling just over the rooftops of an approaching subdivision. "I think so," he said, turning in that direction.

"That's the second set this night."

"Maybe we looped back to the mall? We didn't, of course. Just sayin'."

"Gonna take a look?"

"Yeah," Gus answered. He crossed the lanes and caught himself about to switch on the indicator. He swung into the suburb, passing a green sign with *Legion Road* stamped upon it. He knew the area. New houses rose on either side in carefully measured lots. SUVs and other assorted vehicles were parked in their driveways. Little, well-maintained lawns scrolled by the Brush-It truck. A trampoline with netting stood on one front lawn. A discarded hockey net lay on another. An abandoned soccer ball appeared in the middle of the left lane. It was a nice neighborhood, one where young families might settle down.

"We painted some houses around here," a fidgety Toby recalled.

Gus nodded. "Young neighborhood. Lots of kids."

"Yeah."

A few night joggers darted along the sidewalks up ahead. Except they weren't jogging. They were sprinting. Sprinting hard.

"Holy shit." Toby said, leaning back in his seat.

As Gus slowed to a crawl, a second pack bounded along the sidewalk, past what might've been a low hedge, and darted into a gap between a pair of houses.

Then they were gone.

Another crash of metal somewhere to the east, and a car alarm went off, chirping like a hysterical cricket. The sound was far off, but nonstop. Gus drove on, trying to see everywhere at once. There was no traffic. Up ahead, the cruiser's lights swept the sky.

"Gus," Toby said, pointing.

Gus saw the house, its picture window smashed, coating the front lawn in jagged shards that glittered under the nearby streetlights. Curtains hung in tatters while sheer drapes were yanked down entirely. Lamps remained on inside the dwelling, further uncovering the struggle that had occurred within the home. On the other side of the road, a different house with the same level of destruction, as if a gigantic boot had kicked in the home's teeth.

"Holy shit," Gus whispered.

Some twenty meters or so ahead, the road snaked to the left, disappearing around the corner of a two-story house. The police cruiser's lights grew stronger, larger, whisking across the seemingly deserted neighborhood in a psychedelic spin cycle—an unclean, miasmic swirl portending badness. The cop car lay just out of sight, and a part of Gus wasn't so sure that he was going to see anything he wanted to see. He eased the truck forward, the way lit by streetlights. A hockey stick lay across the road. The tires went over it, and they heard the clatter, felt the bump. More house windows had been smashed, the damage becoming more noticeable in the neighborhood. Garbage bins upended and strewn about. A door hung ajar, allowing half a peek inside.

"Shit's long gone down, Gustopher," Toby said, pressing himself back in his seat. "Maybe we should go. Go find that cop station."

Tammy. Gus exhaled. But he wanted to check on the cruiser first. The lights from the unseen car swelled with intensity, but they weren't the lights of a law enforcement officers' ride anymore. Now they were alarm klaxons warning of unchecked radiation, or a hidden reactor on the verge of explosion.

"Stop," Toby ordered, looking to the right.

Gus did so, causing both men to lurch despite only creeping along. The pickup's engine idled, sounding impatient.

"What?" Gus asked.

"In there," Toby said, pointing at a split-level home with its windows still intact. Pinkish vinyl siding covered the exterior, and lights were on inside. Drapes hung behind the glass. "Upstairs. Someone moved past the windows."

"What?" Gus said, hunching over to better see.

"Right up there."

"I can't see anything."

The indicated window remained empty.

Gus got the truck moving. "No time for this. Cop car's just up ahead. We check that and then boot."

"Where the fuck is everyone?" Toby asked and settled back, watching the gaps between the houses.

The line of vision widened as the truck edged toward the turn. The lights became dazzling.

"Christ almighty," Gus said, turning the wheel. "Those things are bright."

They moved into the full glare of the cruiser's light bar, some twenty meters back. The colored lights flashed before their eyes. The vehicle had stopped in the opposite lane, just a nudge over the white line. The doors were wide open, as if both officers had bolted, but Gus couldn't see anyone nearby. And if that wasn't interesting enough, runnels of black glazed the road, as if someone had emptied cans of motor oil in the middle of the asphalt.

"Can't see shit," Gus said into the dark magic glare of the light bar.

"Drive alongside it," Toby said.

"The door's in the way."

"Go up over the sidewalk then if you have to."

The truck edged forward, the engine hissing with distaste. The cruiser's crushed windshield drew Gus's attention, revealing a little more of what had happened on Legion Road. The indentation marked the point of impact in the center of the glass. Gus's mouth hung open as the truck crept past the cruiser's open door. The whirling lights were blinding.

He stopped the truck and looked inside the car.

Toby leaned over the cup holders. "See anything?"

"Nothing," Gus reported.

But something caught his attention.

There, just over the cruiser's roof, a flicker of movement on a front lawn, in a walkway just out of the reach of those lights. A black shape dragged itself along and stopped, dragged and stopped, uncovering itself.

"Gus," Toby said.

Gus didn't answer, his eyes fixed on that stop-go motion of the lump on the lawn. A lump pulling itself toward an open gate that led around the back. The shape became a body from the waistline up, crawling toward the gate. Except the body didn't have any legs.

"Gus," Toby repeated and slapped his co-worker's arm.

Gus turned.

A figure appeared in the smashed-out picture window of a house across the street. The person was adult-sized, sexless, with arms by its sides. But that wasn't the worst. More people were emerging from the house's backyard. Tall and short shadows moved with drunken purpose toward the pickup. The dismal light revealed disturbing white faces, but that was only secondary, because a crowd was materializing *behind* the truck, a straggly line of people colored stove-burner red by the tail lights, creeping out of the October night. Their summer clothing looked damp and in disarray, their faces long and indistinct. The mouths …

Gus tore his eyes away from the scene in his side mirror. He accelerated, the truck responding with a roar that sounded like *finally*!

More shadows appeared on front lawns, emerging from pathways, drawn to the engine's enthusiasm. The streetlights revealed a road slick with oil, but Gus no longer thought it was oil. Not really. Not when the gang in his side mirror started to chase him seconds after he sped up.

"Holy shit," Toby said, pushing himself back into his seat, bracing for impact.

Up ahead, a group of people clustered around a person lying on his back in the middle of the road, just inside a streetlight's range. The group fussed over the unmoving individual and were giving mouth-to-mouth. The surging engine distracted the lot of them, and a collection of faces turned toward the truck.

The sight robbed Gus of all speech. Toby was equally shocked.

The pack gathered around the body in the road weren't administering mouth-to-mouth resuscitation. Far from it.

They were eating the person's face.

Shivering matter dribbled and sprayed from masticating jaws. Black eyes stared and twinkled. Gus drove around the mess in the road, knowing full damn well he was going to have nightmares of not only quivering flesh, but the body's open torso as well.

"Holy *shit*," Toby exclaimed.

The truck swung past the feeders, but more people were coming out of their houses, sticking their heads out of broken windows, straightening their postures in doorways. The road curved to the right, and Gus drove, managing to keep control of the vehicle while spotting the horrors flashing past his windows. Three people rose from what appeared to be a dead dog on the sidewalk. Chunks of organic mud dropped from their hands. Another small meeting of figures stood in the road's left lane, all turning as Gus sped by doing fifty. And that viscous tar still coated the road, as if a fire hydrant had doused it with syrup.

"Oh, my fuck," Toby ejected, clawing at the dash, staring straight ahead.

The headlights flashed left and right with every jig of the steering wheel as Gus maneuvered around abandoned vehicles and surging zombies. More undead were turning upon the sight and sound of the speeding vehicle. Some figures ran from their houses as if chasing an escaping ice cream truck.

The pickup turned left, zipping past a guy in shorts and a blood-drenched shirt. A dripping beard of gore hung from the lower part of his face. The thing pawed at the truck as the vehicle shot by, just before the side mirror smacked it away. The impact spun the zombie in a violent pirouette.

The two painters traded frightened looks before focusing on the road

"Look out!" Toby shouted.

Gus saw them.

He drove up over a front lawn to avoid a collection of chest-high children charging the truck from the right, the feral glee in their expressions frightening. Something in Gus wouldn't allow him to run over kids.

Not even zombie kids.

The pickup bashed a lawn chair, destroyed a hedge, barely missed a fire hydrant, and crossed a pair of driveways before hitting the subdivision's road again. Debris flew up and over the truck. The men screamed and bounced in their seats, but Gus retained control of the steering wheel. He slowed, righted the vehicle's course, and took a left.

He glanced in the side mirror.

There, running as if they'd just left a starting line, was an animated crowd in pursuit. The sight shivered his entire frame.

"*GUS!*"

He looked to the road.

Ahead, cars and SUVs mashed together as a result of a panicked escape. The wrecks blocked the street, creating a very dead end.

Gus turned left, tipping the rig dangerously. Toby, God love him, uttered not a word as he was thrown into his door. Gus held on, zip-lining a very fine wire between all good and disaster. They bounced over a curb, ran over a series of garden gnomes that popped like ceramic light bulbs, and came to screeching stop in front of a Camaro.

Broadside in someone's driveway.

The truck settled down on its chassis as the collective populace of Legion Road closed in from all sides.

Gus saw the neighbouring house. Saw the driveway on his left lead into a backyard. Saw a work shed and a fence.

He looked at the hundreds of Annapolis residents sprinting for his truck.

Gus hit the gas, the rpm needle almost doing a trampoline loop, the accelerating engine loud in his ears. His teeth hurt from clenching as he missed the corner of the nearby house by inches. Toby held on without a word. The truck blasted through the driveway, headlong for the work shed at the end of the driveway. The shed's front doors raced toward them with a spectral quickness neither man appreciated.

"*Ahhhh, fuck!*" Toby cried out, bracing for imminent impact.

And Gus turned the wheel.

The Brush-It truck missed the corner of the shed by the narrowest margin. The vehicle ran through a garden patch with enough force to martini-shake the living shit out of both men. They missed a wheelbarrow by a foot. Avoided a picnic table. A lawn chair crashed over the hood with all the grace of a cement beach ball. Then the outline of a rapidly approaching fence materialized out of the dark, perhaps six feet high, just before the Brush-It truck torpedoed through the barrier with a clap and clatter of wood. Planks rained across the windshield. Toby was screaming. Gus was screaming. A pair of posts snapped across the hood and what seemed like an honest-to-God manta ray crashed down atop the truck roof with a boom that shook the entire vehicle.

And then the world dropped out from underneath them.

23

There was a crash, a blast of black water that smashed into the windshield, and the dashboard exploded, halting the forward momentum of both men. Gus tasted metallic dust, felt water around his feet, and looked around in semi-daze. It was dark, wet, and he swooned against the airbag keeping him upright. The deploying safety device pretty much socked the wind out of him, and it took him precious seconds to get his bearings. Water flowed into the truck, from unknown breaches, sobering him to his stationary situation.

When he lifted his head, he couldn't see. Anything.

But he could hear.

And everything he heard was bad.

A raucous concert of voices from beyond the night, oddly muted, but out there, just beyond the black veil of reality enveloping the truck. The dashboard lights were off, which didn't help.

"Muh," Toby muttered. "*Muhhh.*"

Gus flailed an arm in his co-worker's direction and connected with a skull. "Quiet," he stressed, and then listened again. There were splashes, *loud* splashes, and that woke him up to the fact that he and Toby had crashed through the fence and into someone's backyard pool. The truck was on the bottom, or so it seemed. Gus strained to see around the airbag, and saw nothing beyond the windshield.

"What's going on?" Toby asked in a low voice, regaining his senses.

"Don't know," Gus whispered back. "Just—"

Feet clattered over the roof, except it wasn't the truck's roof. Gus looked up with narrow-eyed wonder, hearing the mosh-pit stomping overhead and unable to locate what exactly was making that sound. A Neanderthalian grunting and yelling grew in volume as well.

Gus held up a hand but realized Toby was probably just as blind as he was.

The footfalls increased.

Then the splashing.

"Gus," Toby pleaded.

"Shut up, Tobe. Please ..."

More splashing—a watery thrashing that put Gus's nerves on edge. Things crashed into wood just beyond the truck's crew cab, and Gus struggled to breathe because of how close the zombies were. The dead were in the pool as well, splashing around on Toby's side like a bunch of kids. Something connected with metal in the back, scrubbing the truck's box, but it didn't last long. Thunder rolled overhead, a regular beach party of wide-eyed cannibals searching for the two meat puppets that inexplicably disappeared.

At least, that was how Gus saw things.

Water flowed into the cabin, but not from the sides. It reached his knees, cold but not uncomfortably so.

But how deep are we? Gus asked himself. When would the water level off? And how did they manage to drive up under a wharf?

That bare-belly smackdown of water tapered off into lesser splashing, a sound which befuddled the hell out of Gus. His mirrors revealed nothing.

Water touched the fabric and skin of his upper thighs. It pooled at his crotch. Seconds later, cold water cupped his already drawn-up testicles.

"Gus," Toby whispered. Gus barely heard him over the feet walking overhead.

"Yeah?"

"We in a pool?"

"Yeah."

"How deep?"

Good question. "We'll find out. Now, shush."

Toby shut up, but as the water increased to Gus's navel, his level of anxiety did as well. He thought back, back to when the pickup went through the fence. They hit posts, he remembered, thick ones, and then something clamped down on the truck's roof.

But what. A deck? Could they have swept the support beams from someone's second story deck and have it crash down atop of them? Didn't seem plausible to him, but there was *something* keeping those carnivorous masses away from them.

"Gus."

Toby again.

"What?"

"I gotta pee."

"Go ahead." *What the hell*, Gus thought, and let go himself. Wouldn't be the first time he pissed in someone's pool. It was just a coincidence, but the water level rose faster as he took a leak. By the time he'd finished, his stomach was submerged.

"Gus."

"Goddamnit Toby, *what?*" A little too loud, and Gus cursed himself for raising his voice.

"What do we do?"

"You wanna get out, be my guest."

Toby didn't say anything to that.

The water rose to Gus's chest. Things were no longer good.

"Never thought I'd die in a pool," he whispered. "And not by drowning."

"I hear drowning's real peaceful," Toby whispered back. "Like going to sleep."

"Yeah, and that's why the CIA uses waterboarding to get information from prisoners. Relaxes them all to fuck."

Toby shut up, not appreciating the tone of voice, but Gus no longer cared. There were still a ton of people walking overhead, just standing there, while the pool water slowly rose to dangerous levels. The pressure grew on Gus's chest, and he became aware of his own breathing. Something slammed down just to his left, but there was only blackness there. More unseen things fell, and Gus watched the dark on his left, fully expecting a horrible face to appear just outside his window.

The water touched his neckline, creeping along like a silent, fleshing-eating glob.

Toby whimpered on the other side.

"Toby?"

The man squeaked a reply, as brazen as pinched-off fart.

Gus took a breath. "Shut. The fuck. Up."

Displaying a considerable amount of willpower, Toby complied.

The water caressed Gus's Adam's apple.

And he realized he wasn't going to find Tammy after all. When the water filled the cabin, he was going to open his truck door, and step outside if he could, and the zombies overhead would hear that, locate him, and that would end it all right there. They find him and devour him like greasy chicken, or so he pictured his death. So, he tried to think of other things in his last moments, tried to think of Tammy on the phone, tried to think of brave Rebecca the zombie expert and wondered if she and Walt had escaped. Then there was Anna and he wondered if she was anywhere near Falmouth. He hoped she was. Hoped they were somewhere safe. Even that dickhead guy with the camera and that bitch Mel what's-her-face.

A muttering inside the truck caused Gus to look at Toby.

The man was praying.

Gus left him be. Might even be a good idea. One way or another, he figured he'd soon find out if God was watching.

Leaning back in his seat, Gus tugged at his submerged crotch and inadvertently jabbed a thumb into his balls.

Christ. He mentally groaned and took the sick pain. Just his luck. He'd dinged himself good, at the worst possible time, so he leaned against the airbag and rode out those debilitating waves of nausea. The suffering distracted him. And when the pain finally receded, Gus opened his eyes, realizing he'd squeezed them shut.

The water wasn't any higher than his Adam's apple.

He waited, waited, and then became aware of the second miracle.

The stomping overhead didn't seem as heavy. In fact, it seemed like half-strength.

"Gus?"

"Yeah?"

"They moving off?"

Gus didn't know, but the animalistic groaning seemed to taper off as well, as if the mob were growing weary of the party and decided to look for something more interesting.

"Seems like it," he finally said.

"Thank you, Lord," Toby whispered.

"Yes, thank you," Gus agreed, eyes on the ceiling.

Sputtering on Toby's side, as he blew out water.

"Stay quiet," Gus warned him.

Toby stopped spitting water. "For how long?"

"As long as it takes."

"That could be all night."

"Probably will be all night."

Water lapped at the inside of the windows. Gus shivered. It wasn't a violent one, but unpleasant all the same. He hoped it was just the water.

They waited.

Gus woke with a jolt, his face mashed against the airbag.

The glass outside his window was no longer black.

Not two feet away from the driver's side, a squished triangle of unbroken sunny gold was stretched to the left and out of sight, illuminating aquatic blue patterns on white tiles. Gus took in the sight, leaned back, and relaxed. Toby's side, however, was still dark. Not completely dark, but dimmed by whatever was resting on the pickup's roof. Toby had fallen asleep as well, his head looking toward the door.

"Tobe," Gus whispered.

The guy didn't respond.

Nothing tramped overhead. Nothing moaned. Gus rubbed his face, wondering how he managed to fall asleep at all, given the conditions, but he did. He reached over and shook his co-worker's shoulder.

"Toby."

"Mm."

"Wake up."

And Toby did, explosively, jacking upright with a gasp and splashing water.

The blast of movement startled Gus. "You okay?"

The other man blinked and pressed his palms to his cheeks. "Yeah."

"It's morning."

With a mighty intake of air, Toby looked out his window, then Gus's. "On your side, it is."

"Well, it's brighter."

"Always brighter on the other side."

"Listen," Gus pointed to the ceiling. "Hear anything?"

Toby shook his head.

"Wanna get out and take a look?" Gus asked.

"You think that's safe?"

"You wanna stay up to your neck in water?"

Toby did not.

"See if I can crack open the door." Gus said. He gripped the handle. With a click, it opened, and he waited for a reaction from above.

Nothing.

Caution on his mind, Gus pushed. The water pushed back on the door. The poolside prevented him from opening it all the way, and the airbag made things even more awkward. When the gap was wide enough, he struggled free from behind the wheel and waded into the dusky marine blue. Light twinkled on the water and along the edges.

He turned and inspected the covering above. "Well, fuck me."

"What?" Toby asked.

As an answer, Gus motioned for quiet and waded out of sight, keeping his head above the waterline.

A vaulted roof comprised of tightly fitted tongue and groove boards rested above the truck. The structure was slanted all the way back to the tailgate, where it lay on the pool's tiled edge. There was a bright sliver perhaps half a foot wide on his right, but Gus wasn't going to weasel his way through that. He'd be like a fat gopher sticking his head out. He glanced around. The rear of the truck was submerged. It wasn't pretty, certainly wasn't flush, but in their blind flight the night before, the truck swept the support legs out from the roof and carried it to the pool.

Where everything went into the drink.

"Wait for a minute," Gus told Toby, and waded to the tailgate. He refrained from drinking the water, mindful of them both pissing in it, and he remembered all that splashing as well. Zombies had dunked themselves all through the night. Who knew what bacteria might be swimming around the deep end.

Gus stopped at the back, causing water to lap against the truck and poolside. He couldn't detect any movement above. A gap between the truck's tailgate and the edge of the pool was a little more than a foot and a half, so he turned broadside, sucked in the gut, and sloshed to the other side of the vehicle.

Holy shit, he thought when he reached the tailgate's end.

The roof didn't cover the whole pool, but it covered the truck, enough to grant him and Toby protection to survive the night. Gus felt along the woodwork, appreciating the tight construction, until he reached Toby's door.

"Everything's okay?"

"I think so," Gus reported. "Listen."

Nothing to be heard.

"I'm getting out of here," Gus said. "You coming?"

A frantic nod.

"All right, let's get you out."

They opened the door together, and Toby wiggled his way free.

"Pass me my bat," Gus asked.

Toby did as told and retrieved his own. Neither man was hurt, escaping injury in the crash, though their clothes were soaked, and their hands resembled bleached raisins. They went to the roof's edge, sloshing water with every step, and shared a look.

Gus went under first.

He came up face-first into sunlight, warm and bright.

Gasping, he swung himself around, scanning the area and seeing nothing threatening. He reached underwater, and gestured for Toby to join him.

Seconds later, both men pulled themselves up a short ladder and onto dry land. Shivering, dripping, and standing in a backyard, two things got their attention.

First, a broad roof covered in black shingles rested on the truck, covering it completely. Taking in the rest of the surroundings, they saw that the roof belonged to an outside barbeque pit and bar, which seemed oddly naked standing on the tiles. The Brush-It rig had swept the outer beams, took the roof down, and pulled the other support beams off their concrete bases. They'd missed the barbeque and bar entirely. A set of lawn furniture was stacked against the back of the house, near a stair pit ending with a basement door. October moving, Gus figured. The owners were getting everything inside before the weather turned bad. If the zombie outbreak had happened a few days earlier, perhaps he and Toby would have collided with those backyard fixings as well.

The other thing they noticed was the backyard pool in which they'd parked the truck. The pool was L-shaped, where the pickup's nose rested across the letter's lower stem, like a big old mechanical dog resting its chin across its master's slippers. The rest of the pool remained clear, and while they had used a ladder, the upper section was the shallow part, allowing people to wade out if they wished. Though there was a tree line and a small copse of woods behind the backyard, there were no fences, so the mob dispersed as they pleased, drawn off by whatever.

"They followed us in here," Gus nodded, replaying the chase, "walked around scratching their heads, even up on the roof since it's not much of a step. And muddled around, not knowing they were right on top of us. A few dropped into the pool, but the roof edges kept them away from us. And when they stood, they splashed around, finding the path of least resistance, until they got out of the water."

"And they didn't bother looking under the roof," Toby added, "because they're zombies. With zombie shit on their zombie minds. They were walking over everything, falling, but getting right back up."

"Maybe they didn't even see us go into the pool?" Gus whispered. "We had a few seconds' jump on them. Maybe when they came around the corner all they saw was ... a roof in the pool. If they even recognized that at all. Maybe to them, it was just solid ground to walk over."

Water dripped off the two men as they stood and marvelled in stunned silence.

"We should get outta here," Toby finally said.

"Yeah," Gus agreed. The back doors of the house seemed intact, but the flowerbeds near the baseboards had been trampled, not that it mattered. Gus walked to the entrance, waterlogged sneakers farting all the way.

No one appeared home, at least he couldn't see anyone from a quick peek through a window, so he tried the door.

It opened with a click.

Gus traded looks with a nervous Toby before sticking his head inside the house. "Hello?" he asked warily. "Anyone home?"

No answer.

"Go in," Toby urged, looking around.

Gus wavered, and pulled the door open. The two men entered a kitchen, brown cupboards undisturbed, the island set and ready for a meal for two. A covered pot rested on the stove. Toby closed the door and locked it while Gus moved into a living room.

Where he stopped.

Before him was a cozy-looking living space. Brown sofa and matching chair. Big television. A coffee table of glass with a remote on it, along with a bunch of magazines, and a tablet of some sort. A trace of pipe smoke, faint but pleasing, scented the air. Above a gas fireplace was a painted picture of a Spanish galleon on the high seas, the sun setting in the background. Family pictures were on the mantle. A couple and their three kids. Smiles at graduation. Smiles at Christmas.

The real thing that got his attention was the picture window.

It was intact, with curtains and drapes that presented the world in a static white.

And outside of that window was a man walking along the street, along the edge of a square lawn. He walked as if he were somehow stricken, as if he'd forgotten to take a month's worth of arthritic medicine.

Then Gus saw the knife sticking out of the guy's back. A butcher knife, probably, big enough that Gus recognized the household chopper some forty feet away. That didn't stop the man, however, as he plodded along, from the left side of the window to the right, as if wandering across a wide stage.

As he reached the end, two more people came into view. A woman was looking up at the sky, the man was gawking straight ahead. The man had his shirt hanging off his torso, ripped down to a jelly-like chest. The guy with the knife in his back exited stage right while the new ones continued to the left. A pale and sullen kid, perhaps no more than fourteen, wandered into the picture not ten feet behind them. He dragged a fishing rod across the pavement and plodded along as if he'd just run a marathon on an empty stomach. More zombies wandered through in twos and threes, going nowhere, waiting for some stimuli to catch their attention.

Gus stood there, watching, part-scared of moving, part-mesmerized with the show.

Toby stopped beside him, and together, they dripped water on laminate flooring, the spattering loud in their ears.

"Holy fuck," Toby whispered.

"Holy fuck," Gus repeated in weary awe.

"The street's crawlin' with them bastards."

"Yeah. Listen, don't move. I'll check out the rest of the house."

"You do that."

Gus didn't hurry, although his heart was revving in his chest. He walked into a hall, where his whole frame froze.

The front door was open wide, with shoes scattered across the floor.

A pair of kids walked—no, *stalked*—past the front of the house, not forty feet away.

Gus didn't like seeing zombified kids. The kids were the worst.

Though his insides raved at him to do something, he had the presence of mind to belay those impulses. He eased himself to the wall, slowly, to not attract attention. Once out of sight, he nudged the door closed with a dripping foot, with all the concentration of a bomb expert disarming an explosive device.

The door shut with a soft click. He composed himself and flipped the three locks. There was a curtain, and he pulled it across, dimming the hall.

"Toby," Gus said.

His co-worker was still in the living room. The man glanced over.

"Slowly ... get the fuck out of the living room."

Toby nodded.

Gus looked down a bedroom hall and noted the stairwell heading into the basement. Bat in hand, he squished his way along. The bathroom was clear. Two of the bedrooms were plastered with posters. Baseballs rested on a chest of drawers, and stuffed animals relaxed on bed covers. The master bedroom was different. The queen-sized bed looked like a tornado touched down on it. Pillows and sheets were strewn about. A dark patch that looked mighty suspicious spilled over the side and onto the white carpet. Gus didn't go near it, but he checked the en suite and the two closets. All empty.

"Clear?" Toby whispered from the hall.

Gus nodded. "Now the basement. Gotta check that out."

"What do you think happened?"

"Someone was sick. Maybe turned. Maybe, I dunno, maybe one chased the other out the door and into the street. Let's check the basement."

Toby wanted Gus to go first, so he did, with an unimpressed frown. His sneakers hissed and slopped along the floor, getting on his nerves, but Gus figured the house was empty. Just needed to confirm.

A rec room with a fireplace and a wrap-around sofa set. Very cozy. A drum set filled a corner. A laundry room was off that, with a stainless-steel washer and dryer. There was a small bathroom with a shower and a storage room filled with a deep freeze, tools, all manner of stashed garden supplies, and firewood. There was a solid door as well, which Gus figured opened into that stair pit and led directly into the backyard. A stuffed red squirrel covered in dust sat on a shelf, ignoring him.

"Bedroom back here," Toby announced. "One window. I covered it up."

Gus glanced at the two windows in the basement, both opened, but both set low in the foundation. The window offered a ground-level view. He pulled their curtains across, but didn't close them completely. The basement dimmed.

"What do we do?" Toby asked.

Gus frowned with wet misery. "Get the fuck out of these clothes."

24

They located a pair of fluffy bathrobes and peeled off their sneakers, painter duds, and underclothes. The house had in-floor heating, so they cranked the heat upstairs and draped everything wet across the laminate flooring. The back door was locked, and the two men retreated to the basement, feeling a little more secure below ground.

At least until Gus felt the need to use the bathroom. The owners had almost a new roll of toilet tissue on the rack, which he greatly appreciated. One could never have too much bum wad on hand.

Fifteen minutes later, he returned to the rec room, where Toby had turned on a television, the volume set low.

The images on the television screen stopped him cold.

The CBC was broadcasting images of cannibalistic savagery and police counter attacks while a scrolling message below the picture ordered people to remain inside their homes, lock their doors, and not to venture outside. A state of emergency had been declared across Montreal, Ottawa, Toronto, as well as the other major cities. The news anchor, appearing more than a little unhinged but still holding things together, reported that cities south of the border and across the Atlantic pond were well into a state of emergency. Army units had been mobilized. Detroit and Boston were mentioned, but by that time, Gus had plopped down on one end of the sofa and watched. Interviewed scientists speculated on the origins of the outbreak, and by that time, the enormity of the situation smacked him between the eyes.

"Looks like it's official," Toby said.

"Yeah," Gus said quietly.

"It's happening all over the globe," Toby said. "They were even showing video out of Tokyo and Hong Kong. And that's all I got while you were on the shitter."

"What are we gonna do?"

"Dunno," Toby said. "But it might be an idea just to hang on here. Keep an eye on the news and the street. Unless you want to go out back and see if you can get the truck out?"

Gus made annoyed side-eyes at his co-worker.

"What about the phone?" he asked.

"Phone's dead, I checked." Toby nodded at the company device on a coffee table. "The pool killed it. Land line too. No service at all. First thing in a war, the enemy knocks out communications."

"That's a thinking enemy, you dummy. These things don't think."

Toby half-shrugged, not commenting. "What do you want to do then?"

Gus sighed in resignation. "We're here for a while, at least. I'm exhausted."

"Sleeping in a pool will do that."

"Yeah, so how about we bunk out here for a while? Rest up. Let the clothes and sneakers dry?"

Toby studied his companion. "You okay?"

"No."

"Wanna talk about it?"

Gus scowled reproachfully at the other man.

"Just asking," Toby said. Then, "Y'know, I was thinking. You know the reason why something like Ebola hasn't wiped us all out? Wanna know why? It's because it kills the people it infects way too fast. Melts them down before they can spread. Three days I think, from exposure to when they finally drop. These days, anywhere in the world is just a flight away. Thousands of people are in airports, all going somewhere, all landing in other airports to connect with other flights, passing by more people going in different directions. All it takes is one sick person to go through an airport, and the fuse gets lit. This thing has been around for a week already, and we thought it was the flu. Only now we know different. And now it's probably too late. This bug doesn't melt people down, it just takes over their minds and makes them crazy, and they want to spread the love. You know what I'm sayin'?"

"Yeah," Gus said. "We're in the midst of a zombie breakout. And there's a good chance my girlfriend is gone. My friends are gone. Maybe my ... my family is gone. Oh, God."

Toby kept his mouth shut.

Before any more emotion leaked out, Gus got to his feet. "I'll take the bedroom," he muttered, voice breaking, barely holding the panic back. He left Toby on the sofa without another thought, while the fright and emotion clawed at his throat and guts.

The bedroom door closed behind him with a firm click. The window had the curtain pulled across. The bed itself, neat and unused.

Gus flopped onto the mattress.

He closed his eyes, took a deep breath, and let himself go.

It was dark when he woke.

Gus lay there for a moment, staring at an unfamiliar ceiling. He wiped his eyes and his face, and listened. His ears teased him with murmurings that might've been the rec room television. Unfortunately for him, he woke up knowing he was firmly entrenched in reality and that the world probably had changed even more in the time he'd passed out. For the worse.

Adjusting his robe, he sat up and hung his head. He felt a little clearer of mind, so he stood and walked to the door.

The TV was off, so Gus told his brain to fuck off with the imaginary voices.

The lights were off and it was dark, both inside and out. Toby was on his feet, arms crossed on the window sill, still dressed in his bathrobe. A weak light passed through curtains parted just a sliver. Toby peered outside, the lower part of his face faintly illuminated.

"Hey," he said, sounding exhausted.

"Hey," Gus greeted. "What time is it"

"Just a little after holy fuck."

"What's that in real time?"

"5:30 in the evening. Well, really nighttime."

"You eat anything?" Gus asked.

That sliver of night light showed Toby's sad smile. "Nah. Been watching TV. Until it got dark anyway."

"Any news?"

"All bad. CBC's gone. CNN's still on, but the other stations are gone. They're now saying they think that it's a mutated virus, a mix of Avian and Swine Flu, SARS, and a few others. There's a lot of different theories."

Gus located the corner of the couch and sat down. Toby remained at the window, looking outside. The man was a ghost.

"You sleep any?" Gus asked.

"Nah."

"You should."

Toby didn't answer, didn't look away from the window.

"You eat anything?" Gus asked.

"No."

Gus rubbed his stomach, feeling the urge. He could do with something. He remembered the drying clothes. "Clothes dried?"

"Didn't check."

Figures. Gus thought, but there was something in Toby's demeanor that wasn't right. "You been upstairs at all?"

No answer.

Gus waited for seconds, counting them off, watching his co-worker and, dare he say it, good friend, at the window. The guy didn't move, watching what lay beyond.

"Tobe?"

"No," the man replied.

"Tobe, you okay?"

That made Toby look away from the window, but that didn't make Gus feel any better. Toby's face was a shadowy thing, a sepulchre shade of gray-black in the pale glow from the outside. The man's eyes were two tiny glimmers of light, located deep within the black cauldrons that were his orbital cavities. Toby watched with a post-mortem silence that stretched well beyond a comfortable pause. A hand came away from the window sill, slow and deliberate, and drifted to his side as if he were reaching for a holstered sidearm. The action made Gus remember the old black and white flick *Nosferatu,* where the vampire's every movement was a silent, spidery nightmare.

Toby still didn't answer. He scratched at a hip.

"Toby?" Gus asked. "You hear me?"

"Yeah."

"And?"

No response, and no sign of having heard. Gus blinked a few times, but he wasn't sure if Toby did, because those tiny lights in the tar pits of his head hadn't wavered.

"Sorry," Toby finally whispered. "Just a little stressed out, I guess."

"You're stressing me out," Gus said, lying through his teeth. Toby was, in fact, frightening him.

"Sorry, dude," the co-worker said. "Been a long day."

"You better get to sleep."

"Yeah."

"I mean it," Gus insisted.

Toby went quiet again. A white spider moved on the window sill, and Gus realized with a start that the man's hand had returned there. That subtle, soundless stirring sent paralyzing sub-zero splinters through Gus's chest and brain. Toby stood there, a baleful ghost harkening to things best unheard. He looked outside and stared, his hand poised and ready to leap—or so it seemed to Gus, and Gus was having doubts now. He was having grave doubts that the guy was simply stressed out. In the hours left alone, gazing upon a rapidly changing world while alternate televised realities winked out behind him, Toby's own mental fortitude just might have crumbled a little. Crumbled and then rebuilt hastily, with whatever reasoning and assurances he had to use to cement and duct tape his sanity back in place and keep it there.

"Did you sleep?" Toby finally asked.

The question caught Gus off guard. "Yeah."

"Did you dream?"

The answer took a while to surface. "No. Luckily enough. No."

"That's good."

On impulse, Gus stood up.

Toby's face locked onto his movement, in much the same way a deer might have when poised to bolt.

"Toby," Gus said evenly, paying very close attention to how he spoke to the man. "Listen now, you've been up a long time. A long time. And a lot of shit's gone downhill in that time. Ever since we stepped into Mollymart. How about I head upstairs and take a look in the bathroom? Maybe there's some sleeping pills or some—"

"Don't wanna sleep," he said sternly, without any opening for discussion.

The answer left Gus dangling. "Well, okay, how about a drink or—"

"I mean," Toby cut him off again, sharp enough to draw blood, "I know I should. And I feel myself dozing off, right here at the window. But every time I relax …" And at that point, Toby's gloomy face broke into a horrid smile that quivered around the edges, "I see … I see Gord having his face ripped off."

That brought Gus back, to a time and place he didn't want to revisit, and he stood there and listened, going cold below the neckline.

"I mean, I was staring out the window of the truck," Toby explained in a strained whisper. "And those things were all over him, at his face like they were eating … great big swaths of cotton candy. Every time I relax and close my eyes—drifting off, y'know—that's what I see. That's what's waiting for me. In my dreams. And that's when I jerk awake, knowing that if I go any further, I'll see more. And I'm pretty sure I wouldn't be able to wake up then. Oh, I could try, but you know how nightmares are, once they really dig in. Nothing you can do except ... take it. And I, well, whenever I have bad dreams, I scream, right? I mean I scream. Loud. And considering what I've been seeing outside today, it's best I don't scream. Which means I don't sleep. At all."

That quiet, pleading explanation hit Gus hard and left him speechless. "Tobe," he finally got out. "I'm up now. You could use the bedroom. Try and sleep. I'd be out here, keeping watch. If I hear you screaming, I'll come running. Wake you up. Really."

Toby spoke, but his mouth didn't seem to move. "I don't know, Guster, I don't know. You know what's going on out there? I mean, really going on?"

"People are walking around."

"They're not people anymore, Gus. It's official. They're not people anymore. I've seen shit. A wide variety of shit. And all of it bad. It's frightening. In a fish tank sorta way. But you're right about them walking around. They're on the move, all right. It's deep water out there Gus. And you and I are stuck in a cave at the very bottom while the sharks prowl overhead."

"Listen," Gus said. "Just come away from the window. Sit down at least. I'll be right here. I'll stand guard. Nothing will happen. Not with me on the job. I'm wide awake now, anyway."

Toby seemed to think about it. "I'll dream. I know it."

"Maybe. But I'll wake you first thing if I hear you or see you twitching. First sign of twitching, and I'll fuckin' smack you one in the balls."

"Ow," Toby said, sounding like the man Gus knew. "Christ, Gus. Don't do that. That would be the worst. My fuckin' reflexes would be sleepin' too. I'd be all exposed and shit. You could really hurt me."

"All right, no ball smackin'. Just sayin' is all. You should really get some sleep. Or try to. Right here if you want. The couch is big enough. Let's swap places. You camp out here and I'll take up position where you are now."

Toby looked from the window to Gus, and back again, clearly thinking things over. "You sure?"

"Sure, I'm sure."

More silence, dreadful and swelling with sound, until, a very quiet, "Okay."

That single word took a lot of tension out of Gus. Toby stepped away from the window, arms falling to his sides as if he'd been holding them up for hours. His shoulders sagged, and he stepped heavily, exhaustion hitting him hard. He inspected the wrap-around couch.

"You need a blanket?" Gus asked.

"Yeah," the sleep-deprived ghost said. "Please."

Gus went to the bedroom and pulled off one of the thin blankets. It was warm downstairs, but there was something comforting about pulling a blanket up around one's neck and ears. And right now, Toby needed all the comforting he could get. When Gus returned, the guy was already splayed on the couch.

"I'm back," Gus said, approaching the relaxing mass.

"Yeah."

"Just gonna spread this over you, okay?"

"Yeah. Sure."

Gus covered him up, dropping the blanket edge around the guy's neck. Toby hauled it in close, covering half his head. "Thanks."

"You're welcome. Just sleep. If you can."

Toby answered with a sigh.

Gus retreated from the couch, watching his friend get comfortable. Once the rustling died down, he assumed his post at the window. Streetlights were on, weak and just out of sight, hidden by bushes on the lawn and failing to fully reach the basement's interior. The light was brightest beyond the greenery, yet he could see well enough before him, right to the darkened front of the neighbour's split-level across the street.

There was more than enough light to see what was happening outside.

People walked.

With a slow, almost shell-shocked lack of purpose, as if recovering from a massive sensory overload of some kind. *A fish tank*, Toby had said, and they wandered into Gus's field of vision from both sides, their hands rubbery and dangling at their thighs, their faces lifted to the heavens or staring straight ahead. And there wasn't just one or two. He tracked seven lurching through his line of sight, the figures steadily replaced by others ambling into view. Some limped as if stricken with arthritis or somehow wounded. There was a soundtrack to the scene, a low moaning, a disconnected muttering, as if they struggled to talk and couldn't remember any words.

A woman moved into sight from the right, dressed in knee shorts and T-shirt, and walked straight for an overweight man dressed in a sleeveless tee and jeans. Like a pair of small ships, they walked toward each other, grunting warnings about their imminent collision. The zombies bumped into each other, belly to belly. They rebounded and collided again. The second hit twisted them both, the woman awkwardly bouncing off the man's greater mass like a dinghy spinning off an iceberg. They didn't fall, however, but righted themselves and walked out of the picture.

Only to be replaced by more zombies.

And as the show went on, it went from a rating of PG to straight up XXX for graphic imagery.

A man with his bicep chewed away to the bone. Only a few dull sinews kept the appendage from dropping into the dirt.

A woman had her throat half-devoured, and the resulting spectacular blood loss was displayed on her dress.

A guy had one end of a pickaxe buried in his neckline, but he strolled along as if looking for his car keys.

An elderly lady walked along dragging a cane, looking perfectly normal, except when she turned just a bit to the side and showed off the shocking damage sustained right down to the bones of her face.

Another man, tall and built for powerlifting, didn't have his right arm at all. All that remained was a short sleeve caked with blood.

Those were the most memorable amongst the pageantry of horror, and Gus would indeed remember them unless he found a way to exorcise the images from his mind. At times, he looked away, just before they swayed to reveal hideous wounds. Some didn't have any telling injuries at all and presumably those were the ones contracting the bug in the beginning, but then there were the victims.

Those were the worst.

Minutes ticked off into hours. The hours dragged on, and Gus watched. And watched. And attempted to remember individuals, just in case he was seeing one twice. He wasn't, however, and gave up as the zombies saturated his memory, and his anxiety rose to flood levels. There were a *lot* of people walking around outside the house. It occurred to him that it was more than an entire housing division, and wondered if the extra zombies were wandering in from other parts, following whatever impulses or currents that pushed them along.

And it was while he was watching all those corpses go by, right at the very point of being desensitized to the horror, when a pair of feet stopped directly in front of his window and damn near made him scream.

Gus froze at the pair of cheap sneakers, ankle socks, and the hairy legs accompanying them. The legs stayed there, swaying ever so slightly in the night air, as if the owner was working off a night of drinking and struggling for balance. Between those legs, figures continued on the lawn and road. They were suddenly secondary. This individual had left the street and walked along the house until he stopped for a rest.

At least Gus hoped it was a rest.

He slowly drew back from the feet framed in the window, not daring to take a step himself, for fear of the thing outside hearing. Gus's head filled with mini-movies of the zombie dropping to its chest and peering inside the window, its face lighting up with discovery. He didn't appreciate the thought and, again, told his brain to fuck off.

The feet stayed. The legs continued to sway, the movement more noticeable the higher up. He couldn't see the knees, just those meaty, hairy calves. Not that he wanted to see anymore. After what he'd witnessed in the last few hours, who knew what operated those legs.

So Gus stood there and waited, watching the zombie parked right in front of him. God must've left the room or something, because the undead bastard standing outside the glass not two feet away from Gus's face, showed no inclination of moving. For a moment, he wondered if the thing was taking a leak, but he didn't even want to think about that.

He licked his lips, needing a drink very badly. Just a drink of water. Or a coke.

The zombie abruptly stepped away from the window, moving to the right and out of sight. The sudden departure took a few seconds to sink in. Gus leaned forward, angling to see where the legs had gone, but he couldn't see. He glanced at the road.

Well, shit.

He scowled in disbelief, and his temples ached from the sudden intake of blood.

There, walking up the middle of the street and still wearing his painter duds, was Gord.

Gord walked very well for a man in his undead condition, as all his limbs were intact. His painter clothes were saturated in blood, however, so that wasn't so good, and his face had been removed down to the red bone. Despite the lack of facial features, Gus had no trouble knowing it was his old friend. He recognized the outfit and sneakers, and upon greater scrutiny, even recognized the man's remaining hair.

Chest hitching, with his eyes welling up with water and feeling lightheaded, Gus backed into a corner.

And on the couch, Toby moaned.

Loudly.

25

Gus lurched for the couch and grabbed Toby's legs. The man kicked out in reflex, and the moan became a yelp. Gus groped for his friend's face, clamping both hands across a mouth. Toby's nostrils flared with a mighty intake of air, and his head bounced on the cushion. His eyes snapped open while his mouth flexed beneath Gus's palm. An expulsion of air blasted out of Toby's nose as he grasped the hands holding him.

"I'm okay," he said, the words muffled.

But Gus wasn't.

"Shhhhh," he released into Toby's ear, hard enough that the man flinched. Gus pulled Toby's head close in a *don't-fuck-around* test of strength.

"Not a sound," Gus warned.

Toby's bright eyes locked onto his. Toby nodded, fully awake, so Gus let him go, cautioning him with a finger.

He pointed to the window.

From the angle where they were, the window appeared as a slanted portal with its curtains parted a ghostly inch. An eerie afterthought of streetlight peeked through that gap. There was no way of seeing if anything was outside, no way of seeing if anything approached the house, and certainly no way of knowing if anything was looking into the basement.

But Gus figured caution to be the wise course of action. So they remained there, Toby laid out on the couch with Gus on one knee and locked into place beside him, staring at that window. Waiting. Waiting. Counting off seconds.

The light faltered, blocked by something unseen.

A mass pulled itself along the length of the house, testing the vinyl siding, clattering, unrelenting. It was as if a person was dragging an uneven rock along the home. That wobbly nail-head scraping positively petrified Gus.

Toby remained still as a coffin's corpse, eyes flickering in the dark, tracking the sound as it passed by and headed toward the window. A hard slap punctuated the house-length noise coming from the other opposite side, causing both men to flinch. Gus might've whimpered, but it was lost in an off-key twang of a couch spring.

The light fluttered, darkened, and stayed dark.

Another hard blow struck the house's siding, mere feet above the basement window. A third smack then, but it wasn't as forceful as those before it. The scraping sound ended, and for a moment, Gus wondered if the two noisemakers hadn't collided with each other like the rest of the undead dummies out in the street. Whatever had happened, the noises didn't repeat.

The two men waited. Gus rubbed sweat off his face and forehead. He felt his chest, his heart racing faster than a drunken snare drum. If he got out of this alive, he promised his ass was going to drop a few pounds.

The light flickered, wavered, and alternated between going dark and back to normal. There was no further noise, even though Gus waited for another hit, or worse—one of the doors being battered aside, followed by the rapid deployment of feet across the floor overhead.

"I don't hear anything," Toby whispered.

"Me too," Gus replied in an equally hushed tone.

"Think it's safe?"

"I dunno."

"Wanna check?"

"Fuck that."

"Yeah, fuck that," Toby agreed.

Gus looked to the ceiling, waiting for the inevitable assault on the doors. Minutes passed.

"Gus, I gotta pee." Toby eventually said.

"Hold it."

"I gotta pee real bad."

"Tobe," Gus bit back in a harsh whisper. "Tie a knot in it or something."

"There ain't enough there to tie a knot in it. Besides, it wouldn't help anyway. I had to go five minutes ago."

"All right, go." Gus moved back from the couch, allowing his friend to gently roll off and slink toward the downstairs facilities. A door softly closed. He shook his head at the sound of Toby relieving himself, the tinkling coming through in the absolute stillness. Then a squeaker of a failed attempt of suppressing gas, which quickly escalated into a full-blown balloon flutter of escaping wind.

Sighing, Gus crept to the window, hanging back enough to hide himself, yet peeking outside.

Zombies moved about the lawn.

A cluster of zombies, seen through several sets of legs.

A small army right on his doorstep.

Slowly, then, as if the town meeting had been adjourned, the zombies moved off, restoring light to the basement.

Gus watched them. Toby stood a few feet away, returned from the bathroom and awaiting an update.

"They're moving off," Gus whispered.

"Many of them?"

"More than I need."

"Like Mollymart?"

Gus thought about it. "Not quite, but close."

They listened.

"That one's on me," Gus said contritely. "My mistake. Said I was going to wake you and I didn't. Got caught up in what was outside."

"That's okay."

"Should've been paying more attention."

"Did I snark?"

"No, you didn't snark. Just moaned."

"Oh man," Toby said.

"I ... I saw ..." Gus hesitated, wondering if he should say anything at all. "What?"

"I saw Gord," he said, unable to contain himself. "I saw Gord. Gord was out there. With the rest of them."

"What?" Toby said in disbelief, his hands holding his head.

"He was out there."

"How far is that?" Toby asked. "From Mollymart to here?"

"I dunno. Fifteen, twenty klicks."

"God *damn*."

"Goddamn." Gus repeated. "He had all day to get here. He might've just followed a pack or something. Or hell maybe the fuckin' wind just blew him along."

"That's fucked up, Gus."

"It is fucked up."

"How'd he look?"

Gus studied his friend. "He was ... pretty bad."

"Dead?"

Oh yeah, Gus thought, and nodded.

"Poor Gord," Toby whispered and looked to his feet.

They stayed that way for a short time, holding the silence for the departed Gord Munn.

Then Gus's attention went back to the zombies moping around the neighborhood.

"Go on back to sleep," he said to Toby. "I'll stay up."

"Think I can sleep after that? No way."

"Might as well. You can take the early morning shift."

"Gus," a worried Toby said. "What are we going to do? We can't stay here."

"We can't go out there either."

"Well then what?"

"Let's just …" Gus paused to collect his thoughts. "Let's just get through the night first. Okay? Think on things, then compare notes in the morning. How's that sound?"

"Okay," Toby answered, and to Gus's surprise, he went back to the couch and lay back down.

Gus stayed at the window, watching the traffic.

Toby took over watching about an hour before dawn, allowing Gus to sit down and doze for a while. He didn't really sleep, however, as the recent dead plagued the corners of his dreams, reaching for him just before he opened his eyes. A deep-down body weariness set in, his internal clock tossed for a loop and wondering what was going on. Gus knew it was going to be a long day.

"You up?" Toby quietly asked from the window. He hadn't budged from the spot.

"Yeah."

"Sleep?"

"Not really."

"Come take a look."

Sunlight beamed down from overhead, the dew sparkling on the grass. Bushes dotted the lawn in no particular pattern. A fat spider worked on a web stretching from the window's corner to a nearby bush, replacing the one destroyed from the night before.

Zombies wandered the street.

Where there had been a pack of them during the night, the current numbers hovered around ten or an even dozen. It looked like a day along a busy strip out there, or a community event of some kind, except everyone was dead. The wounds weren't as haunting as they were during the night, but they were still disturbing. People had bites taken out of them. Dark splotches stained their clothes. A guy walked by missing a couple of fingers. An old man pulled himself along the street like a gray grub sensitive to the sun, his pant legs streaming behind him, the fabric baggy around his shins and bare ankles.

"They just keep on moving," Toby quietly observed. "Keep on walking or crawling."

"I can't watch anymore." Gus turned away.

"What're you gonna do?"

"Check the perimeter."

The stairs led up to the hallway and living room. Gus reached eye level and looked around. He continued to the picture window curtains and located a string. Slowly, he pulled those heavy red drapes to, hoping the dead outside wouldn't take notice and storm the house. He doubted the glass here was five-eighths of an inch thick. The thought stuck with him, and he hoped again that the Mollymart people had made it out alive. Hoped that Anna was somewhere in Falmouth. The room became dark, but Gus's spirit improved. He left the bedrooms and went to the kitchen, where he stopped at the sink and the window there.

Zombies walked around in the backyard.

Some stood on the roof covering the submerged Brush-It truck, staring in almost all directions. One had slipped into the pool and was in the process of circling the wall to the stairs. Gus shook his head at the display. They weren't smart, as far as he could tell. They just bumped along, looking for the path of least resistance—unless you stood in front of them.

Whereupon they'd try to eat your face off.

Gus edged out of sight and closed the blinds. He proceeded to the back door and checked the locks, closed the curtains as well.

He peeked into the backyard again and mentally groaned.

The sonsabitches were everywhere.

Christ almighty, he thought. He and Toby were surrounded. Trapped. No way out. And this wasn't Mollymart. It was a much smaller scale with less security, and certainly less robust building materials, but with more dead people circling them. And if the dead discovered the two men inside, they would pound their way through the doors and windows in very short time.

He needed the wall to keep standing, dazed by the situation.

When the moment passed, Gus checked on the clothes arranged around the floor and found them dry. He gathered up everything except the damp sneakers and went downstairs.

Toby hadn't budged from the window. "See anything?"

Gus dropped Toby's clothes on the couch. "Lots."

"Yeah? Like what?"

"Not sure how to tell you this ... so I'll just tell you."

"Okay. Go ahead. I'm ready."

Gus paused, organizing his thoughts to best express their situation. "We're fucked."

That didn't go over well, and Gus could tell. So, he started again and told Toby everything he saw surrounding the house. When he finished, Toby leaned against the wall for support.

"Shit," he whispered and regarded Gus. "What do we do?"

"Hell if I know. But we can't go outside. Not like it is now with them out there. The way they move, if they saw us we'd be swamped in seconds."

"We can't stay here forever," Toby whined, the color draining from his face.

"We won't," Gus assured him and plopped down on the couch. "But we're going to be here for a little longer. Until things die down or we see a chance to, I dunno, get to a car."

"There was no car in the driveway."

"I know," Gus said, his voice rising just a little. "Think with me here, okay? Okay?"

Toby nodded that he would try.

"Now, there was a Camaro in the next driveway over," Gus said. "Remember that? We could get to that and hot-wire it."

"Can you hot-wire a car?"

"No. You?"

"Fuck no."

Gus held his chin. "Okay, maybe there's a set of keys in the house."

"So, we'd have to go to the house and get inside."

"Just next door."

"Dude, I don't know," Toby said while shaking his head. "I mean, my legs are about to go just thinking about cracking a window here. I don't think I can go outside."

"It's just next door," Gus explained. "If they clear out the back, we can creep over there. Nighttime if you like. Just sneak on by."

"I can't ninja-walk."

"You're gonna have to."

"My ninja-walk sucks donkey cock."

"So you want to stay here? 'Cause a few seconds ago you said we can't stay here forever."

Toby fretted with indecision, looked to the window, and nodded fearfully.

"All right," Gus said, not used to seeing the guy in such a stressed-out state. "We hold here. Stay quiet. See what happens."

"Maybe they'll burn themselves out," Toby said hopefully. "Like Ebola."

But neither of them believed it.

26

Around 9:30 a.m. or so, Gus's stomach shuddered, wanting sustenance.

He patted his considerable gut, sighed, and figured he go take a look. He felt hungry enough but wondered if he could keep anything down—especially after the sights of last night.

"Where you headed?" Toby asked when Gus rose from the couch.

"Upstairs. Gonna get something to eat."

"You can eat?"

"My gut's telling me it can. You want anything?"

Toby shook his head.

"Any change out there?" Gus asked.

"No, nothing. They're still walking."

Great, Gus thought. He went to the kitchen, mindful of the windows and curtains. The fridge was stuffed, luckily enough. Someone had gone for groceries before the zombie shitstorm broke out. There was an assortment of fruit juices, four liters of two-percent milk, a Brita full of water. Meats and leftovers of chicken stewing in a congealed pink sauce occupied a shelf, but Gus left that. He picked out a loaf of bread, an unopened carton of milk, salad dressing, and a pack of assorted lunch meats. He got a cutting knife from a collection hanging on a wall, and transferred everything downstairs in two trips.

Toby watched him as he set everything up on the coffee table. "You really gonna eat?"

"Yeah."

"What if some of that's contaminated?"

"How so?"

"Well, if they drank from the carton or something?"

"Who?"

"The people who lived here."

"Oh." Gus held up the unopened milk, then the meats, also unopened.

"What about the salad dressing?" Toby asked. "Someone could've licked the knife before scooping out more of that goop, and whatever might be on their tongue is now in the salad dressing."

"Who does that?" Gus asked. "No one licks the knife until after they're finished with it."

"I do it."

"And you're a freak. Anyway, regular folks don't do that." All the same, Gus took off the lid and inspected the half-empty jar.

"How much you got there?" Toby asked.

"Half empty."

"You mean half full."

"No, I mean half empty."

"Try and be positive here," Toby said.

"Well, considering the circumstances, I am being positive here."

"You're being negative. You said the jar's half empty."

"Which it is."

"I said it's half full."

"Say what you like, but the stuff comes out of the jar, thus *emptying* it. When it goes in, filling it and it stops half way or wherever, then it's half full. But in most cases, people don't go around filling shit up halfway. Comes out, half empty. Goes in—"

"I'm talking about the state you first found it in," Toby countered. "When you don't know if it was being filled or being emptied."

"Look," Gus faced him. "I'm not gonna fuckin' argue with you about a fuckin' jar of salad dressing and the state I found it in, okay? I saw that same fuckin' movie you did and that guy was wrong. That whole half-full, half-empty Zen enlightenment shit doesn't apply to a glass of whatever. Just doesn't. Water goes into the glass, that's half full. Comes out, that's half empty."

"He was talking about when you look at it for the first time," Toby explained. "Without any preconception about who placed it there, and you don't know whether it's been left in a state of being filled or emptied. It simply is. It's symbolic of your reflective state of mind. Of being."

"As far as I remember," Gus countered, "he was drinking it in a bar. And if he just picked the glass up—and I can't remember the scene exactly now—

but guess what? Doesn't matter. Does not matter. That water didn't just appear on the counter. Someone asked for a drink of water and he got a full glass of it and drank half and left the rest. No one gets a half glass of water in a bar. And even if they did, using that in an analogy of a person's state of mind or existentialism and yak philosophy about it how it applies to a person's character is poppycock. The water was given to that initial person, fuckin' full, and he drank half of the goddamn thing and left the rest. If anything, it's a waste of water. Guy should've asked for half a glass if he wasn't so thirsty, which would've been just a better conversation piece about how we waste water or take it for granted."

"You're missing the point, there."

"Oh, I got the point. Some people would look at the glass and say that's half empty, others would say that's half full, and that would somehow reflect on what kinda person they are and how they look at life. I'm saying it's not that simple, that there's more to it than that. More going on than what you might think."

That discombobulated Toby completely.

"Yeah," Gus said before he could recover. "I've been hanging around you too long."

"You're a pessimist," Toby told him.

"I'm not a pessimist," Gus grumped, his nerves getting to him. He got to work on making some sandwiches. "If anything, I'm a fuckin' realist."

"Realists invented that term because they don't like to be called pessimists."

"Yeah, well, dingbats don't like to be called dingbats, but they get called that. All the time. And it's all better than being called a dick knob."

"I'm pretty sure you just validated my point."

"Toby, I'm making a sandwich here. You want one or not?"

The smell of a freshly opened pack of assorted meats wafted over to the guy, and the gears went to work inside his head.

"Okay," he eventually said. "But let me go see if there's another jar of that salad dressing upstairs. You know they call that shit mayonnaise down in the States?"

Gus let him go, thankful for the lull in conversation. He thought he won that round. Usually, Toby would talk his ass off until he was right, but at least he made a showing that time. Anything was better than the one-word replies Gus was getting last night. He hoped that Toby was just having an episode thing, and hoped Tobe kept a grip on his own nerves.

That was being positive.

Pessimist my ass, he thought to himself.

And as luck would have it, there was a new jar of salad dressing in an upstairs cupboard.

They made sandwiches and ate like a couple of guys on a work site somewhere. CNN was still on, so they watched that, the volume a whisper. The screen showed footage of religious nuts holding their hands to heaven, praying for intervention and appearing positively jovial that they finally got one end of the world scenario right. Then the feed switched to riot gear police in some United Kingdom public park, retreating in mass from a wall of oncoming infected.

Lunch paused after that one.

Then the feed shifted again to another story. One reporter stood before a low hill cleared of all vegetation except grass, with a formidable steel door in the background. Security guards were flanking an older gentleman in a business suit. The guy was identified as sixty-eight-year-old founding minister of the Church of Green Pasture. An innocuous-enough sounding name, until it was revealed the Green Pasture congregation believed in the coming apocalypse and intended to survive it. Survive it and then repopulate the earth, through the guidance of one Father Tommy Throttle.

Gus sat up for that one.

Old Tommy was a self-professed doomsday prophet and went into action when people were getting sick worldwide. He contacted and gathered up selected members of his considerable flock. In this case, fifty or so women. The reporter turned the microphone over to Tommy, who went on to explain how he intended to wait out the plague, weeks if necessary, and then work to reclaim the Earth in the Lord's name.

Except Tommy didn't say that exactly, as CNN went off the air around that time, leaving the two men staring at a black screen with a message reading "Unable to locate signal."

Without a word, Gus switched off the TV.

"So much for that," he muttered.

Toby didn't comment, and neither man was interesting in talking about what they'd just seen. So, they sat on the couch, bent over their food, chomping away. The TV going dead didn't seem to bother Toby. All Gus could hear was the man chewing.

And Toby chewed like a cow.

They finished their brunch and sat back, hands on bellies, nursing mugs filled with milk. Neither man spoke for a while.

"I bet there's cookies up in those cupboards," Toby finally suggested.

"Cookies."

Interesting way to change the subject, Gus thought. "I bet there is too," he agreed.

"Want me go look?"

"Go ahead. Just keep your head down."

Toby quietly went upstairs, his socked feet barely making a whisper on the laminate flooring. When he returned not five minutes later, he had half a bag of Oreos, half a bag of Chocolate Chip, and an unopened pack of Purity Fancy Biscuits.

Gus's face lit up at the cream-filled cookies. "Where'd you get these?"

"From the cupboard."

"Excellent."

"Hey. Guess what."

"What?"

Toby reached into the bag of Oreos. "Found this little darling upstairs. I stashed it in here to surprise you."

He pulled out a cell phone and charger.

"Nice," Gus said.

"I'll plug it in," Toby said, setting the cookies down. He located an outlet and plugged the device in. "Maybe that thing'll work after an hour or so."

"Maybe," Gus agreed. "Ah, how'd things look up there?"

"I didn't look," Toby said, plopping down on the couch and reaching for the Oreo bag.

"Don't blame you," Gus said and went into the Purity cookies.

They had dessert, the sugar doing them wonders, and when they finished, Gus went to the basement window and peered out at the world.

Zombies patrolled the street, the sun bright and harsh on them.

"How's it look?" Toby asked from the couch.

"Shitty."

But at least Gord was gone. Gus wasn't sure he could handle seeing him walk around.

The usual assortment of dead people paraded out front. Most looked normal, at least as far as normal went for a goddamn undead creature of the night. One went by looking as if he'd been scalped, the top of his head shorn of hair and covered in a crusty black. Bone peeked through the covering.

"Hey," Toby said. "What's worse ... a bad dick or a bad back?"

Gus thought about it. "A bad dick ..."

"Naw, man. A bad back."

"How you figure that?"

"If you got a bad back, you can't use a bad dick."

"Point taken."

"Think about it."

"I shall," Gus assured him. "In the hours to come."

He went back to watching the show outside the window. Toby relaxed on the couch. In short time, his chin drooped and he dozed. Quietly.

Somewhere just after noon, Toby woke up. He even smiled at Gus when he looked over.

"Morning Sunshine," Gus greeted, standing at arm's length from the window.

"Morning."

"Sleep good?"

"I did. No dreams."

"That's good."

"Anything new?"

Gus shook his head. "They just keep walking."

"Any of them running?"

"No."

Toby thought about that. "Maybe they don't have any reason to run. Maybe there's nothing for them to run after."

Gus looked to the window and the parted curtains. Every now and again, one or two of them would swagger across the lawn, but no closer. The majority kept to the road.

"Maybe," Gus said. "You wanna take a shift here?"

"Not really, no."

"One of us should."

Toby didn't say anything to that.

"Don't want to?" Gus asked.

Toby shook his head.

"All right, I'll hang on a bit longer."

"I think it'll be okay if you didn't."

Gus didn't agree. "I'm the other way. Y'see, if there's a lull out there, or they clear out, whatever, and there's room to move? I wanna be up those stairs and out the back door. Head for the neighbor's house and find a set of car keys."

"For the Camaro?"

"You go it."

"Probably other cars around."

"Nothing as close," Gus said. "Best to go with what's handy. Searching driveways along the street for a ride is dangerous, exposing yourself. But we'll probably have to take the chance eventually. The Camaro next door is closest. It'll do until we find something better."

Toby sat and thought about things.

"Take it easy," Gus told him. "Anything happens. I'll let you know."

"Thanks."

Nothing happened.

Toby tried the charged cell phone. He called people he knew first but no one answered. Then he tried the police, the fire department, even city hall. Nothing. He even called Benny, but got only the boss man's voice mail. That put him in a funk.

Things got quiet in the basement.

Until around three thirty in the afternoon or a minute or so afterward, when Gus straightened at a window

Gunshot.

A series of gunshots.

A popcorn rattle of firearms far and away from Legion Road, but close enough to be heard.

"You hear something?" Toby asked from the couch, laid back and staring at the ceiling.

"Shooting," Gus said, shifting from left to right, trying to gauge the direction. "That's nearby too."

Seconds passed from the last *pop*. "Close," Gus said, "I think that was back toward New Minas, but that's too far to go on foot."

"The zombies move any?"

Gus took greater stock in what they were doing. When he heard the gunfire, he was more focused on determining where the shooting was coming from.

He looked to the road and his heart leaped.

Zombies were moving left to right. A lot of them were hurrying along in the same direction, but they weren't running. Gus watched them shuffle along, noting how they seemed to be moving slower than two nights ago, as if each one were shackled in ankle chains. The sight puzzled him, and as he stood there, he realized the gunfire had ceased entirely.

"Something going on," he said.

Toby looked up with a question on his face.

"They're moving slower," Gus informed him.

"Slower?"

"Yeah, slower, like they're clenching ass cheeks or something."

"Are they moving away?"

"They're ... wait ... shooting's stopped," Gus leaned toward the glass. "Looks like they're losing interest."

"Or just forgot about it." Toby suggested. "My short-term memory is bad enough. Fuckin' zombie's can't be much better."

Gus smirked. The guy had a point. Outside, the zombies clearly weren't hurrying along like they were seconds earlier. They'd lost interest or just up and forgot. That interested Gus. If the gunfire had continued, he suspected whatever was hanging around Legion Road would have left to investigate.

"How about now?" Toby asked.

"How about you come on over and see for yourself?"

Toby shook his head.

"Tobe, look," Gus said, figuring he best explain the facts. "We're stuck here for the next little while at least. We're a two-man team here, and we have to look out for each other. Sooner or later, you're going to have to take a shift."

"I'll do anything else," Toby said. "I'll barricade the doors. Move furniture around so those things can't get in. I'll cook. I'll clean. I'll clean the toilet and make sure there's plenty of bum wipe on the roll. You'll never have to check again."

The little outburst worried Gus. "You okay?"

Toby fell silent. He met Gus's gaze and gave a sheepish little shrug. "It's just that ... I prefer you keep an eye on things there. Keep watch. I, ah ... seeing them bothers me. I mean, bothers me a *lot*. And ... when you saw Gord out there, well, that bothered me even more. I don't think I could handle that, Gus. I don't think I could handle seeing him out there. Like that. And it's not just Gord. I mean, Annapolis isn't a big town. And I only live maybe twenty klicks from here. Chances are, sooner or later, someone I know will walk along the street out there. If I saw that, I think I'd break down. I'd lose it. So maybe in a day or two, maybe, but until then, I'll just do other things. How's that sound?"

Gus didn't answer right away.

"Okay," he finally said.

27

Gus remained at his post, observing the world from the ground up.

Toby crept upstairs during the afternoon. He brought down more food and placed blankets over the windows, hanging them off the curtain rods. He didn't speak much, except for reporting on the most recent work detail, so Gus left him alone.

Guard post duty was monotonous. The zombies drifted along like they did, but they walked slower. Gus pondered that. He remembered that once people died, the heart stopped pumping blood, and rigor mortis set in. He wondered what happened if the blood wasn't being pumped, wondered if the blood collected in the lower extremities, where perhaps it stewed and thickened and became rancid weight. Then there was rigor mortis. How did that work? The zombies looked dead enough to Gus, so would that mean their joints would eventually lock up until, well, whatever? Any or all those factors might affect the zombies' speed, even their strength. If anything, it gave him a flicker of hope.

The dead weren't streaking along like before, and that was a good thing.

They remained plenty numerous, however, and even though they walked slower, that only meant Gus had more time to size up each one in greater detail.

Sooner or later, someone else I know will walk along the street out there.

Those words stayed with Gus a lot longer than expected. And Toby spoke the truth. As the sun pressed itself into the horizon, squeezing out evening light, Gus thought he recognized one face out there, moving amongst the masses, struggling to go nowhere in particular.

Toby was in the bathroom at the time, so he didn't see Gus's reaction.

Walking along, wearing a shirt and cargo shorts and looking like shit, was

Barney Jones, who graduated high school with Gus. He wasn't a friend, just an old classmate who worked as an assistant manager at the Handy Redwood Hardware Shop, owned and operated by a Ron Thames. The Brush-It crew didn't purchase their supplies from Thames. The guy was an obnoxious asshole.

Barney, however, wasn't a bad person. He had two kids, last Gus heard, and was married to Marilyn Jones. There was no sign of his family, however, and for that, Gus was grateful. Barney strolled alone, walking as if he'd been clubbed and suffered traumatic head damage. He didn't have a mark on him, not even a drop of blood, but he didn't look good. In fact, Barney looked damn right terrible, and that was from a distance.

The family man walked into Gus's field of vision and shambled right on by, exiting the stage.

See ya Barney, he thought, watching him stumble off into the unknown. A part of Gus's brain, the protective part, suggested that perhaps Barney was just fine, that, yes, he was obviously sick, but he'd get over it. They all would. Just wait.

He then understood Toby's reluctance to take watch.

The sun went down, and the light in the basement went with it.

As the shadows deepened, Toby went into the storage area and brought out a pair of flashlights that worked.

"Can't use those," Gus told him.

"Huh?"

"Can't use them. Too risky man."

"But the windows are covered," Toby protested.

"Yeah, but who knows," Gus explained. "They might see a glow outside. They might see light around the edges. It's too risky, Tobe. Maybe just settle down for the night."

That didn't go down well with the man.

"Jesus, Gus, we can't just sit around in the dark down here."

"That's exactly what we have to do."

"The nights are so long."

"Yeah," Gus agreed quietly. "I know. Well, maybe if you just keep it away from a window. Don't move around with it. Like if you wanna read a book or something."

"Or something?" Toby choked out with a sad smile. "Oh man. This is bad."

Yeah, but Gus didn't say that.

Toby planted his ass on a couch, with the flashlights nearby. "You gonna sleep tonight?"

"I'll take the bedroom again, if you don't mind."

"Go ahead. I'll stay out here."

"Gonna take a shift?"

Toby shook his head. "I'll just listen."

Gus figured that would be okay. "When you get tired, come wake me up, okay? I'll cover the night shift. Keep an eye on you while you sleep. Although you didn't freak out last time."

"That's good. Probably because I'm not looking out there."

"Maybe."

They quieted.

"You want this?" Toby held out the cell phone.

"Yeah." Gus walked over and took it from him. "Remember then, when you get tired, give me a shout. And if you use those flashlights, keep them away from the windows. Focus them toward the wall or corner or something. Okay?"

"Got it. G'night, Gus."

"Yeah, g'night."

Gus walked into the basement bedroom and settled back onto the disheveled mattress. He thought about his brothers out west working the oil patches. His parents were gone, killed in a car accident six years earlier. He couldn't think of his brothers' phone numbers, so he went with anyone else he could think of. Neighbors. Friends.

Like Toby before him, no one was answering.

Gus switched off the phone.

Despair welled up in his chest, but he fought back against it. People could be hunkering down just like he and Tobe were doing. That's all.

He lay back, got comfortable, and stared at the ceiling.

The room seemed that much darker.

For the next two days, those decomposing bodies lurked and shuffled just outside the basement window, at times no more than mere feet away from the glass. Curtains or blankets concealed that morbid reality, but it was still out there. Gus and Toby alternated shifts, keeping watch (though Toby mostly listened), hoping to see a drop in the zombies' numbers. There wasn't.

At one point the zombie count observed rose to about two dozen or so before thinning out.

What was worse, the zombies were changing.

Their flesh sagged just a little more, and the color had noticeably seeped from their faces, leaving the flesh a disturbing anemic white. Many were slack-jawed, their mouths opened, as if pleading, or gasping last breaths like dying fish. But there was definitely a paling of the skin going on, a degrading, bleaching process, which left them resembling the true, risen corpses of book and movie.

Then there were the flies.

Flies buzzed and pitched on their faces and heads, crawling over their features in that hyper-frantic stop-go motion, sampling the goods. They flew off at times, perhaps disturbed by the slow but steady lurch of movement, but the zombies didn't shoo them away. The zombies didn't care in the least. The flies sensed that. One guy's bald forehead seemed alive with the vermin for some reason. Flies crawled and buzzed over his white dome like they were bees working on honeycomb.

That one was hard for Gus.

Toby became increasingly demoralized by the situation, and being trapped in the basement wasn't helping. Worse, there were only two rolls of toilet paper left in the house, and that wasn't going to last long between the two of them.

There was no one to call on the phone, but Toby, being more apt with the device, did find plenty of people on social media. Pockets of survivors all across the globe, trapped in some improvised fortification. Facebook was alive with messages and pleas for help. Twitter was giving blow-by-blow accounts of zombie activities. Feeds became live world-wide reports. Toby had even found a website for the Armed Forces, and he texted in their location for a communications officer located in Greenwood. He even chatted with an officer briefly, giving his and Gus's name and their general vicinity and the degree of infected activity (the officer called it) in their area. The last item the officer offered before going silent was a phone number, but when Gus attempted to call it, all he got was a busy signal, or a voice recording asking him to leave his number and address.

Despite that, Toby's spirits lifted somewhat at the contact, relieved that there was someone out there in a position of authority to listen.

They searched the house while their hopes remained high.

And discovered that the place they'd taken refuge in had to be the least prepared for a zombie outbreak.

There was effectively nothing to really help them. Most of the goodies were probably outside, secured in the shed. Besides their bats, the only weapons they could find were a set of large kitchen knives, a heavy-duty screw-driver, a hammer—which made them both miss Gord and the company whammer—and that was it. Rubber gloves for cleaning were in abundance, so they took those. They found a pair of winter parkas, both a little too big for Toby and both too tight for Gus. They stashed them at the foot of the basement stairs all the same. Toby laid claim to a single set of swimming goggles, but there was nothing else of note. A mosquito mesh in the form of a jacket was in a closet, and both men refrained from cracking jokes.

Gus tried the army number a little later in the day and got the same recording. Tried again that night, and yet again the next morning.

The army seemed preoccupied.

After failing to make contact, Toby returned to one-word responses, when he decided to respond at all. A palpable vibe of dread and despair emanated from him like a fallen power line. Gus was at a loss as to how to deal with him and wished he'd watched more episodes of *Dr. Phil* instead of Blue Jays games.

"Gus?" Toby said one night from the couch, lying down, and nothing more than a voice in the dark. "You think any of the others got away?"

"You mean the Mollymart people?"

"Yeah."

"I don't know."

"I hope so. I liked some of them. Except for that bitch."

Mel Grant. "Yeah," Gus agreed.

"You think we're gonna get out of here?"

"Good question," he said quietly. "I don't know."

"Come on now. You're the realist here. With shades of optimism."

Gus smiled sadly at that. "You're just saying that."

"Maybe I am. Doesn't matter though."

"No. I guess not. I say chances aren't good."

"That so?"

"Yeah."

"Like how much not good?"

"Like really not good."

"Can you give that to me in a percentage?"

Gus wanted to tell him to fuck off for even bringing it up, but that might not go over well with his friend's current state of mind. Instead he said, "No."

Toby digested that, and for a while, nothing moved in that basement bunker. Shifting, staggering figures moving outside. "Yeah," he finally said. "Thought so."

"But hey," Gus said. "I've been wrong before."

"So you have."

Another bout of silence.

"What are we gonna do about the toilet paper situation?"

Gus sighed. "Use regular tissue."

"And after that?"

"Any newspaper we can find. Catalogs included. Just like the old days."

"Not looking forward to that," Toby admitted.

"Me neither."

"What happens when the power goes off? I mean off. Like, blackout. Or the water stops running?"

Gus pinched the bridge of his nose. "I don't know, Tobe."

And he didn't. Truth was, he'd been thinking of the same things and was at a loss as to how to deal with those problems. It was an unthinkable situation.

"I miss Gord," Toby said, the sadness unmistakable. "I miss Monday night hockey. Jay and Dan and their sports talks in the mornings. Driving to work and shooting the shit. Break-time coffee. Slapping on that first coat of paint ... everything."

"Me too," Gus agreed.

But most of all, he missed Tammy.

Light bled into the room, spreading out from the blanket-covered windows in a rectangular halo. Gus studied it for a moment, and realized he'd slept through the wee hours of the night. Toby hadn't summoned or disturbed him at all, and that made Gus sit up straight in bed. The air was cool, the temperature having dropped noticeably, and he shivered. He got up, wincing at his joints, and went into the rec room.

"Hey," he greeted.

Toby was up and stationed at the window's corner, peeking out at the world.

That surprised Gus, remembering the explanation from before. He decided not to make a thing out of it. "You didn't wake me up?"

Toby shook his head.

"You're not tired?" Gus asked, coming closer.

"Wanted to see the sun come up," Toby finally said. "Couldn't resist. Had to look."

Gus watched his friend warily. "Any change?"

"Yeah."

A pause. "Okay, what?" Gus asked.

"Come see for yourself."

Curious and more than a little anxious, Gus went to the window.

At first, there wasn't anything to see. The sun was up and bright yet again, but the temperatures had indeed tumbled into the single digits, signaling autumn was ready to resume regular programming. The zombies walked. Areas around their faces, their mouths, in particular, appeared unshaven, even amongst the women. Three of them, going about their business.

"Holy shit," Gus muttered, his eyes narrowing.

There were only three zombies in sight.

28

They gathered at the base of the stairs and geared up.

Towels from a bathroom closet went around their faces, and Toby snapped on the extra protection of the swimmer's goggles. They pulled on the gloves and winter parkas for extra protection, but Gus didn't think the coats would fare well if shit really went south, if a zombie really latched onto them. Still, the coats were all they had in the way of body armor, so they wore them.

Once they were ready to move, Gus and Toby exchanged looks, the rising tension palpable.

"You ready?" Gus asked his goggled friend.

Toby nodded back, tucking the cell phone in his pocket.

"You sure you can do this?"

"I'm sure."

"We creep for the car, check it out, and if there's nothing there, we go for the house. Get inside and look for keys. Sound good?"

"We creep for the car, look inside for keys, and go for the house if we got to, and repeat. Got it."

Gus nodded and held out his bat. Toby clacked it with his own.

"Here we go," Gus said.

He waddled up the stairs, his added bulk actually swishing against the walls, giving them a dusting. He was already sweating, and hoped he didn't get lightheaded or sick from the extra layers.

At the backdoor they stopped and peeked out.

Two zombies were present. Both on the deck roof, standing at attention like a couple of wingless gulls.

Nervous energy raced through Gus's system, giving him a huge boost. Mentally preparing himself, he cracked open the door and stepped through.

The zombies on the roof noticed the emerging men. One started shambling toward them while the second slipped and went ass first into the pool with a rattle and a splash. The upright zombie stepped onto tile and then grass as he increased speed, gunning for the two painters.

Toward Gus.

Gus hefted the bat, cocked it, and faltered at the white face charging him, the arms lifted as if going for a hug. A smattering of black-tipped skin tags covered the corpse's mouth, lending an unwholesome five-o'clock shadow.

And in the seconds before contact, Gus couldn't bring himself to bash that dead's man face in. He ran them down at night and did so repeatedly, but he hesitated at delivering a more personal blow.

The last few feet and the zombie lunged, turbo-boosting toward the stricken man.

Only to have a bat slam into his face.

The blow whipped the zombie off its feet and onto its undead ass. The blunt connection startled Gus, and he drew back in horrified wonder as Toby got into the picture and clubbed the downed zombie. He destroyed the thing's head, smashing it apart like a revolting flower pot, spilling pulpy organic tissue over the ground. Some speckled Toby's coat.

"Oh God," Gus said and backed into a flower bed, where the house stopped his retreat.

Toby hit the thing twice more, ensuring it was finally dead, and looked to Gus. "You okay?"

"Yeah. Thanks—"

But Toby was racing across the open space. He closed in upon the second zombie rising from the pool. The creature moaned a question before a rock-hard length of ash wood clubbed its head with that same punctuating crack. The blow spread the zombie back into the water and Toby stood at the poolside, clearly wanting to finish the kill, but not so keen on getting wet.

The zombie didn't rise again, however, so Toby jogged back to the house.

"You okay?" he huffed, eyes concerned behind the goggles.

"Yeah," Gus nodded. "You killed them both."

"Fuckin A, I did," Toby whispered, impressed with his work. "Goddamn face-chewin' sonsabitches. Those were for Gord. You saw what I did? Nothin' to it, dude. Just line up the head and swing for the fences."

"You got some on you."

Toby inspected the spatters on his coat. "That's nothing. Got the coat, right? C'mon let's get moving."

Gus followed Toby to the end of the house, not bothering with the debris scattered around the property or the work shed. Toby stopped at the corner, peeked, and held up a hand.

A zombie ambled around the house.

Toby popped its face, dropping the thing. He then proceeded to deliver a second powerful strike to the head, shattering the bony bauble. He reset himself, waited a split second, and bashed a second zombie arriving on scene, the force splaying the thing against the house.

A third zombie appeared, actually reaching for Toby's shoulder, but the guy kicked out a leg, staggering it to its knees. In a second, Toby whirled and smashed the skull of a *fourth* zombie, knocking its head into its shoulder in a spray of black. The house painter bounced back with a boxer's grace, hefted his bat, and went-over-the-shoulders in a two-handed chop to the zombie rising from the ground. Two more bashes and the thing ceased to be.

Two more zombies emerged, closing in on Toby, their hands contorted into fleshy claws.

And the painter put them both down, kicking out legs to buy enough time to hammer the bat into unprotected heads.

"C'mon!" Toby cried out, taking charge.

That unlocked Gus's paralysis. He sprinted for the Camaro in the next driveway over, a teal green muscle rocket just begging to shit fire and rock n' roll. There was something special about the car, and it wasn't the machine's overall mean design, but the impressive upgrades on the front. There, protruding like the jawline of some primordial predator, was a rack of white curved horns. Gus had no time to marvel at the pointy attachments, however. He registered movement along his periphery vision.

He reached the Camaro's door and opened it with no trouble while Toby bopped and weaved alongside, facing all challengers.

And there were plenty.

A pack of zombies, spaced out like a sloppy arrangement of bowling pins, zeroed in on Toby as if he was an invading organism.

No keys in the ignition. Gus went around the front of the car. "No keys, Tobe, no keys!"

Toby backed up with him, holding his bat samurai ready.

"No *keys* Tobe!" Gus urged him.

"*I hear ya!*"

The closet zombies reached the painter, and Toby went to work.

He dispatched three of them with chopping block precision, almost impossibly bending and weaving and somehow avoiding the hands clutching for his jugular. Toby took the legs out of another and upswung the bat, taking a zombie that had to be eighty in a past life off its feet. He crushed the temple of another and smoked one reaching for his shoulder, sending the attacker into the cement covered driveway.

Gus stopped at the door to the neighbor's house, just underneath a roof that shielded the final few feet of the driveway.

The house was open.

"Toby, I'm in," Gus shouted and held the door.

But Toby wasn't listening.

Speckled as if he'd shoved a slab of bloody beef sideways into a meat cutter's band saw, Toby waited for the street zombies to attack him. The driveway was covered in dead and unmoving bodies.

"Toby *come on!*"

"Get the keys!" Toby shouted back and grunted while clacking a head square with the sweet spot of the bat, barrelling the undead onto the lawn.

"Jesus Christ," Gus muttered, half-frantic, and charged into the house. *Keys.* Where would the keys be? He was in a small entry room with a walk-in closet with racks of heavy coats and lighter jackets. The kitchen lay ahead. He raced inside, sides grazing the doorframe, and looked to the walls.

Key hanger.

Right there.

Next to the questioning stare of a brunette mother-type zombie, hissing through a mouth that only had a pair of incisors in it. A darkly stained tank top covered her torso, and the black ink flames that raced up her arms seemed just as infectious as whatever sinister virus powering her.

The thing lurched for him, and Gus retreated with a whimper, rounding the far side of the kitchen's island. He cocked his bat, crashing it against a nearby cabinet he wasn't aware of.

The zombie grabbed for him, the biker-mom's opaque eyes rimmed with what looked like red custard.

Gus ducked, the island corner catching his hip and spinning him around to face his ardent pursuer. With a spurt of desperate speed, he jammed the bat up under the biker-mom's chin, driving that hissing face back. She clawed for him and Gus shoved her off, but only just barely. The thing was strong. He backed around the island with her in pursuit, slobbering all the while. Gus got the bat up but ran into the nearest doorway.

And found himself in a living room.

With a dead man lying on the carpet.

Except he wasn't all dead. He was a large, practically naked individual with a gaping belly wound in his midsection, as if he'd been subjected to a very unprofessional C-section, and things just weren't put back in—in fact, Gus couldn't see where the missing internals were exactly, but he certainly saw the basketball-size hole in the guy's gut, the ghastly excavation that had happened, as well as a pair of thighs eaten down to the bone.

Biker-dad reached out, flailing an all-too-white arm.

Gus spun, swinging the bat, and hit the wife square across the face. The strike was nowhere near the sweet spot needed to put her down, but he did smash her jaw about two grisly inches to the left. The impact drove her back while Gus teetered, momentarily mystified at his total lack of balance.

Just before he fell down a flight of carpeted stairs.

His fat ass crashed into a rack of shoes, and old sneakers flapped about his face. Panting, registering pain in his entire back, Gus flung the footwear away and struggled to right himself. He scrambled onto his side, drawing his legs in underneath so he could stand upon a small landing that led to a basement.

A wild-child shriek almost made him shit himself. Hands gripped his shoulders and yanked.

The parka ripped.

Gus screamed.

He turned, no space to utilize the bat, and drove an elbow into biker-mom's upturned face. The thing was indeed strong, stronger than even him, perhaps.

But Gus had greater *mass*. A little over three hundred pounds worth.

He fell forward, cross-checking the biker-mom's face, turning the head away as he used his bodyweight to pin her against a wall. Red-rimmed eyes covered in cataracts twitched in his direction, and Gus swept a leg.

Biker-mom fell, but not before a hand shot out and fastened onto Gus's knee.

With a piggish squeal, Gus stabbed downwards with the bat, as if driving home a spear.

He caught a cheek, reset, and caught the cheek again, making the already ruined jaw crackle. Skin broke. Blood spattered. Then he mashed an ear, a shoulder—all the while the biker-mom raved and clawed and strove to escape. Gus discovered firsthand that it was hard to bash someone determined to get up.

"*Sweet fuck,*" he gasped and aimed for the thing's platinum-haired head.

Missed and got a derelict sneaker instead.

With its lower jaw askew in a dreadful grin, the zombie pulled itself up by his leg, those steely fingers digging into his painter duds and the jeans underneath. The fright energized Gus to work faster. He drove a knee into the zombie's face, knocking her flat, and retreated onto the stairs he'd only just fallen down.

In a flashing microsecond, Gus immediately judged the distance as good.

Biker-mom rose just as Gus slammed the wooden bat down, across the top of her head.

Shattering his bat.

The barrel bounced around the landing like a super springy ball while Gus staggered back, hands uplifted to shield himself. The biker-mom fell, arms flayed wide as if trying to catch herself, and landed in the corner.

She immediately got up and lunged.

Desperate, stumbling back, and still holding the jagged spear of the broken bat, Gus's arm shot out and sunk the pointy bit into the soft area under her descending chin. That splintered spear tip pierced skin and throat in a crackle of cartilage and a spurt of blackness.

When the bat tip connected with the top plate of her skull, the biker-mom's expression relaxed as if her power cord had been yanked free of the wall. Her form went limp. She half-collapsed on Gus, who twisted and stumbled on the stairs. He fell, landing on the hard edge, his feet pointed to the landing.

The biker-mom lay to his left, face down and unmoving.

With a grimace, he shoved her away—just as a second hand clamped down on his shoulder.

Gus screamed.

The biker-dad eyed him with all the undead hatred of an avenging husband.

Gus flung himself forward, dragging and stretching the biker-dad over the stairs, breaking the grip. Gus located the upper barrel of the broken bat, reduced to a shortened Scotland Yard billy club. He fumbled past the biker-dad, and grabbed the club at the top step. Once again armed, he spun and pounded the biker-dad's head until bone snapped and crackled, and things got spongy.

When the biker-dad and mom were both dead (Gus checked his kills with adrenaline-fueled foot stomps) he dropped the ruined bat. *Jesus Christ,* he thought frantically. *They made it look so goddamn* easy *on television!* He held his chest. Dark sparkling motes floated past his eyes. His heart leaped and banged, not at all accustomed to this level of frenzied activity. Gus slumped in a corner, wheezing uncontrollably, riding out the dizziness, struggling to get a hold of himself. Sweat glazed his face and temples. His vision warped for a bit, darkened around the edges, then leveled out. Cleared.

The thought of Toby got him moving.

Arms and legs afire, Gus hauled his padded person up the steps and into the kitchen, away from the ravenous homeowners. He spotted the keys and staggered to them, sounding as if he'd just powerlifted a ton with the help of some very illegal chemicals. He snatched the keys, pulling the entire rack off the wall.

Gus didn't care.

He had the goddamn keys.

Stage two had been completed.

And stage three consisted of getting the fuck out of Dodge.

He burst out of the house, depressing the push-button start on the key fob. The car chirped and a second later the engine released its mechanical version of *aHAaaaa!*

But that was all secondary.

Because standing there in the driveway, his frame heaving and holding his dripping bat like a sorcerer's staff, was Toby. And at his feet, with their heads cracked open and spilling gray candy, were dozens of zombies. All in various poses of death.

At *least* two dozen, but Gus suspected closer to three, and he wouldn't be surprised if there were four.

"Tobe?" he asked, noticing even more zombies hurrying toward them, crossing the street. More were appearing further down the road, drawn to the painter and his killing field.

"Yeah?" Toby looked over his shoulder.

"You okay?"

"Oh yeah. Just fine. Fuckin' exhausted, but otherwise, hey."

"Let's boot."

Toby nodded and regarded the driveway and then the way ahead. "Gonna have to drive around this."

Gus saw the log jam of torsos littering the driveway behind the car. There was no way the Camaro was going to roll over any of it. He climbed aboard the car and Toby got in beside him, with zombies tripping over the unmoving roadblocks in the driveway. Ominous specks covered both men, as if they were standing behind the screen door just before the shithouse blew up.

"What got a hold of you?" Toby asked, placing his well-used bat between his knees.

Gus sighed. "The fuckin' owners, man."

"You kill 'em?"

"Yeah."

"Where's your bat?"

"Broke it."

Toby looked ahead at a backyard and a white wooden fence. "That's fucked up."

"I know one thing," Gus said.

"Yeah? What's that?"

"If I get outta this alive, I'm getting a better bat." Gus checked the side mirrors and gripped the wheel. He put the machine in gear. "Yeah," he said, breathless, but good enough to drive. He had to be. He wasn't getting out and swapping places with Toby now.

Gus hit the gas and the car rolled ahead. He steered around the backyard, leaving the pursuing zombies behind, and aimed the car's toothy grill toward a dense-looking hedge.

There was no other way out of the backyard, and no way to see beyond the carefully maintained foliage.

"I feel lucky," Gus muttered.

And floored the accelerator.

29

The car blasted through the wall in an explosion of branches and greenery, slamming both men back into their seats. They shot over a cement driveway and missed a huge stone bird bath by a foot. One of the white tusks flew off the car's front, much to Gus's disappointment, but otherwise the machine handled like an exquisite dream, the engine rumbling like an old drill sergeant standing before a microphone with a stogie clamped between his teeth. Red needles jumped and spun on the dashboard displays, providing information Gus wasn't entirely sure of, but everything was working.

Everything was working just fine.

He turned onto the main road, stopping more than a few of the dead things in their tracks. The car sped by them, transforming their ashen expressions into blurs.

The sign for Legion Road flashed by.

"Where we going?" Toby asked.

"Away from here."

The sun beat down upon the road, rendering the horizon in a blinding white. Houses lined the sides, sometimes broken by thickets or small parks. Abandoned vehicles littered the street, and zombies wandered or stood amongst them like decomposing pylons. Gus slowed to maneuver around some of the cars. The zombies that lurched toward the Camaro weren't as speedy as before.

Two zombies ambled in front of the Camaro.

Gus hit them, buckling the corpses mid-thigh and tossing them to the asphalt. A hand slapped the driver's window, causing him to jerk the steering wheel. The car responded and bounced over a sidewalk with a crash and a spine-stropping *thud* that rattled both nerves and back teeth. Both men were whipped forward, their heads almost connecting with the dash.

"Fire hydrant!" Toby yelled.

Gus saw it.

Trouble was, there were thick patches of zombies on either side of that metal speed bump. He turned and went for the least amount of them. The Camaro ripped through the mob. Bodies crashed over the hood before rolling off the sides. One went over the roof with a metal dimpling rattle. The driver's side mirror got smashed away. A face squished itself against the windshield in a burst of blood and teeth, breaking glass in a tracery of cracks before tumbling over the passenger side. The undead pinballed off the Camaro, and the machine took each impact with a chrome smile.

Gus braked, regained control, and drove through the masses and the cars.

"Holy fuck!" Toby cried while straightening his goggles.

Holy fuck, indeed.

Gus drove along a familiar street and hit the brakes, jarring them forward again.

Corpses filled the intersection ahead.

"I know where to go," Gus said as dozens of deceased pedestrians took notice of the road racer. "Greenwood."

Toby glanced over.

Greenwood. There were soldiers there. Even an air force base.

"We need a highway," Toby said.

"Yeah."

The zombies broke into their best run, becoming an animated wall charging the Camaro. Gus checked the rearview mirror and saw the undead they'd already cut through coming after them. The few houses on the street prevented the car from going anywhere but forward, effectively hemming them in.

Zombies ahead of the car.

Zombies behind.

Nowhere to go.

Gus had been through a lot in the last four days or so. He'd lost Tammy, lost Gord, and probably lost most of his remaining friends and family. He'd narrowly escaped death a couple of times and had dead bodies try and eat his ass off, and it only took one instance of that to start a shitty week.

The zombies on the road ahead were close enough to see faces.

Two things jumped out at him and Toby.

Toby said it first.

"Is that …" he said, pointing.

It was.

Though she had pretty much half of her scalp and the left side of her head chewed away, right down to the bone, there was still enough face remaining to identify one Mel Grant. Her eyes were open wide and locked onto the Camaro, as if she recognized the two painters from Mollymart and was about to insist—no—*order* them, to remain where they are until the zombie cops arrived.

"Hold on," Gus said, speeding up to forty.

Not too fast to lose control of the muscular missile that was the Camaro, but fast enough to push through the forces ahead.

Mel Grant was the first to boomerang off the front of the hood, her ass flattening against the weakened windshield and her legs kicking, as if she'd taken it upon herself to stop the car singlehandedly. She didn't however, and the last Gus ever saw of her was the relatively good side of her face, just before she fell off the car and disappeared.

Then the Camaro was in the meat.

Hands and arms slammed the roof and sides in a torrential downpour of flesh and bone and voracious, mindless fury. A couple of ivory white tusks went up over the hood and rattled off the roof. Toby's side mirror got smashed to the street. The driver's side windshield wiper was torn off the car. The roof thundered with hammer blows. Open palms slapped glass while zombies landed flush on the hood but were unable to hang on. The undead piled onto the moving vehicle, effectively blinding Gus. The fists and punches and slaps continued, intensifying as the car plowed through the crowd. The driver's side window cracked into a spidery mesh. The passenger side window followed a second later. Gus increased speed as the bodies became thicker, the hands and arms heavier. The Camaro approved. It was like driving through an undulating mosh pit, where every participant was either taking a swing at the car or using it as a trampoline.

And at the absolute pinnacle of this gauntlet, a powerful hand heel punched through Gus's window just before the car's momentum yanked the attacker off his feet. Toby was cringing, moaning. Gus turned the wheel left and right, attempting to dislodge the boarders from the hood and improve visibility because *he couldn't see shit.* The car rose and dropped over a fallen corpse, and that briefly tossed the two men into the air. The wall of bodies disappeared two seconds before the Camaro went through a fence in a snapping of planks. Cheap lawn furniture got smashed aside, and Gus drove through another fence, back onto the road filled with more undead. He straightened out the wheel and drove on, grateful that the corpses were no longer on the hood and he could see through a small clear patch in the windshield.

What he saw, however, demoralized him utterly.

A marathon's field of zombies clustered together, turning as they detected the Camaro's approach, too many to completely drive through and yet there was no other choice.

"Here!" Toby screamed. *"Turn here!"*

To the right, a road Gus almost completely missed.

He turned, the force heaving him against his door. Toby braced himself as best as he could. The car hit three zombies head-on. One lodged itself flat against the windshield as the car continued forward. The other two were clipped and dropped.

Once again Gus couldn't see anything beyond the dead man on his hood.

"Keep straight," Toby said, able to see over the thing's struggling legs. "Keep straight, it's a line to Port Williams!"

Gus knew it. One of three roads that led into an older part of Annapolis, spanning an area of about two kilometers. He hit fifty klicks an hour, which felt a lot faster when he was receiving driving instructions from Toby. Air blasted across his profile.

The zombie on the hood faced him.

"Gotta shake this fucker loose," Gus said, and toggled the steering wheel.

The zombie shook.

"Stay straight!" Toby yelled with heat. The zombie didn't have any eyes in its head and its mouth was spotty with gold.

Gus turned the wheel right, then left, and miraculously, the thing on the hood rolled off.

A split second before the Camaro hit a guard rail, and a gray thunderbolt impaled the car through the eye.

30

When Gus came to, he leaned back from the steering wheel and gazed ahead in drunken wonder, squinting through the crushed windshield and the smoking wreckage of the muscle car. It took him a few seconds to equalize, for his brain and senses to reconnect and right themselves, but he was aware of stopping. Aware the car wasn't going to run anymore. And very much aware of a guard rail stabbing through the right side of the windshield, passing through the space once occupied by Toby's head, plunging through to the rear, where it exited the back windshield in a very ragged splitting of safety glass.

Gus took a double-take of his friend and co-worker.

The guard rail had decapitated Toby right at the neckline and proceeded to chop the top off the car seat's headrest as well. The steel concealed the damage from the shoulder up, as if it were a flat gray hand ushering Toby aside to whisper a secret in his ear, but it had cleanly taken his head off. Gus knew that, because when he glanced into the back seat, he saw the head there, amongst the glittering pebbles that littered the cushions. The face was turned away, sparing him whatever shocked expression Toby might've had before his unexpected death.

As if very, very tired, Gus slowly blinked at the corpse, studying it, his own shock keeping the well of sadness from overwhelming him.

"Hey!"

The word didn't really connect with Gus at that point, but when his driver's door opened and a man in black body armor pulled him out of the car, the world slammed back into place in one jarring stop. Just for a second, however, and then it sped away.

Three men—three police officers decked out in riot gear—pulled Gus to his feet and herded him to a waiting pickup. They had to carry him along, as his legs weren't up to walking just yet.

The pickup wasn't the Brush-It truck, but it was close enough. They lifted Gus into the truck bed, where he landed on his back. The sky glowed an indigo blue. Someone was shouting and suddenly two of the police officers were firing large automatic rifles, moving in a dreamy slow motion. They weren't going full-Rambo, however, but picked their shots with all the cadence of a winding down clock. Spent shell casings ejected in shiny arcs that seemed to hang in the air. The truck roared in Gus's ear, but it was a calming sound, one that assured him all would be just fine. Don't you worry.

The truck stopped.

More yelling. A clatter of boots to pavement, and things being dragged along.

"Go! Go! *Go!*" a voice shouted, almost next to Gus's ear, and he flinched because of it. He tried to rise but never got off his back, and collapsed on the truck's bed.

The sky. Blue. So blue.

And without a sun.

A popping erupted all around him, reminding him of a thousand sheets of breaking bubble wrap. Men and women were yelling. They were yelling a lot. Gus rolled over onto a side, still wonky from the crash, and studied the inside of the pickup's bed. Blue as well. Imagine that.

People moved past him. Which was strange, because from his point of view, it looked like they simply walked into the ceiling, where they vanished.

Someone was screaming. More shots, a growing storm of bullets.

And suddenly Gus's senses were back, ending that soupy dreamtime where he was a distant observer. He groaned and struggled into a sitting position, where he had a perfect view of what was going down, not forty feet away.

The truck was parked behind a wall of cars blocking the street. In front of the cars was another line of defense, a row of white and red roadblocks, the kind that resembled wooden saw horses, paltry in comparison to the vehicles. And beyond that …

Unchecked dread filled Gus then, as he saw what filled the streets, from shop to house front and all the way back.

A mob.

A concert-sized crowd perhaps in the hundreds.

A patchwork mudslide of walking, decomposing flesh, channeling itself toward a roadblock and police barricade. If it wasn't the entire populace of Annapolis, it was pretty damn close. Gus wondered briefly if the reason he and Toby could escape the basement was because the zombies were advancing on this place. Or were drawn to some other element.

But he only pondered that for a second.

Because the shooting stole all his attention.

The assembled police force hunkered down behind their defensive lines and unloaded their weapons into that approaching army. Brass bounced and sprinkled the ground. There were about twenty or so shooters, in various stages of reloading or emptying magazines, firing with a determination that Gus thought was a last stand state of mind.

The zombies in the front died first as bullets shredded them in bits and chunks. Their faces and heads exploded at times, in little pollinating plumes that spattered others nearby. Those that fell obstructed the second and third ranks, but only as long as it took for the zombies to move around or crawl over the unmoving dead. Chests exploded, as well as shoulders. Some zombies spun before falling from the misplaced shots. A few of them stood high on the mounds of gathering dead, straightening only to be picked off and sent tumbling into that multicolor mass of faded colors.

One cop, a police woman not wearing a helmet and with her red hair tied back into a war braid, assumed a firing range stance and popped off a steady body count of dead things. Her aim was incredible, her poise Olympic, and the destruction awesome.

And yet, the zombies seemed to only get closer, walking without fear into that decimating hail of gunfire. Gus realized then there was no breaking those things. There was only running from them or putting them down, and frankly, arranged against the force bearing down upon them, the police had picked the wrong fight.

"We gotta get out of here," Gus said.

Not one listened.

"*We gotta get out of here!*" he shouted.

Two of the officers looked in his direction, but only a cursory glance before they dropped below the car barricade and reloaded their weapons.

"*We gotta get out of here!*" Gus repeated "*NOW!*"

No reaction.

Gus stood up in the truck's bed, his guts a solid block of ice.

Then, as expected, disaster struck.

The police, for whatever reason, had stopped in a T-junction, where houses and other small buildings lined the sides, creating a loose bottleneck. The zombies of Annapolis marched down that street, but their numbers were so great that they flowed around the houses in a tidal surge. And as they got closer, a smell, a putrid, gas-leaking stink reached out and enveloped Gus and the police. An eye-watering, breath-stealing pestilence that momentarily struck the officers' aim and their resolve. Men and women ceased firing, suffering from the stench. Some were coughing and holding their faces. One actually pitched over to his knees and puked. Others looked around, wondering where that toxic, contaminated gas cloud was coming from.

Then there were the flies.

Swarming over the heads of the dead and speckling their faces black. The insect swarm lavished kisses over the corpses' graying features. In the lapse of gunfire, the buzzing could be clearly heard, coming across like an apocalyptic chainsaw. That flying, buzzing drizzle chilled Gus right down to his boys. He clamped a hand over his face and disturbed a few flies that had attached to the towel still covering him.

He waved them away, only to realize that the towel was soaked with his own blood.

From the car crash, he thought, and tossed the cloth.

Gunfire erupted from the side street, breaking Gus's brief paralysis and the police's too. The defenders on the absolute fringe of the firing line repositioned themselves, squaring off against the walking corpses ambling in from that quarter, where there were no barricades.

Suddenly the firepower was divided and lessened.

"Oh, shit you guys, we have *got to get out of here!*" Gus roared, stomping his foot.

But the police didn't respond. Didn't even look at him.

One finally did, a helmet-wearing individual that finished reloading a very heavy-duty assault rifle. He waved at Gus. "Get in the truck!"

Get in the truck?

Fuck that.

Gus saw the writing on the wall. The police had stopped here, positioned themselves with an escape route in case they had to retreat, except … the one road that continued on, directly behind Gus, was also filling up with zombies.

"*Behind us! Jesus Christ behind us!*" he shouted and pointed.

Some of the cops on the front line heard that. The red-headed Viking stopped and studied the back road with a frown. She then looked to the main drag as if weighing their options.

Gus was about to shout to her when a familiar face appeared in the main mass of attackers. His voice fluttered and died in his throat, and his vision blackened around the edges.

He hadn't seen her in days, but when you're in love with someone, you can just zero in on them in a crowd.

The front ranks of the dead had been mowed down in controlled gunfire, and one zombie dropped only to be replaced by Tammy. Long black bedhead hair, the strands drizzling her features. So many mornings he'd had the pleasure of waking up to that face.

Except now she was dead.

Amongst that concert crowd of corpses, her face and skin tone was just a paler shade of gray. Tammy shambled forward, toward the saw horse barricades, rubbing shoulders with others in her army. She still wore her pajamas, the ones her mother gave her last Christmas, and a stained T-shirt that clung to her torso. Heads cracked back and zombies next to her dropped dead, killed by well-aimed bullets, but nothing hit his Tammy. Tracers of lights zinged and streaked past her head, close enough to singe her hair, but not one hit her.

The worst possible nightmare had come true for Gus, and even as he sighted and identified her, as sure as God was his witness, he was certain she locked on to him. All the while she watched him, watched him as she pushed forward, climbing over the unmoving corpses littering the road. She picked her way over the backs of the dead, moving in his direction, all the while a killer lightshow flared around her person.

"Oh …" Gus moaned, and though there was perhaps a good forty feet or so between them, he was looking deep into those dark eyes of hers, mesmerized for the final time.

Tammy reached out to him.

She smiled.

And rancid filth spilled from her mouth.

That broke something in Gus, and the nightmare suddenly twisted into the worst nightmare of all.

Just before the Viking police officer put a bullet into Tammy's skull.

Gus saw her take the shot, saw the round slam into Tammy's forehead and blow out the back in a rotten spray and a halo of flies. She went down like an abandoned puppet, disappearing amongst that fetid tangle at her feet. Those behind trampled over her body, delayed only a heartbeat.

And though he knew she was already lost to him, forever gone days earlier, Gus got the closure he was searching for.

Even though it killed him, just like he knew it would.

"Pull back!" The red-haired Viking shouted, her voice cutting through Gus's emotional haze. "Pull back!"

The retreat began. The police broke off and ran for the handful of vehicles parked in the street. Engines powered up, started by drivers Gus only then noticed.

But then the runners appeared.

Bolting from the zombie masses and sprinting forward like missiles homing in on pre-selected targets. One officer went down under a single runner. A second cop turned to help, only to be tackled full on by another charging dead person.

Police turned and went to the aid of their companions while the main bulk of the mob, no longer absorbing a punishing amount of semi-automatic gunfire, slowly marched into the outer roadblocks and pushed them aside. Zombies fell, resulting in a ripple of tumbles, but the majority of the undead pressed forward. They trampled the fallen, cresting bridges comprised of backs and spines, and slid toward the wall of cars.

There was time, very little time, but Gus saw the cops going for their rides. All semblance of a coordinated fire effort broke down as the officers dealt with fallen members while firing at the zombies filling up the roads and escape route.

"This way!" Gus shouted and jumped off the truck. He landed heavily, the impact stinging his feet. There were the spaces between the houses, and those were filling with walking corpses.

So, Gus went for the house.

"This way!" He shouted and ran up a walkway splitting a lawn in two. The shadow of the two-story affair fell over him. He jumped the two steps to the porch, his heart hating him for that, and spun about to see if any of the police were following.

What he saw shocked him.

All unity had completely disintegrated. Pockets of zombies were already feeding on fallen officers while crowds of undead completely surrounded the cars attempting to escape. One car, the windshield cluttered by flailing bodies, revved free of a rotting cluster and clipped a light pole with a loud *bang* of collapsing fiberglass. The car stopped, and the zombies swarmed it once again.

A second car sped toward the exit route, smacking into dead pedestrians who made no effort to get out of the way. The cruiser got perhaps fifty feet up the street before it swung up a lawn and crashed through a trampoline set. A beach ball ballooned over the car's light bar and fell out of sight.

The dead closed in.

Movement caused Gus to look back to the pickup he'd left behind, and his eyes narrowed in recognition.

A zombie moved for him, no longer as fleet of foot as it once was, but making time all the same. The thing's face had taken some damage since the last time Gus had laid eyes upon it, rendering its features a red-black smear with glimmers of white, like a chunk of meat left far too long on a barbeque. There might've been eyes or just an eye in there, but he wasn't sure.

But there was no mistaking the crowbar sticking out of the thing's guts.

That's Mister *Crowbar to you*, the thing projected, or perhaps that was just Gus's horror-blasted brain providing an unneeded persona to the corpse.

And worse, as if he needed it to be worse, were the children.

A pack of five of them ran around Crowbar's limping figure and charged up the walkway toward Gus. They were slim, weirdly emaciated, and had moldy-white faces, as if they belonged to a secret gentry that had cast them out into the world. Their clothes, perhaps different colors at one time, were now a filthy black.

They stormed toward him with all the vitality of rabid jackals, anxious faces bright and frightening, and that was all Gus needed—having his ass taken down and chewed on by a bunch of undead twelve-year-olds.

Wasn't going to happen.

He pulled open the screen door and tried the knob.

Open.

He got through the entrance just as little feet hit the porch's wooden steps. He slammed the door a second before bodies crashed into the house. The door shook but held, absorbing the adolescent charge. Gus backed away, glimpsing one of the fleet-footed little bastards pressing his famished face into the window, and he knew that was a picture that he wouldn't soon forget.

A hallway led to a living room, another hall, and a kitchen.

Gus raced into the kitchen, hearing glass break behind him, and that sinewy groan of doors being forced. He didn't hear any gunfire.

The back door.

He stopped only as long as it took to check the yard. There was a fence to the right but nothing on the left. Nothing would oppose or would deter any crowds approaching from the left, and the amoeba-like mass that had curled around the police barricade was moving in that direction.

Unless they were preoccupied with the law and their cruisers.

Gus slammed the door behind him as he bolted outside, making a line toward the backyard of the next house over. Even there, that stink cloud of rotting skin enveloped him. Tall elms grew and offered spotty shade. Sunlight dappled through foliage just turning overhead. He kicked up a few dead leaves. He rounded a picnic table, dodged a barbeque pit, and threaded a path through a collection of children's fire trucks, cars, and tanks.

He spied the back door of the next house, at the end of a patio deck in need of stain. His legs burned. His chest ached. He sucked down air in alarming gulps and he wished he had the Brush-It truck back. He took three stairs in a frantic pitter-patter, tripping on the last, and falling flat. With a huff, he staggered to his feet, sensing—*hearing* movement behind him, as well as the incessant moaning from things that didn't need to rest. Something tripped in the toys behind him and slammed to the ground.

The back door was open.

Two for two.

He charged through a kitchen, failing to secure the door, and it flapped in the frame behind him. He went through a living room and stopped only when he saw an elderly mother-type posed at the top of a staircase. The old woman's face lit up with hungry surprise at the sight of him. Gus whimpered, wheezed, and ran down a short hall while Granny tumbled down the steps behind him like a hundred-pound tumbleweed, whistling a tea-pot shriek all the way.

Front door.

Locked. Gus fumbled with the knob and then clawed at a bolt. Sweat and blood slicked his hands and face and stung his eyes.

Granny rolled to a stop at the base of the stairs.

He hauled the door open, sunlight stabbing him, and stumbled outside just as Granny collected herself and got to her knees, her eighty-year-old plus frame remarkably spry and game for a chase.

That scared the living shit out of him.

In his haste, he almost fell over the stairs of the front porch, where a bannister stroked the inside of his bicep and ribs. Pain sirens flared. Wheezing, Gus hauled himself upright as Granny hit the porch. He launched himself forward, glimpsing crooked shadows coming around the sides of the two-story house. The kids were catching up to him.

Worse, he was slowing down.

That scared the shit out of him even more, and the sudden jolt of fear lancing through his system offered a little extra gas for his labouring frame. Gus chugged over a small patch of lawn, across a two-lane street, and toward a garage, white-painted and resembling a once-successful backyard mechanic business. Husks of vehicles scavenged for spare parts rested just behind the building.

Penny's Service Station said the sign, greeting the morning as if all was still just rosy and pink. The front door was windowless and heavy. Gus approved with a parched croak.

Feet hit the asphalt behind him.

A *lot* of feet.

All moving faster than he was.

All getting louder in his ears.

He grabbed for a shiny gold-painted knob and it opened as an unknown mass collided with something behind him. Gus darted inside, slammed the door shut, and immediately slapped home a pair of bolt locks.

A weight rammed the door, and the barrier shivered in its frame. Gus drew back, his legs like rubber, pushed to exhaustion, the energy his fear had lent him already depleted. He propped himself against a nearby service counter, accidently hitting the silver bell. That single metallic note prompted him to clamp both hands around the little dome, silencing it.

A picture window was to the right of the closed door.

Gus's heart raced, red-lining an overstrained system.

The pack of pre-teens rammed themselves against the door. Even worse, a new group of frightful hunters, fresh from the police battle, had joined them. Old Granny moved toward the garage as well, hurrying along as if not wanting to miss the dinner bell.

And behind them all, Crowbar.

It came around the corner of the house, walking in a bow-legged, gut-shot kinda gait. The crowbar embedded in its guts moved ever so slightly with each step.

A zombie kid—a boy or a girl surprisingly tall for their age—slammed against the window pane and split it down the middle.

Forgetting about Crowbar, Gus dove beneath the cover of the counter.

There, he moved along on screaming knees, cheeks puffing, and located the door to the service bay.

The picture window behind him shattered into pieces.

When the first zombie came through, Gus was already inside the bay and had closed the door behind him.

31

The undead flipped over the thigh-high window sill and toppled into the garage, landing upon a floor of jagged glass. Knife-like shards stabbed cloth and flesh alike belonging to those who fell inside, but the cuts did not immediately bleed. Zombies lingered at the window, their faces set, jaws working. Some expressions were permanently stuck in toothy grimaces, some simply gazed on with early morning stares while others possessed aristocratic sneers, as if not yet convinced about entering such an establishment. Particularly if there wasn't anything of interest to chase.

But the man-thing they were chasing—which they very much needed to bite and chew upon—had gone inside. *Where*, however, they did not know, nor did their blasted, white-noise filled minds attempt to reason. Nor did they truly identify their quarry as a man-thing, but rather as an object very much not them, but very edible.

So, they dawdled, prodding things for a reaction, blindly searching for the trail of the man-thing once so close, but who had up and disappeared.

Crowbar arrived on scene with dozens of like-afflicted brothers and sisters. They walked until bumping into the unyielding mass that was the garage. They slapped the main door and the walls. Some of them moved along the front of the building, and Crowbar went with the flow.

He stopped directly before the bay door, listless, until one of his many companions jostled him from behind. Crowbar fell against the barrier, the impact shoving his namesake deeper inside his abdominal cavity until the claw tapped a lower rib. Crowbar backed away, moaning at the one pushing him to no effect. Others moved along, spreading out, caressing, bumping, searching, and forgetting what it was exactly they were doing there in the first place. More zombies arrived, drifting, muddling around the building, surrounding it.

A sharp metallic clatter from inside the garage got their attention.

Crowbar straightened. His fellow corpses released notes of interest and faced the door. Hands slapped against the side, demanding entrance. The commotion drew other zombies to start flailing at the building, until all the hitting melded into a heavy-handed applause.

Seconds later, the door complied with a clack. It rose, cranking slowly upward, captivating the crowd. The zombies didn't wait. Some bumped against the rising barrier, some slowly ducked inside, their grunts encouraging the others to follow.

Crowbar didn't follow. Like some decrepit, undead baron refusing to bow, he stood and waited for the door to fully open.

An engine flared to life inside the bay, a mechanical, fuel-injected thunder that greatly interested the gathered corpses. That one, glowing shot of gas animated the mob, got them moving even more, and Crowbar himself looked about with a jerky, stop-go curiosity.

Then its opaque eyes narrowed.

The engine's rumbling smoothed out.

A split second before tires screamed against concrete.

Smoke belched from the garage as a chunky black cargo van surged into daylight, smashing through the wood and fiberglass bay door, ripping it away. The lower lip of the door whipped up and caught Crowbar's steel, catching him square, and violently lifted him three feet off the ground before the van smashed him over the shoulders of those behind him. There was a flurry of bodies and flailing limbs, and the zombie ringleader landed atop a tangle of mutually stunned torsos.

The van rolled through them with a revving, eight-cylinder war cry. Bones crackled. Torsos pinched and squeezed until things squirted out. Reaching arms were snapped or rudely brushed aside. Some figures were knocked back as if hooked from behind.

The van blasted through them all, stopped with a squeal of rubber some forty feet later, where it came to a rest on a front lawn. There it shuddered with unsuppressed fury, rattling like a wooden box with a devil trapped inside it.

Then the machine reversed.

Crowbar struggled to rise from the bloody mesh of limbs and slippery organic matter. He sat up as if doing a stomach crunch and heard that killer mass of metal behind him.

Bereft of fear and driven only by a ravenous need to feed, Crowbar turned himself around.

Just before an all-seasonal tire rolled up his spine, flattening him in a very destructive yoga fold, splattering him amongst the others.

Crowbar didn't register the damage done to his person.

And a split second later, a tire crunched though the zombie ringleader's skull.

32

Debris rained and slid down the front of the van. Bursting profiles left ghastly prints against the windshield. Running over bodies tossed Gus left and right, but his seat belt kept him in place. He hunkered over the steering wheel, slowing the machine down as it rolled to freedom. Zombies smacked against the van's front and were either hammered back and away or knocked flat. The machine wasn't the Brush-It truck, but rather a different animal.

A different beast.

A beast Gus very much liked.

And after the morning he'd had, he let the machine's greater mass do what came naturally.

The beast smashed aside the flimsy wall of corpses, battering its way to freedom. But when Gus rolled onto a front lawn, he decided he wasn't quite finished.

Not by a fucking long shot.

Anger replaced exhaustion. Revenge shoved aside sorrow and remorse. Gus shifted into reverse and steamrolled over the pack he'd just burst through. He heard the impacts off the van's ass and scowled with righteous wrath.

He backed up right to the open garage bay door, where he'd jammed a length of steel onto a red button, so he could return in time to the van. Fleeing inside the garage had been entirely instinctive, as he was simply trying to hide from his pursuers, but it was the highlight of the day.

The wonderful machine—with its keys hanging from a nearby rack—had pretty much saved his ass.

Gus shifted into drive, noting that the gears were somehow screwed up. REVERSE was actually forward, and he figured the messed-up labeling was the reason the van was waiting inside the garage. It drove fine, otherwise, once he played with the gears and identified the problem.

He turned the wheel, steered out into the street, and faced a group of zombie reinforcements already facing him.

"Oh no you didn't," he whispered and hit the gas.

The van bashed two undead off their feet.

"Take it," Gus growled as the machine bumped over legs and chests and settled down in time to take the next round.

"Kiss my left nut," Gus swore and rammed a zombie.

"And you—" he said as he lined up another, "can gently suck the right."

The undead thing spattered against the grill and upper windshield with an alarming thud, but it went under the van like the others.

"Like that?" he muttered, turning the wheel, and taking two more off their feet. "Huh? Thought so, y'goddamn ugly cocksmokers."

The road lay ahead, about a dozen or so walking corpses occupying it.

Once again, Gus felt lucky.

And plowed through the works of them.

Like sticks smashing a snare drum, zombies thrummed off the charging beast of a machine. Gore spattered the windshield in great greasy gobs, to which Gus applied wipers and fluid wash.

"*Green grimy gopher guts!*" he yelled, lining up the last zombie between him and the open road.

The van crashed into the figure and a grayish red halo spattered the glass. A crooked arm and a foot appeared in Gus's line of vision for all of two seconds before it fell and went under the tires. He bobbed in the driver's seat, kept his hands on the wheel, and the ride smoothed out.

Open road.

He flicked on the wipers again, clearing the windshield of that last grisly spray of pudding.

The van rolled on, and as Gus flexed fingers on the steering wheel, a well of sadness opened up inside him. For Tammy. But also for Toby, for Gord, and even a little bit for Mel Grant. And in between those sad thoughts, he once again hoped beyond hope that Rebecca and Walt and Nelson somehow got free of the city. He hoped that the librarian named Carol, Vlad whatshisface, willowy John Maple, and the quiet Rene had escaped as well. Gus prayed they all escaped in one piece, even the fuckwad with the cellphone camera, even though he thought the man was a complete dick by recording everything.

And he sincerely hoped Anna Hajek made it to her farm.

Houses flashed by, becoming increasingly farther apart.

Greenwood.

Army base.

Some reason, he doubted the place was any different from Annapolis right now. He knew the road he was on, knew where it was going. Out of the city, toward the countryside.

Toward South Mountain.

Abandoned cars and other assorted vehicles filled the road, but nothing that hindered the van. A sign informed him he was headed the WRONG WAY, and that made him giggle.

Wrong way, indeed.

The drive relaxed him, brought him down, as much as it could bring him down anyway, after narrowly escaping a crowd of flesh-eaters gunning for his fat ass. The sadness hit again, and Gus snorted back snot and swallowed. His throat ached. His eyes watered. He palm-wiped them clean, blinked, and focused on the road.

Where the fuck was he going?

There was nothing behind the city except some small farms, smaller towns, and a dam. Regardless, Gus drove on, heedless of time, feeling the warm light spilling inside the van like a ghostly hand attempting to comfort him.

"Thanks, Mr. Sun," he whispered, sniffed, and winked at that great ball in the sky.

The houses disappeared. The deserted cars thinned out and vanished. The forests, in all their glory, thickened. Shadows lay across the pavement's width in a dark uneven fence.

And during that drive along a lonely-looking highway, the sadness came back with a fury. Gus felt it come on, starting with a deep-rooted hurt in his chest and a trembling in his shoulders. He recognized it and decelerated, pulling over despite no one else on the road.

Engine chugging, he carefully put the machine into park and hunched over in his seat.

Then he dealt with his growing misery and despair the best he could.

33

He saw a gap in the forest wall on the left, some thirty meters away.

Running a hand across his face, Gus focused on that parting of foliage. With his emotional overload dealt with for the time being, he fiddled with the gears and eventually got the beast moving. He pulled alongside what appeared to be a dirt road. The window went down, and he inspected a pair of skid marks spraying the pavement with gravel, as if the people had gotten the hell away exceptionally fast.

Gus wondered where. He also wondered where the dirt road led and if it might be dangerous.

"Fuck it," he decided and checked his mirrors. He drove into the forest. At the very worst, he'd find himself at a dead end. At best, maybe he'd find a cabin he could break into and settle down for the rest of the day, think about what his plans were. Maybe there might be people at the end of the driveway, and they'd bunkered down in a mountain retreat.

Or maybe he'd just drive into a waiting pack of zombies.

He watched the road, taking care with the turns and slopes.

He entered a clearing dotted with short trees, where the road ended in an open gate, hanging off a wall at least ten feet high. Gus stopped the van. He studied that opening, saw the house and its peak beyond. A very nice house. A tall timber frame structure. He'd always wanted one of those.

Cautiously, Gus eased the van forward.

The gate was one of those tall, iron-barred, gothic sorta deals. He passed through, seeing how it was one flung to one side as if someone was in a real hurry to leave the place. Well-kept grounds lay inside, and the road led to a closed garage.

Gus halted the great beast again, brakes squealing that time.

He looked around, studying the empty grounds and the back of the house. No one appeared home. No zombies came around the corners, but that didn't mean anything. They might still have been in the house.

Yet, scanning the windows, Gus didn't see any life or movement at all.

He parked the van and killed the engine.

Birdsong drifted inside. That interested him, so Gus got out of the van. He had no weapon, but he bet there was something inside the house. A bat— preferably aluminum—might be hidden therein, and if not, he made the mental note to get one anyway.

The sun caught him in a beam. It warmed him, those odd high temperatures refusing to leave, but that would change soon enough. Gus realized he still wore his shredded parka. With a grunt, he shrugged off the coat and tossed it aside, studying the burst seams and the gray fabric spilling out.

He'd need a new coat. And he needed a shower. The sweat and blood and whatever else there was clung to him like a dirty second skin, and he didn't like the feel.

"Hello?" Gus called out, figuring that would be best. He'd rather have the zombies come at him from a distance than pop out from around a corner.

"Anyone in there? I'm from down the Valley. Things are pretty fu—hairy down there."

No response. No discernable activity.

"Hello?"

And he listened. Wind rustled the trees and the birds had stopped singing. That might be a bad sign, he thought, and looked around. The wall cut off a good chunk of property, he noticed.

Gus went to the front door. A white buzzer awaited him and he jammed it with a thumb.

Waited.

Two minutes later he buzzed again.

Two minutes after that, he looked fearfully at the van behind him, saw that it was twenty feet away. If he had to, he could make twenty feet at good speed.

The knob turned in his hand, and the door opened.

"Hello?" he asked, widening his field of vision and taking in a very clean mud room.

"I'm coming in, just because I'm worried here. Worried you're either alive and can't answer or are being prevented from answering. So please don't hurt me."

Gus thought about that last bit. "Or shoot me."

No response to that either.

"Okay, then," he shrugged and listen. No shuffling of feet. No moaning. And no eighty-year-old Granny tumbling down a staircase. He waited and gazed past the short hallway, into an open area. "I'm coming in now."

And he did.

No one was home. He walked through a very posh living space, marveling at the high-end finishes and expensive furniture. There were stairways leading up and below and he went upstairs first, exploring the bedrooms and en suite baths. Sweet fixings, subtle earth-tone colors. Laminate flooring and carpets.

Someone was rich.

And someone wasn't home at all.

The basement wasn't occupied either, but the many rooms impressed Gus even more. The place was a castle. An abandoned castle. He returned to the main floor and wandered into the kitchen. Modern. Spacious. With a generous eating area and all the appliances one could ask for. Gus opened a cabinet door, and his eyes widened at the food stores. Canned goods. Pasta. Jams. Bottled beets and prunes. Peanut Butter. Cookies. Chocolates. Chocolate bars. He spotted the Cherry Blossoms right away.

But no people.

That got him to rub his chin, feeling the thickening stubble. Perhaps the owners had arrived only to leave. Or something spooked them, although Gus couldn't think of what, other than the collapse of civilization as they all knew it. Perhaps someone called them away, but the open gate suggested they rushed.

A mystery. And one Gus wasn't capable of puzzling over. His puzzler was overworked.

There was a wall phone, but the line was dead. That made him think of the cell phone, and he realized then the device was still with Toby.

The thought of his dead friend depressed him.

There was another cabinet, and after a moment's consideration, he opened it.

The sight that greeted him stopped him cold.

A bottle of Captain Morgan's white rum, the captain's smiling face plastered across the front. It was a decal. A fabricated brand name and logo, but right then, at that very instant in time, it was the next best thing to a smiling, friendly face.

And Gus badly needed a smiling, friendly face.

"Howya doin' buddy?" he whispered and gently took the bottle by the base. "I think you and I are gonna become good friends. You too, Uncle Jack."

He winked at the whiskey bottle. There were other brands in there as well, but the Captain and Jack Daniels were a couple of his father's favorites.

Gus wandered back out into the living area, holding the rum close to his chest. He stopped before a bank of wall-length windows. There was a sliding door, and he went to it, opened it, and slid it across.

"Jesus," he muttered, the sun warm on his face.

He walked forth, dazed and amazed, over a deck and past a swimming pool and lawn furniture. There was a cliff out here, with a yet undetermined drop. The deck extended partially over the cliff, but that wasn't what got Gus's attention.

There, in the distance, was the dull face of Annapolis, as brilliant as a full moon.

The mountain retreat offered a spectacular view of the city. The sky was a deep blue, unstained by exhaust or any other smoke or pollutant. The city itself appeared dormant, but Gus knew dead things plagued its streets.

He stopped three strides away from the deck's edge and stared, as if the sight of it tested the straining fabric of his mind and reality. The events of the last few days froze him, rendering him speechless. He knew life had changed. Even wondered how he was going to make it on his own.

Birdsong returned in the background, but he didn't hear any of it.

Gus hugged the rum bottle closer to his chest.

And he gazed, red-eyed and unblinking, upon the cityscape.

About the Author

Keith C. Blackmore is the author of the Mountain Man, 131 Days, and Breeds series, among other horror, heroic fantasy, and crime novels. He lives on the island of Newfoundland in Canada. Visit his website at www.keithcblackmore.com.

DISCOVER
STORIES UNBOUND

PodiumAudio.com

Printed in the USA
CPSIA information can be obtained
at www.ICGtesting.com
JSHW082200140824
68134JS00014B/335

9 781039 449909